PERFECT TIMING

What if you found the right guy at the
wrong time...

By Robin Mellom

ISBN-13: 9781505688030

Los Angeles County Juvenile Detention Intake Report

Name: Tori Wright   Age at booking: 16

Eyes: HAZ   Hair: BRN

Height: 5'5"   Weight: 124

Sex: F   Charges: Infraction 240; 594

Charging Officer: Ortega

Court date/time: To be determined

Intake Notes:

Suspect is out of sorts, slightly belligerent. Agrees to explain why she was found in establishment, underage, and charged with battery/ stalking.

Before proceeding, suspect makes a request for a grape soda. Specifically Fanta.

Three days before

CHAPTER ONE

I had a feeling this would happen. It's usually the best friend who is first to sense the shift—that moment when a guy falls out of love. Unfortunately, I'm right yet again.

Shannon is sitting on the floor of my bedroom, crying even harder than the time Josh Gardner broke up with her. That was three and a half months ago. But Brent—she thought—was different. And given all the playlists he made for her, I thought so too.

Until last night.

She's waiting for me to say all the right things to make this easier. To pull out the perfect blend of inspiration and attitude and salty snacks that will help her move on.

I just wish the signs Brent had given hadn't been so sudden. We didn't have much time to anticipate this breakup.

I lie on my bed, head propped in my hands and try to come up with all the right words to make Shannon feel better. And even though I feel incredibly sorry for her, I also feel a little grossed out.

She's blowing her nose in my T-shirt. Really hard, too.

Luckily, I'm not wearing it right now.

Gosh, I love her. But *come on*. Did she have to grab my vintage Betty Boop V-neck? Category: favorite.

I scramble to find a replacement.

"Here, sweetheart." I hand Shannon a slightly crumpled Dairy Queen napkin sitting on my nightstand. It's leftover from last night, when the four of us went out for our Friday night routine—Blizzards and onion rings.

But not anymore. Obviously.

Shannon blows her nose in the crumpled Dairy Queen napkin and looks up at me with tear-stained cheeks. "What do I do, Tori?"

I prop myself up and sit cross-legged. "First, you call him. Tell him to come see you. You need to hear it in person."

"But I tried that." Snort. Blow. "He won't pick up—didn't even answer my texts."

"Then I'll call him," I say. "Maybe he'll pick up if I—"

"He won't answer. Don't even try. Why. Even. Try?!" Shannon wails as if an asteroid sent to destroy mankind is about to crash right here in the middle of my purple shag rug.

"He'll answer," I reassure her. And Shannon definitely needs the reassurance because she's now doing that crying thing where you get the dry heaves and make those little choky sounds. I pat her back with one hand while I dial with the other.

He doesn't answer.

This is bad.

Being that Shannon is my best friend, the realization that Brent had a change of heart tore me up inside. We're the best-friends-since-first-grade type: practically sisters and annoyingly inseparable. We laugh until we're almost choking and usually over some inside joke that we didn't even describe with words and everyone around us just stares in confusion.

Yeah, we're *those* girls.

Her heartache is my heartache.

However, in the interest of full disclosure, we aren't the type of friends who share clothes. The Pisces in me values comfort. I'm the girl in a lacey skirt, flower print shirt, floppy hat and boots—purchased because of the give in the leather. (But also the cuteness of the silver buckle, I can admit that).

While Shannon, on the other hand, prefers all-things-blingy. And heels. And hair extensions. And rhinestones in place of buttons.

She's a Sagittarius.

You may have guessed that.

Brent is (was) her boyfriend of three-point-two months. And last night when we were out on a double date, in mid dessert, I sensed it: their imminent breakup. A change in the force, if you will.

He was doing that thing where he flicked his eyes back and forth between her shoes and the EXIT sign. And then, just to top off that Fudge Sundae of Rudeness, he talked about the weather. The *weather.*

I heard it was going to be foggy in the morning and clear by the afternoon.

He'd suddenly turned into Bob "The Man" MacKenzie, KZOY meteorologist. The change in him was so quick it was nauseating. I clenched my stomach and tried to choke down my Oreo Blizzard.

Adorably oblivious, Shannon never sensed a thing.

So I knew she'd show up here. *Here* being the purple shag rug of my bedroom floor on an unannounced visit, a heap of a mess. Not that I mind—she's family. But honestly, I didn't think it would all fall apart *this* soon. Maybe few days of back-and-forth phone calls, late night texts, and then one final meeting where he breaks her heart without any eye contact. That's how I thought it would happen.

That's how it *always* happens—eventually...to everyone.

But a mere twenty-four hours later? In a text? Who breaks up in a *text*? Brent White, apparently. And with such a lack of creativity. Did he see the text-breakup in a made-for-TV movie? If he wanted to breakup in a predictable fashion, there are far less cliché ways. Research, my friend.

Without Brent around, it means our ritualized double-dating has been obliterated. All with one immature cliché text. And that means it's solo dates from now on for me and Joel. Not that I have any complaints.

A little over four months ago, Joel and I met while in line at Pinkberry. "You can go ahead of me," he'd said. I replied with, "Dang, aren't you the gentleman." We talked about our favorite toppings and I stared at his long eyelashes and we've seen each other every day for the past four-ish months. I had no idea I would completely fall for some guy the moment I he said "chocolate sprinkles." With those fluorescent lights? Lord.

But he wasn't just "some guy." I'd studied my yearbook enough to know the names of all the available upperclassmen. This was Joel Metzer—junior, left wing on the varsity soccer team, and on the honor roll. He'd recently gone through a break-up with Carly Watson, his girlfriend of almost two years. *She* broke up with *him*, unbelievably. It explained why he was going through a dark phase. Hoodies, shaggy hair, shoes untied. But I liked it—a guy who grieves is strangely attractive. No. *Completely* attractive.

So, sure. I knew who he was.

And that night, when he placed his hand on the small of my back just before saying goodbye, I felt this energy—a shot of electricity that raced through every fiber of my body.

I fell for him instantly. And I fell hard.

And looking back on all my relationships (all two), they've started the same way. A touch. A touch that shoots a pulse of energy through my body that sends me into a dizzy state where I can hardly talk or move, turning me into pudding. Love Pudding.

Shannon looks up at me, her eyes bloodshot. "Pictures. I need those pictures of us from the lake." She pops up on her knees and clamps down on my arm, giving me a look like she is certain this— THIS—is the answer. "I'll burn them. We can make a fire pit in your front yard. Come on."

I pat her hand, trying to calm her down. "You're going to take control of the situation and keep your dignity. A Sienna Hart movie marathon. Pretzels. Scented lotion. Got it?"

She looks disappointed. "No burning stuff?"

I reach into my top drawer and pull out my favorite bottle of Jasmine Forest Fairy lotion, sitting next to the picture of me and Joel at the beach—he's wearing his cap backward, his shirt's off, he's tan, and wow, I can't stop looking at him. "No fire pit. You're starting with lotion. Slather it on, it smells like a Christmas tree." I lift her chin to make her look at me. "It'll make you new and fresh and foresty, like some kind of woodsy nymph. Frolick through the trees in a chiffon gown, sweetheart. Forget Brent...we'll start with Sienna's first movie—The Vampire Chronicles, Part One, Dawn of the Un-Dead."

She nods.

After our Hannah Montana phase, Shannon and I became devoted Sienna Hart fans. She's sparky and gorgeous and could kick in a guy's teeth all while taking a drag on a cigarette. In eighth grade, we both even dyed our hair platinum blond to match hers. Unfortunately we'd used drugstore hair dye in a box, having been taken in by the overly optimistic advertising. It took two $90 visits to a real hairstylist to get my hair back to its natural color: turkey gravy.

Shannon squeezes out some lotion in her hand and gazes down at her palm as if it holds the answer to all of her problems. I'm pretty sure it does. Or at least it's a start. She has to take control of the situation, and Jasmine Forest Fairy is made for that.

As she settles next to me on my bed and begins slathering her legs, I can see a slight smile start to form on her face. A feeling of satisfaction rolls over me, knowing she just might be on the road to recovery without resorting to pitiful depression behavior. There is no need to scarf gallons of ice cream. They always do it in movies, and it makes me want to throw my overpriced Diet Coke at the screen. Not all women cope with heartache through dairy products.

I tuck Shannon's hair behind her ear, but my attention is taken away by a buzzing sound.

My phone. My phone is buzzing.

I snatch it off my nightstand and look at the screen. When I see the words, my stomach plummets and I gasp.

It's a text from my guy—Joel.

And completely cliché.

CHAPTER TWO

I press my palm against my forehead. "Whoa. WHOA."

"You okay?" Shannon asks while happily applying lotion to her elbow.

My hand quivers as I cautiously hold the phone away from me like it's a tarantula. "I think Joel just sent me a break-up text."

"Naw, that boy worships you."

I hold out the tarantula and let her read the message.

ULTIMATE FRISBEE SEASON STARTING. INSANELY BUSY. LET'S TAKE A BREAK. YER STILL GORGEOUS. LATER, J

Shannon's jaw drops. "What?!"

I slide off the bed and flop down on my shag rug in disbelief, my stomach doing flips but not in the love pudding sort of way. Shannon joins me and I rest my head on her shoulder. "Why would he do this? No explanation? Just a stupid break-up text?"

Shannon pats my head and does her best to soften this news. "You know...maybe he didn't mean it the way it sounds. 'Taking a break' could mean that he just wants to take a day off."

It is, I guess, entirely possible that he meant take a day off while he plays Frisbee. But even *that* didn't make sense—over the past few months we hadn't gone for more than a few hours without calling each other.

I double-check my phone to see if he's texted back to explain it was an auto-correct typo or something. That's reasonable.

But nothing.

Not in a million years did I think he was capable of such cliché crap. And he broke up with me...without warning? There are *always* signs. But with my guy? Apparently, not a one.

"Get my car keys." I scramble to my feet. "We're going to pay a visit to Joel Metzer's house. I'm going to get some eye contact. And an explanation."

· · ·

As we rush down the driveway to my car, Shannon lingers behind because she's hop-walking while she slips on her flip-flops. Flip-flops with *heels*. Who invents this stuff? Clearly it's not someone who understands the need to slip shoes on quickly when you're helping your friend jam over to her guy's house who has just used the lamest breakup technique straight from a made-for-TV movie and *ohmygod* I can't believe this is happening to me. "Hurry, Shan!"

I pop open the passenger side door for her and sprint around to the other side, briefly considering a hood-slide ala Dukes of Hazzard. But I'm wearing a skirt and my thighs could get hood burn. I'm sure that's a thing.

Plus a hood-slide on my car could result in a visit to the Med-Plus since it's covered in rust spots. No doubt I'd require an emergency tetanus shot. So for now: desperate sprinting.

Shannon and I both breathe heavily as we fall into the car seats. I pat the dashboard, shut my eyes tight, and—as usual—say a quick prayer. "Please start. Please start. As God and Shannon as my witnesses, I promise to wash you if you just fire up right now, Margaret."

I call her Margaret. Short for Margaret Thatcher. She's a yellow '73 Volkswagen Bug with rust spots (as I mentioned). I named her Margaret Thatcher because she's old and not super attractive and sometimes I don't like what she does, but she's tough enough to be Prime Minister to all cars, so there.

I turn the key in the ignition.

Only a sputter.

Gripping the steering wheel tightly, I pump the gas and whisper positive messages. "We have a boy to see...you can do this, darling."

I turn the ignition again. Sputter. Sputter. ROAR.

"That's my girl!" I tap on her roof.

We're off. Not exactly zooming down the road, but a form of forward movement is happening.

Almost the entire two and a half miles there, Shannon chats about how she's already feeling better about breaking up with boyfriend number six. Clearly she's ready to move on since she's already referring to him as a number.

But then she spills more details and admits that he's been talking about the weather for quite some time.

"Why didn't you tell me?! Weather-related talk is the first sign. I could have told you that."

She shrugs. "I just thought he'd become *really* interested in humidity. The Discovery Channel has a way of making boring stuff super interesting. I figured he'd been sucked into some new series."

I shake my head. "No, I'm pretty sure it's Shark Week."

Just so you know, this is not new territory for me: the "figuring out relationships" thing, not the Shark Week thing. Quite a number of girls at my high school have come to me at one point or another for my insight on their relationship.

Should I break up with him? Is he into me? Am I into HIM? Should I date a guy with terrible taste in footwear?

(With that last question, the girl already knew the answer going in.)

They come to me because my track record for predicting relationship success is pretty stellar. It's not a gift or some mystical power I acquired from my mother who is the descendant of Aphrodite, the Greek goddess of love.

That would actually be interesting.

But the truth? It's sort of…weird.

Let me explain.

I know how to find a guy, keep a guy, dump a guy, or get a guy back. I know the rules, the guidelines, and the lists of what to do and *not* to do. Part of it is the Pisces in me and part of it actually *is* because of my mom. I learned it from her last November, when she got the stomach flu. (I guess the truth is also sort of gross. Sorry, but stick with me here.)

Here's one thing you need to know: my mom (the lovely Nancy Wright!) writes a blog called I'M NOT DEAD, I'M JUST DIVORCED. You may have heard of it—or your mom has. She started it up a few months after she and Dad split. I was twelve and only interested in all-things ballet and/or the Hannah Montana movie soundtrack.

But Mom was full-on lonely. She even showed the classic signs: withdrawal from social situations, lack of keeping up her personal appearance, no longer obsessively recording *The Bachelor*. I tip-toed around her like she had a life-threatening illness, not bringing it up: The D-word.

Even though to me, divorce seemed like a good choice. This is weird—I know. The majority of sane-minded kids would never *want* their parents to split. But I was pretty matter-of-fact about it because the fate of their relationship seemed so obvious to me.

The thing is, I love both of my parents, just…separately. Because together? They're a flipping mess. Fighting, silent-fighting, loud-fighting—all kinds. *Every* kind. (But not the fist-to-face kind, thank God.)

Since they made each other miserable, I just didn't see the point. Isn't your partner supposed to make you feel better on a regular basis? Make jokes. Rub your shoulders. Perk you up? Isn't that what we're supposed to be looking for—that one person who lights up when you enter a room, simply because it's *you*?

That's my plan anyway.

I'm not sure when Mom and Dad's relationship turned sour. Was it before I was born? Or did the stress of hauling me around to all my tap-dance lessons as a toddler get in the way? (Tap, by the way, is the gateway drug to ballet.)

Whatever the reason, Mom and Dad had stopped seeing the awesomeness in each other. So...I told them. When I was twelve. I came home from practice, changed out of my ballet uniform, casually walked downstairs and told them I think they should split. While eating a banana. I was *that* relaxed. And by my third bite, I had even explained how I thought the custody split could work, printed on a calendar. Color-coded and everything. This, I'm sure, was an obscenely obnoxious move on my part. But I was a pre-teen and oblivious to anything not related to pointe shoes and my music collection.

You would think that twelve-year-old-me presenting a color-coded "Divorce Plan" would cause my parents to be furious. But holy pirouette, I'd never seen more relieved looks on their faces! It was like I'd pulled a thorn from their eyeballs. Such relief.

Mom got the house, Dad got a city loft, and I finally got the quiet home life that every only-child is accustomed to. I assume.

But the quiet was short-lived. Within a week, behind Mom's closed bedroom door, I could hear her crying. Every night.

So I promptly googled: divorce and depression. I found an ad for Dr. Jan Nelson, PhD. I knew she was the right choice because her ad had a picture of a heart with a band-aid on it. "Therapist and heart-healer," she called herself.

Perfect.

So it started out as an assignment from Dr. Jan. "Write through the pain" was Mom's task. She enjoyed it so much that she decided to share with other people. Within the year, Mom's blog had almost 25,000 followers and women from all over the country sent her questions about their relationships on a daily basis.

Mom is quite a good writer, an avid reader of self-help books, and one who greatly benefitted from therapy. So that's why the blog took off. And that's how she healed from the divorce.

She tackles on-line dating and breaking out of your shell and even sexually transmitted diseases. (Lovely, I know.) Her readers write to her as if she's the expert on EVERYTHING even though she doesn't have a doctorate or anything and works as a nighttime news assistant at The Gazette.

But last November, she caught that stomach virus, poor thing—the one where you feel so sick you're pretty sure you're dead and living in hell where you are nauseous for eternity and you can't even bear to look at an ice cube.

She asked for my help (as soon as she realized she was *actually* alive). "Please...the blog," she'd said weakly. "They expect me to post...questions need answering...how can I—"

I shushed her and got her some Gatorade. Then I promised her that she didn't have anything to worry about because my grade in creative writing that semester had been an A-minus. I could totally pull it off.

She nodded and pointed to a stack of books on her desk.

Her self-help books.

So I started reading...

The Rules of Love

Girls Guidelines to Dating

And my favorite go-to (believe it or not): *The Total Idiot's Guide to Relationships*. There's actually some really good stuff in there. Just be sure to skip the chapter on "seductive one-liners." It's ridiculous.

So on a Friday night last November, I wrote my first blog post on "How to Tell if You're The Rebound Girl." A short excerpt, for the curious:

Give your new relationship space. If it's been thirty days or less since his break-up, run in the other direction, ladies! Otherwise you'll be nothing but a fill-in fling! A way he passes the time. But you are no substitute!! Thirty days…that's all it takes!

Yeah, I overuse exclamation points. But it still set a record—the most hits on a post that mom had ever written. Or *not* written. They had no idea it was actually done by her sixteen-year old daughter.

When she got well, Mom took over the blog again, but said I could guest post every week. And no one knows it's me. Well, *one* person—Shannon. She's the only person I've told about it.

I've learned pretty much everything there is to know about dating and love and how to spot a jerk from a mile away. And that's why so many people come talk to me when the "signs" start to appear. The lack of interest. The stammering. The weather talk.

Please. Jerks are so easy to spot.

So the fact that I'm currently bombing down the road to my boyfriend's house to see if he's now my *ex*-boyfriend is…embarrassing at best.

I grip the steering wheel and pop up straight as the memory of last night becomes vividly clear. Oh, no. No, no.

While I was choking down that Oreo Blizzard as I analyzed Brent's interactions with Shannon, Joel had leaned over to talk to me. "It's humid tonight," he'd said. But I'd waved him off so I could hear every syllable of Brent's weather forecast. But all the while, my own guy had actually whispered the word 'humid' in my ear. And I didn't listen.

Dang it!

Please don't think that I don't see the irony here. It's pretty much all I can see, as if the letters are a neon sign floating just above my head.

IRONY (blink…blink…)

Here she is—Tori Wright—daughter of popular divorce blogger, Miss Nancy! and wildly successful at determining the outcome of relationships, seen here mourning the unanticipated break-up text from her boyfriend, despite his weather talk warning—the blond on Good Morning

America might say. And then they'd flash a picture of me blowing my nose in my Betty Boop T-shirt.

But that's not going to happen because there Will be no tears here. There must be something more going on and I intend to find out what it is.

Up ahead, I see Joel's street and my stomach clenches. What if he meant exactly what he said? That we'd take a break. Because according to *The Sistah's Guide to Bros* (not my favorite of Mom's self-help books but there are cute drawings), if a guy says 'let's take a break' it means, undeniably: "A break-UP, girl." (Gross, right?) And then there's a drawing of a guy squealing away in a hotrod car drinking a beer. Horrible message, cute picture.

Anyway.

"You nervous?" Shannon winces. She has brought the lotion with her and is vigorously rubbing it on her shoulder.

"No. Yes." I grip the steering wheel. "What if it's over?"

"It's not. Go talk to him. He'll explain it all and you'll have a good laugh over it."

Maybe.

Maybe not.

His mom's SUV sits in the driveway right next to his truck— his nearly new four-door Toyota where I've sat in the passenger seat and spent many hours alone with him. So, right now just the act of looking at the license plate makes my heart flutter.

Suddenly, I don't want to do this alone. I press my head against the back of the seat. On the way over to his house, I was ready to tackle him with questions. But now, just the presence of his truck makes me wilt. I can't help but wonder if we can fix this, and I'll be sitting in that front seat tomorrow night. The Woodward exit beach trail parking lot is where we managed to find ourselves practically every Saturday night. Talking. Laughing. Kissing. Wow, I need to stop thinking about this.

I turn in my seat to face Shannon. "Come with me?"

She pulls a breath mint from her purse and presses it into the palm of my hand. "Go by yourself. And don't worry—he adores you." She shoves me out the door. "Talk to the boy."

I spill out of the car and readjust my blouse.

Okay, Joel Metzer. Here I come—get ready for some eye contact.

Each step up to his door feels like wading through thick maple syrup.

Three weeks later, I finally press the doorbell.

His mom answers with an adorable smile, and she's holding a half-eaten cinnamon roll in her hand.

Good lord, this smell. So intoxicating. Mrs. Metzer regularly bakes cinnamon rolls because she wants to enter The Iron Chef, a TV cooking show contest on the Food Channel, and I'm one of her taste-testers.

"Tori! You're here just in time. I pulled a new batch out of the oven—this time I added a tablespoon of vanilla extract. This could be a winner, honey." She pulls me into a tight hug.

My nose crams into her collarbone, and I lift my eyes to get a peek over her shoulder.

Joel is standing in the living room with his hands shoved into his jean pockets.

Looking gorgeous.

CHAPTER THREE

Mrs. Metzer leads me to the living room—directly toward him— and she leans in and whispers, "I need you to taste test my cinnamon roll. Joel says he doesn't have much of an appetite for some reason."

I swallow what's left of my mint and manage to eek out, "Sure, I'll try a roll."

She smiles and trots off to the kitchen. I take a long, deep breath, then step into the entrance of the living room and wait for our eyes to meet. But he doesn't lift his gaze at all—just stands there staring at my boots. He looks like a Labrador retriever after he's been severely shamed for eating the trash. But from the hands stuffed in his pockets and the lips pressed together tightly, I can tell...this is not an "I'm sorry, I want you back" kind of look. It's just him being only one thing: uncomfortable with me here.

Sigh.

I have a seat on the couch just as Mrs. Metzer returns with the cinnamon roll. "An honest review, darling," she says as she walks away. I feel awful that she's calling me darling at a time when her son is in the process of ripping my heart out.

He sits down next to me and suddenly, we're alone. On this couch. Whoa, the memories of this couch rush in...cuddling when we watch movies. Still cuddling when the movie is over. Him playing with my hair when—

Aaaand enough of that.

Quickly, I hop up and move over to the brown leather recliner—absolutely no romantic memories were created in this man-cave of a chair, so I feel more in control over here. I chew and swallow in silence as Joel sits back with his fingers laced behind his head. He has now moved on to the endearing act of staring at the remote control.

It's Shark Week—I get it. Sheesh.

Finally, I say, "Let's talk about the text you sent me. It sounded like a break-up text, Joel." I lean forward trying to catch his eye. Unsuccessfully. "Your *text*."

But then he briefly flicks his eyes my way. "Okay, I know it was pretty stupid to do it that way."

At least he knows it was stupid. Half a point awarded. But he has a long way to go. Especially since I glance down and notice he's not wearing the flip-flops I bought him for his birthday. He knows how much I love to see his feet in anything sandal-like. So the fact that he's wearing Nike's feels like a statement.

I nervously grip the fabric of my skirt. "Just say what you mean...are you breaking up with me?"

"I...I just. Man, this is hard. Um..."

Oh, no. The stammer. Number three on the list of ways to know if you're the Rebound Girl.

Please, please don't let me find out I'm the Rebound Girl—I don't want to be just a way he passed the time until Carly took him back.

"You're great, Tori. And that's sort of the problem. You deserve a really awesome guy."

I study his face, looking for any indication he's not being honest. But he has a pretty steady look—no strange twitching or anything. So maybe it's not a rebound thing, but I definitely don't like where this is going. *I'm* the problem?

"Don't turn this into the whole..." (I even lower my voice here to sound like a guy)..."'You're too good for me—you deserve better' thing." And now I realize I sound stupid. "That's total crap, Joel," I add—normal voice.

He scoots up to the edge of the couch and faces me, *really* faces me. His distracted-by-The-Discovery-Channel demeanor has now turned into something that resembles attentiveness. The way he looked the night we met.

I find myself longing to be sitting next to him on that couch-of-memories—where one touch would turn me to pudding.

But that text.

Just let me say this: it is truly a frustrating feeling to want to punch him while simultaneously wanting to make-out with him. Thank you, hormones.

"You are so cool and gorgeous. We've been spending almost every day together..." he takes a deep breath before continuing. "But the seniors have that Ultimate Frisbee League." His knees start to bounce. His knees are annoying me. "And they invited me to join. I'd be the first junior on the team... ever!"

"So you've already contacted the Guinness Book of World Records, I'm guessing?"

He ignores my sarcastic remark. "They asked Brent to be equipment manager. So we'll be at practices and games four times a week. And every Saturday night there's a party after at Sam Clark's house. You know how epic those parties are."

I do know. I'm told going to Sam's parties is like being in a fraternity—consider yourself lucky to be there and do whatever they say. Also, they're dicks.

Even though I don't want to go to a Sam Clark party, I ask anyway. "No girlfriends allowed?"

"It's not..." he's now looking at a non-existent spot on the carpet. "...it's not that kind of thing."

At this point, our conversation devolves into uncomfortable silence and staring at walls on opposite sides of the room. I have no idea what to say. Which is unlike me because I can always come up with a witty response for a girl to say to her guy, or *any* guy. I can even come up with better lines of dialogue in romantic comedy movies—a quality that Shannon says is a little irritating.

But right now? In this moment of *my* life? Nothing. No comeback.

Tick-tock.

Wow, I never noticed before how loud the clock is that hangs on the living room wall. It's 5: 57: three minutes until *Fashion Police* comes on, a show we usually watch together. I love the "who wore it best" segment and he loves the snarky comments. Man, I adore that about him. That he would enjoy my favorite show and not complain.

Why am I already back to daydreaming about his luscious qualities? I slyly pinch my leg to snap myself out of this dreamy mess.

He scrunches his eyebrows and looks serious, as if he's about to make final statements in a legal proceeding. Aw, crap. I know exactly where this is headed.

"You deserve to have a guy who's around all the time."

I was right.

"And I'm not going to be the boyfriend you want. It'd be selfish of me. You deserve better."

I cram the last bite of my cinnamon roll in my mouth, giving myself time to think before I speak. (It tastes pretty good, but not her best.)

Though this break-up is gnawing at my heart, I can't help but be a tiny bit relieved that it's because he thinks I deserve more. Of all the break-up excuses, it's the most tolerable. And even though he's (sort of) giving me eye contact and looks all sorry about the situation, I'm *not* going to beg him and pressure him into staying with me. Plus an embarrassing "begging scene" certainly won't advance woman-kind very much. It's the part of a romantic comedy where I fling popcorn.

I stand up.

He does too.

"Well, I guess this is goodbye." I stick my hand out to shake his. As you can imagine, it's more than awkward.

But, strangely, he bypasses my hand and smothers me with a hug. "How about we just say 'see you later.' I like the sound of that better, Tor."

Oh, lord. He's using his nickname for me, he's hugging me, *and* he smells amazing. This is torture.

I pull back and force a slight smile. "See you later. You're right, it does sound better."

No it doesn't.

He walks me to the door, but just before I step out, his mother rounds the corner. "How was the cinnamon roll?" She clasps her hands together in anticipation of my review.

"Great. But next time you could probably add even more vanilla," I say in a flat tone. Then I look directly at Joel. "I like sweet things."

He blushes. And so do I.

"Thanks, Tori. Great suggestion," his mom says with excitement—a woman who has no idea her son just tore my heart out and it's now stuffed in his pocket. "See you later, hon," she says and gives a little wave.

I can't respond to her with a "see you later" since I'm not sure I will. My voice is low and crackly. "Goodbye," I say, then turn and head down the driveway before they can see the tears falling down my cheeks.

Los Angeles County Juvenile Detention Intake Report

Name: Tori Wright   Age at booking: 16

Eyes: HAZ   Hair: BRN

Height: 5'5"   Weight: 124

Sex: F   Charges: Infraction 240; 594

Charging Officer: Ortega

Court date/time: To be determined

Intake Notes:

Suspect states she was simply making an attempt to determine if the text her boyfriend had sent was a break-up text. It was. Suspect claims this is the reason she ended up on the internet, making a bad decision

CHAPTER FOUR

Sputter. Sputter. ROAR.

I jam on the gas and Margaret bombs down the road. The wind whips through our hair and Shannon chews on a stick of red licorice.

"What'd he say? Are you still together? What happened?!" All this said while she gnaws on licorice and dries the tear streaks on my face with the back of her hand.

Talented girl, that one.

"He said he's going to be busy and I deserve better." I take a quick breath. "So he ended it."

"No. Way." What's left of her licorice stick hanging from her mouth breaks off and falls to her lap. "This is a joke, right?" She replaces her licorice stick with a new one and holds out the bag offering it to me.

I shake my head—licorice isn't what I need right now.

"I wish it was a joke. Apparently, both Joel and Brent are going to be on the seniors' Ultimate Frisbee team. Well, Brent is going to be equipment manager, but you get the point—they're both too busy for girlfriends."

Shannon calmly clasps her hands together and gazes out the car window. "You mean that jerk broke up with me...so he could retrieve Frisbees?"

"I'm so sorry," I squeeze her hand.

We silently drive down back roads not saying anything. It's hard to figure out exactly what words, if any, we could say to each other to help us out at this moment. Usually only one of us is in a situation, never both of us.

My tears finally dry up, and I'm having a feeling of—dare I say—clarity. "Here's what we'll do. We'll stay away from any parties so we don't have to run into them and we'll hang out at my house, or better yet—"

"Tori—"

"Your house, we'll go to your house. And we'll start our Sienna movie marathon. Every night we'll start a new one."

"TORI—"

"We'll even dive into Sienna's older stuff...from the 90's. When she was that little girl on Days of Our Lives and she didn't have legs."

"TORI, LISTEN!" Shannon twists her whole body to face me. "I'm starting drill team, remember? I'm busy four nights a week. We talked about this."

Darn, she's right. We *did* talk about this, and I remember not giving it much thought because I knew I could just hang out with Joel instead.

But not anymore. Clearly.

Which means I'm going to be spending most of my nights alone. With mom's job, she usually has to work until eleven at night. Apparently someone has to be at the newspaper to listen to the scanner so they can report on the criminals who don't keep regular office hours. Mom chose to switch to the evening shift because it gives her the daytime to write blog posts and catch up on The Bachelor.

But *I* mind because it means I'm left completely alone. So we miss out on dinners together. Conversation. All sorts of basic human interaction.

Except I wouldn't tell her that I want her to be home at night because for the first time in her life since the divorce, she seems utterly happy. No more crying behind closed doors. Nothing is more important than that. I guess.

And no, this isn't a case of me not being able to be by myself. I've gone to plenty of movies solo and often eaten at the deli section in Whole Foods all by my lonesome.

I am a totally capable person, thank you.

It's possible this is the point in my story where you're thinking I'm crazy. Any sixteen-year old true American girl would love to have limited supervision and access to a car. The options are endless. But I don't go to parties by myself and trolling the mall gets boring. The creeps show up at night.

It never occurred to me that there would come a time when my best friend *and* my boyfriend would be gone. I could kick myself for never investing in a second tier of friends. There is a group of close acquaintances that I have, but they're more the type that you meet up with at parties or the mall. I couldn't exactly call them and ask if I could melt into their family. Feed me. Shelter me. Reassure me when I hear creepy noises coming from the washing machine.

But there is *one* other person in my life I can lean on. Someone who will give me pure, unfiltered, honest ADVICE.

"Do you mind if we go to your house. You know...maybe we could see if..."

Shannon shoots me a wink. "Sure—let's go see if he's home."

I love that I don't even have to explain myself. She knows exactly the person I want to see.

CHAPTER FIVE

Taylor.

He's Shannon's brother, a little older than us—nineteen—and he works as a "bar back" at a nightclub. (He washes glasses.) Taylor has given us fashion advice and romance advice and book-selection advice since we were little. I blame him for getting me hooked on Nancy Drew and the color periwinkle. Also, he's gay. Otherwise, I'd be married to him, even at this tender young age, because he is PERFECTION.

Three more turns, then we whip into Shannon's driveway.

"He's here." She motions toward Taylor's bright red Mini-Cooper.

We rush through her kitchen door but stop in our tracks when we find her dad sitting on a stool, reorganizing the pantry. We always stop and talk to her dad. In the Murphy household, it's just a given that you stop to chat, no matter how much of a rush you're in.

Shannon's dad is usually at home since he runs fly fishing tours and not many people in the greater Los Angeles area seem much interested in that. He used to take me and Shannon to the lake when we were little (Taylor refused to go with us). He taught us how to fish—decked us out in fishing vests and everything. Shannon would stand on the edge of the water with her purse draped over her shoulder because a girl can't be unprepared. (Man, I love her.)

But we always took a different approach: Shannon was only concerned with the numbers—she'd peer into her bucket full of fish, count them...1, 2, 3...7, 8...then, "Daddy! I caught twelve of those little fishes!" She didn't care if they were minnows or sword-fish—she just cared that there were a lot of them. But as soon as she was done counting and getting high-fives from her dad, she'd dump them right back into the lake because deep down she hated fish and thought they were slimy.

I—on the other hand—didn't care how many I'd caught. I'd squat down by my bucket, hold them, study them, count their fins, rub their wounds.

I never wanted to let them go.

And here we are, ten years later, using the same approach with guys. I wish I was the type to dump them and never look back. But my Pisces side won't let me. Deep down, I can't help but want to find a way to fix things with Joel.

Rub his wounds.

"How's it going, girls?" Mr. Murphy says with his back to us. He's a bit of a perfectionist when it comes to things that have the potential to be organized—even stuff you didn't know *could* be organized.

Shannon peers inside of the closet. "Nice noodle section."

She's right; it's organized by width of the noodle. Impressive.

"I'm moving on to aluminum foil and other types of food stor-age next," he says.

"You got this, Mr. Murphy," I call out as we hurry up the stairs to Shannon's bedroom.

He's there, sitting at her desk, calmly flipping through Entertainment Weekly. The sneaky grin on his face tells me he knew we were coming for his help.

Taylor takes one look at our faces and shakes his head. "Girls. Sit down. Time to get this out, whatever it is." He gently folds down the corner of a page and closes the magazine, then turns to give us his full attention.

It's not hard to give *him* attention: tight polo shirt, perfect-fit-ting jeans, hair that hangs over one eye and dyed platinum blonde. Winner of the World's Most Adorable Boy Award. Sheesh.

Some guy is going to be a lucky person when he lands Taylor. I just hope it's sometime soon—Taylor has the "approach" down, but can never seem to seal the deal.

"Explain your faces," he says. "I don't want the two best girls on my planet looking miserable."

We both plop down on her bed and take turns telling him the whole story.

Brent. Joel. Frisbees. Made-for-TV text messages. Cinnamon roll. Shark Week.

He takes all this in as if he's a newspaper reporter—disregarding the blubbering emotional parts where we moan about the lack of fairness and decency and general HUMAN KINDNESS, and instead he just focuses on the facts.

"*Your* guy," (he points to Shannon) "is a complete tool for not calling you back and explaining himself. My sister deserves the truth—always, no questions. So you're done with him. Close up the station—that boy is dead to us."

Shannon smiles and her face seems to fill with relief, as if Taylor telling her exactly what to do was all she needed to hear. I'm pretty good with advice, but Taylor…he's best at *telling* us what to do, and he's usually spot-on.

"That's right," Shannon says. "My station is now closed. I don't know what that means, but I like the sound of it."

He grins at her then faces me and bites at his lip. Oh, boy. This is going to be intense. "Now you, Miss Tori. Your story is a little more complicated."

Complicated? I cringe at this word. It means I may have a choice to make—and it's not going to be an obvious one.

He narrows his eyes. "Joel is a jerk, but he's trying to *not* be a jerk. Those guys are the confusing ones, sorry to tell you."

I flick my eyes up at him. "So you're saying I should try to get back together with him? Give him another chance?"

"Not necessarily. It's not clear. He was right about one thing though...you deserve better. I won't argue with that." He picks at a piece of lint on his sleeve, then continues. "And I don't like that he's taking a break because of a ridiculous *sport,* or whatever it is. Is it *that* hard to catch a Frisbee *and* have a girlfriend? But then again, he did say 'see you later.'"

Taylor glances up as if the answer is hidden on Shannon's ceiling fan. "Sounds like the guy has a time management problem. He'll have a hard time when he becomes an adult. I'm barely one myself, but all I do is manage time, and...speaking of which..." he glances down at his watch. "Crap. Crap! I have to get to work in fifteen and I still haven't found my car keys. Shannon, start the drill!"

It's a drill they've done many times.

She hops up and heads for the door. "Refrigerator?"

"Already checked," he says.

"Inside a shoe?"

"Good thinking, but no."

"Fruit basket?" Her voice trails off as she runs down the stairs in search of his keys, placed somewhere obscure. As usual.

"Wait!" I jump up, clamping down on Taylor's shoulders before he can escape me. "You haven't told me what to do."

"Aw, Puppy." He taps my nose.

I love it when he calls me that. And I always love a good nose tap. From him, anyway.

These fleeting moments when I catch him actually at home are golden; it's pretty rare nowadays, and I miss the years when we were all in high school together and I had access to him whenever I needed advice. Or just time with a guy friend. Getting a boy's point of view is one of life's essential. Every girl deserves at least one truly perfect guy friend. And I feel like I'm losing mine.

Taylor cradles my face in his hands. "Move on for now. Do your own thing and stay busy, sweetheart."

I shut my eyes tight, a tear falls, and he wipes it away.

"Found 'em!" Shannon yells from the bottom of the stairs. "In the pantry...next to the plastic bags—the small snack section!"

"Of course," he whispers to the ceiling. Then he plants a kiss on my cheek and hauls it down the stairs. "Stay busy!" he calls out as his footsteps fade away.

I collapse in Shannon's desk chair. That's the only answer I get from Taylor—to *stay busy*? I never tried out for drill team with Shannon because it coincided with yearbook meetings. But those are only once a week for half an hour so that still leaves me with lots of excess hours to deal with.

I could throw myself into studying for class, but I already do that anyway and still have plenty of time to spare every night. And committing myself to a new series on Netflix will inevitably result in my gaining of ten unwanted pounds; I have a bad habit of scarfing bags of "movie-style" buttered microwave popcorn when I watch TV.

I spend a few minutes staring up at Shannon's ceiling since Taylor acted like all the answers were up there. And yet, nothing.

But I know one thing: seeing Taylor run around busy like this makes me jealous. His job keeps him crazy busy and...whoa. WHOA! I just got my answer from Taylor after all!

I'm sixteen, totally legal. I have a semi-dependable car, hours to spare, and a boyfriend I need to get over.

The answer is simple.

I, Tori Wright, need to get a job.

Two days before

CHAPTER SIX

I sleep on it. I don't want to make a rash decision about getting a job. You always hear that sleeping on it will give you a clear answer when you wake up, but for me—on this morning after being dumped by Joel Metzer—all I have is knotty hair, bad breath, and an aching heart.

I sit on the side of my bed detangling my hair with my fingers (*ow!*) and try to figure out if everything that happened the previous day was real or just a nightmare. Glancing at my phone on the nightstand, the "realness" of what happened with Joel bangs me over the head. His text is still there, threatening to steal all my self-confidence.

I hit delete.

Are you sure you want to delete this message? The phone asks. Even *it* is confused.

"YES, DELETE," I yell at it as I jam the delete button hard with my finger. I'm slightly drunk on power now.

But just before I lay it back down, my phone buzzes with a text. It startles me and I flinch. I always do this: jump a little whenever my phone rings or buzzes. You would think I'd be acclimated to my phone just doing its job. But no, if I'm to be honest, there's usually even a squeal involved.

Reading the message, I realize my sleep didn't help me decide whether I should get a job, but this text sure does.

It's from Shannon.

LOTS OF DRILL TEAM PRACTICE THIS WEEK. LET'S DO A SIENNA HART MOVIE FRIDAY NITE?? SOMETHING WITH FANGS AND LUSTY BOYS!! LURVE YOU!! XOXO

A Sienna Hart movie. Friday night. That's super fabulous except for the fact that today is TUESDAY. So that leaves me with days of obsessing over whether or not Joel showed me signs and thinking about all the memories we made in the front seat of his truck. And that couch.

Nope, not gonna do it. My mind is made up. I'm going to get a job. I will keep my mind on something—ANYTHING—other than that last hug Joel gave me. And the fact that he said 'see you later' not 'goodbye.'

Enough, Tori. I'm just going to put my feet on this cold hardwood floor and start this day.

Who knows what it will bring.

The halls of Lincoln High School are confusing, crammed, and make you want to swear—not too unlike the Los Angeles highway system. So I spend my day routing and re-routing so that I don't run into him in the halls.

I've memorized his class schedule because pre- breakup, I had created an elaborate route to maximize our face time (kissing), even if only for a moment in between classes. But now with this new direct route, I'm surprised at how close my classes actually are to each other. I am the first person to arrive at each class. I'm not rushed. There's no heavy panting due to 'haulin' it', and there's even time to ask the teacher a question or two.

It feels like I'm witnessing how the other half of the world lives. Like a CNN special.

For the entire day I manage to successfully avoid Joel. Except once I catch a glimpse of the back of his head as he ducked out of the lunchroom. Probably to avoid me.

So, yay.

After the last bell, I calmly stroll up to Shannon's locker, hoping we can chat about my decision to get a job. But there will be no supportive "Woo-hoo, you fixed your life!" talk happening. Instead, I am witnessing a girl in mid panic attack as she frantically tosses around her textbooks, hunting for drill team clothes.

"Shorts. T-shirt. Shoes. Isthateverything?!"

"Socks." I throw out there, just before she slams her locker door.

"Aaack! Socks!!" She snatches them and quick-hugs me before bolting down the hall. "Call you later, Tori!"

And she's off to engage in her deliciously busy life.

Darn it.

My house is empty, not surprisingly. Mom's always gone on Tuesdays. And Wednesday and Thursday and Friday. We get a long weekend together, which is when we try to go see a movie together and eat Italian. But even when we do go out, it's always one-point-five miles from our house to the oh-so-suburban strip of chain restaurants. We rotate between Chili's, Applebee's, and Fridays. I've eaten so many quesadillas I'm starting to hate anything in the shape of a triangle.

Even though we only live twenty minutes from downtown Los Angeles, we hardly ever venture there. Mom and Dad lived in an apartment near the city before I was born, and someone broke in and stole their TV, DVD player, and her flip phone. (Back then, phones *flipped open*. Adorable, right?)

After the robbery, they moved out to the suburbs and Mom refers to L.A. as the place where evil lurks. She forbids me to drive into the city alone, unless it's one of my bi-monthly visits to go see my dad. But even then I'm only allowed to drive on the 110 freeway, exit, turn into his apartment complex and PARK. She doesn't know that my dad loosens up and actually lets me drive to the Thai restaurant and back. And then there's my secret spot where I like to sit and think, but it's only a block away. So, if you're keeping track, I'm familiar with a whopping three streets in L.A.

Mom has no idea though that every few weeks Shannon and I drive to Club Bump! to meet Taylor for under-21 night. That's more glamorous than it sounds because it is in a small shopping strip and it's only two exits past my Dad's. So a correction for all you mathematicians: four. I know four streets in L.A.

This may sound pretty reasonable…that I'm only sixteen and I get to drive into the city and eat yellow curry with my dad and sometimes sneak off to go dancing with Shannon and Taylor. And I would agree that it is pretty stellar. But I've never even been to Beverly Hills. I've only seen the sign for it in movies and one time when I caught a glimpse of it through a dusty school bus window on a fifth grade field trip to the museum. Just once, I'd like to go there and experience it myself. Experience what's outside of this protective suburban bubble.

When she took Dr. Jan's advice to write through the pain, Mom focused so much on herself that all the details of *my* life became a number on her list. And my number was way down that list. When she does want to know about my world, it's almost always about my safety. Did I lock the door? Am I driving the speed limit? Did I put on sunscreen? Floss? Bug repellant?

She never used to be so safety conscious before the divorce. But now I think she feels responsible for all the parenting. And making sure I'm cavity-free and not murdered makes her feel better—like she's doing enough.

Sometimes I think it wouldn't be fair of me to ask her for more. And sometimes I do.

On the kitchen counter is a ten-dollar bill Mom has left for my dinner. That may seem like a lot, but it can easily be used up at the Whole Foods deli. Sushi and a bowl of miso soup can quickly add up. But I love going there because it's my only chance to eat something interesting, and not in the shape of triangle.

Paper clipped to the ten-dollar bill—as usual—is a note. Sometimes it's a list of chores. Sometimes it's a reminder to record tonight's Bachelor. And once a week it's my blog topic. According to her note, this week she wants me to write on the topic of "Finding Ways to Cope With Disappointment."

No problem, Mom.

Her note also includes a reminder to double-check the locks on the windows and make sure my bear mace is in my purse. I'm not sure why she thinks wild animals might attack our suburban home but she claims an article popped up on Yahoo! about a cougar attack in Sacramento so now she has me prepared for a bear-apocalypse. Fine. Let's do this, Yogi.

I stuff the money in my pocket and head up to my room to put my plan into action. It's not all that hard: I log onto jobs. com.

Scrolling through, I see that Applebee's needs someone to wait tables. No way, I'm at that place enough.

Vons needs a shelf stocker. Handling all those canned goods is just...whatever, it's a no.

Kinko's needs a night floor manager. Maybe when I'm thirty. And even then, I'm going to pre-decide right here and now and say: no.

And then it catches my eye. *The* job. It's perfect for a sixteen-year old girl going through a breakup.

THE GAP IS LOOKING FOR AN EVENING SHIFT WORKER TO FOLD JEANS. APPLY IN PERSON. PROFESSIONAL ATTIRE.

It's not just a mind-distracting job...it's an easy job! I won't be handling canned goods or managing people or serving quesadillas or even *talking* to people.

Just. Folding. Jeans!

Quickly, I wash up and get ready. Black pants, crisp white button-down shirt, patent-leather flats, hair in a ponytail and a dash of lip gloss. Totally professional.

Margaret sputter-bombs down the highway and since this is the only time of day where traffic is bearable, I pull into the West Pointe Mall parking lot within ten minutes. This mall is one of the spots on Mom's short list of exotic faraway locations that she'll let me drive to. This and the Jiffy Lube because it's cheaper than the Volkswagen dealership near our house.

It's one of those fancy malls (Neiman! Marcus!) but I only come out to this one occasionally so I'm unsure where to park. There are rows of reserved spots. I drive and search, drive and search. The detailed signs are done in cursive (intense cursive) and almost illegible. Even the lettering on the parking lot aisle numbers appear to be handmade and done in gold leaf—wow. I finally find an open spot.

G5.

I jot the number down on the back of a Whole Foods receipt in my purse. Margaret is parked in between a black Mercedes with darkened windows and a black Jaguar with darkened windows. What is with the dark car obsession? Surely not *everyone* is being chased by the paparazzi.

I walk away—head high—proud of my yellow-with-rust-spots statement. Sometimes, when I glance back at her, I swear she winks at me. It may be weird to love a car. But I am weird and PROUD.

I rush through the crowded mall full of people overdressed for the occasion. Shopping in four-inch heels? Really?

When I enter The Gap, a perky girl behind the counter beams a smile at me. "Can I help you?" Her perky bob haircut matches her personality. I notice her thick eyelashes that aren't real. And her arm full of gold bangles that *are* real.

I step up to the counter and say in a soft voice, "I'm here for the job advertised online."

Her smile drops off the planet. She tilts her bobbed head and squints, but says nothing.

"For the evening jean folder?" The words sound weird coming out of my mouth. I mean, I do have *skills*...I practically run our entire yearbook staff myself. Maybe I should be applying for something like "Senior Sales Associate—Since July" which is the badge I'm reading pinned to Perky Girl's shirt.

She looks me over then thrusts her hand out and says, "Resume?" Her voice is flat and cold.

Pretty rude. Don't they *want* people applying for jobs? Isn't that the point?

I hand her my resume—the one I'd quickly put together before leaving. It didn't take me long because my work experience consists of "attending classes" and "pretty much putting the yearbook together myself because my peers are slackers." Though I worded it a bit nicer.

And hobbies? "Jogging." Which is what I used to do when trying to make it to class on time after sneaking in a quick kiss from Joel. Also, "fine cuisine." A hobby I engage in by regularly eating at Whole Foods by myself.

Unfortunately, I can't include that I write a weekly internet article on the woes of breakups for a readership of over 25,000 people. Mom doesn't want it out that she's not always the one writing the advice. So it'll never be a line on a resume for me.

Perky Girl flips my resume over then commences with more squinting. "Isn't there more?"

I shrug. "Nope. That's it. My life all on one page in Times New Roman."

"It isn't even *half* a page."

Man, I knew I should've chosen 16-point Helvetica.

She motions to a girl on the other side of the store who is wearing a navy pantsuit and also sporting an enthusiastic bob haircut. She's folding jeans. Happily. "Annabelle works in our denim department, and she just graduated from UCLA with a degree in finance and international politics."

I swallow hard.

"And Brandon over there is tagging our clearance T-shirts. He just finished an unpaid internship with Goldman-Sachs in New York."

"That's...um...Wow."

She leans over the counter, her sparkling gold bracelets jingling against the glass counter. "It's 2014. The *only* work they can find is at The Gap."

"So you're saying..." Gosh, I'd really like to disappear right now.

"Unless you're being recommended by the CEO of Prada—like I was—then you don't have a chance."

Did she just say those words out loud—inside THE GAP—and *no one* laughed?!

I'm not qualified to fold jeans. That's super. I cannot believe it's this competitive just to stay busy. Way to go, America.

I snatch my resume back from her. "Thanks anyway. And congratulations on being a *senior* associate since July. You must be proud."

She rubs her badge and smiles. "Thanks!"

Aaaand she actually thinks this is a compliment. Wow.

I glance into my purse at my receipt: G5. Time to get out of here and launch part B of the plan.

CHAPTER SEVEN

I don't actually have a plan B yet. That sentence explains why I'm currently parked in front of Sunshine Donuts, scarfing down the raspberry jelly donut I just bought. And truthfully, I didn't buy just one. I bought a set. "Six" is considered a set, right?

Halfway through the second one, my stomach starts to hurt and it hits me that this is not the answer. I don't have enough money to eat donuts nightly and the added pounds would be a bummer. Plus, resorting to fatty snacks like they do in the movies is not helping the feminist movement move forward ONE BIT.

So I bomb home to my empty house and rush up to my room. When I glance at my computer, I'm struck with a light bulb of an idea and suddenly I have it: my plan B.

Basically, I do what everyone does in moments of extreme desperation...I search Craigslist.

If you're thinking that's gross or dangerous, I wouldn't disagree. Because scanning through the jobs available, I can't find anything that's a match, much less anything that's outside of insanely bizarre.

- Personal assistant needed for elderly woman. One hour per day. 8-9 a.m. Please wear a suit and tie.
- Deliver orange popsicles! Must have own refrigerated truck.
- Litter box cleaner. Will trade for pancakes.

But then my eyes land on something.

NIGHTTIME ASSISTANT FOR PHOTOGRAPHY BUSINESS

I click on it and read the ad.

My husband and I run a photography business and employ twelve fulltime photographers. We need an evening assistant to run errands, deliver important documents, and bring food as needed. Knowledge of donuts a plus. Cell phone provided. Must have a dependable car and openness to handling a very hectic, busy schedule.

Huh. Run errands at night in downtown LA? A cell phone? Knowledge of donuts? Busy schedule?!

Bingo, baby!

I hit reply and explain my love of the city (not mentioning my knowledge is limited to four streets and what I've seen on school field trips) as well as my love of running errands, especially those that involve chocolate éclairs. Also, I share my desire for a busy schedule.

I push send and then, out of nowhere, my chest tightens. Oh, no. What have I done? Mom will kill me if I go into the city by myself. And at night? She'll kill me all over again.

But I don't have much time to spiral because within minutes, I get a reply.

Dear Tori,

You sound ideal. We'd like to meet you. Are you available this evening? Our former assistant quit unexpectedly and we are in need of assistance immediately. In fact, if the interview goes smoothly, you could start tonight. If you are interested, please be here by 8 p.m. And bring a backpack.

520 Highlands Avenue

Cheers,

Lizzie

I rub the back of my neck as I pace the floor. What do I do?

But I'm interrupted when my phone rings. It's Shannon. I check the time: 7:30. She must be home early from drill team practice.

"Get down here," she screams before I can even say hello. "We're at Wingers!"

Quick background info...Wingers: a place to eat hot, spicy chicken wings, get unlimited refills on Cokes, and hang out during the week when there aren't any parties going on. Also: a place where the manager gets very annoyed by loud swarms of high schoolers with our notoriously bad tipping.

I haven't been there in a couple of weeks. Maybe I should skip the job idea—it's possible my social life might not be as void as I thought. I reach for my keys.

"Brent and Joel are here!"

And then drop them. "What? They're *both* there?"

"They're here with the whole Ultimate Frisbee team. Our drill team cut practice short to come here and "bond" or something. We had no idea they'd be here, too."

"Did you say anything to Brent?"

"No way. I'm staying as far away from him as possible. But I did talk to Joel."

"You did?! What...who...what did...whoa." Some girls shouldn't talk and mourn at the same time.

She giggles at my stammer attack. "He asked where you are," she says calmly. "He wants to know if you're coming by."

I bounce on my toes. "What did you tell him?"

"That I was about to call you. But you should get here quick. Carly's here."

Oh, no. His ex. Senior captain of the drill team and recently single since she dumped Alan Forrester, which only lasted a whopping three weeks. She'd dated several guys since breaking up with Joel so I never worried about them getting back together. It was clear she had moved on.

Except now she's there. In his vicinity. And single.

But even with her there...Joel is asking about *me*.

"If you want to get back together with him, now's the time. Don't worry about Carly."

I'm conflicted, to say the least. It would be so easy to go up there and wrap my arms around him and tell him we can work this out.

But no. No way. If he wants to get back together, he needs to come to me.

I've done enough relationship research to know that him begging me to take him back will only happen if he thinks I've moved on. Which is exactly what I'm going to do.

"Tell Joel I won't be there."

"Tori! This is your chance!"

I glance at my computer screen. The words catch my eye again. *Very busy schedule.*

Mom will be livid. But if I'm going to give advice to people on how to handle heartbreak, I need to start following it myself. "Sorry, Shan—I'm not coming. I'm going to get a job."

"You, wait...what?!"

The last thing I want is for her to talk me out of this. I mean, I did sleep on it so technically I'm not making a rash decision. I'm not convinced it's the right decision, but it's my best option at this point. 'Best' is a term I'm using loosely here. "I'll explain tomorrow. Love ya!"

I hang up before she can say anything to change my mind. I rush around my bedroom, gathering up a skirt, top, and a pair of my favorite boots. My "professional wear" didn't get me anywhere at The Gap, so I'm changing back into me clothes. I get dressed then quickly print out another copy of my resume (the other one has jelly donut smeared on it), along with directions to Lizzie's house.

Within minutes, I'm back in Margaret again and bombing down the road as I listen to my very favorite radio station—107.5. It's not the music I love, it's the DJ, Jo-Jo Lopez. He's hilarious and soothing, like a cool uncle.

Gripping the steering wheel with one hand, I hold out the directions with the other and read them out loud like a full-on crazy person. The last thing I want to do is make a wrong turn because—as Mom says—in L.A. you're always two turns away from being in East Jesus or in jail. She even looked proud of herself when she said it, as if paranoia was an enviable personality trait.

It isn't.

But I would agree that it wouldn't be ideal to get lost, so I follow the directions exactly. When I turn onto Sunset, suddenly every muscle in my body relaxes, I loosen the grip on the wheel, and there is no stopping the whopper of a smile that fills my face.

Because I see the sign. The brown one with gold lettering that I've only seen out a dusty school bus window.

Beverly Hills.

Los Angeles County Juvenile Detention Intake Report

Name: Tori Wright   Age at booking: 16
Eyes: HAZ   Hair: BRN
Height: 5'5"   Weight: 124
Sex: F   Charges: Infraction 240; 594
Charging Officer: Ortega
Court date/time: To be determined

Intake Notes:

Suspect states she took a night job in Los Angeles. She admits to not knowing all the details of the job and wishes she had asked the right questions. Suspect drops head and states that it was through this job that she met him. Suspect unable to state his name due to heavy sobs.

CHAPTER EIGHT

Bouncing in my seat, I drive slowly as I glance down every street to catch a glimpse of all the houses. The neighborhoods have wide roads that are lined with palm trees spaced evenly apart and all of them identical—clear evidence that this was put through a planning committee or something. The cohesiveness!

Mesmerized, I turn down one of the streets that's not even in my list of directions, but it's so enticing I can't help but want to drink it all in. If feels as if I've busted out and started a new part of my life.

With my windows rolled down, I study the houses, which are lit perfectly, like a movie set. They are of every variety: boxy and modern, traditional with columns and porches, Spanish with tile roofs, and one that looks like it should be on a cliff in Greece. All unique and gorgeous.

But then there's one that's pink—intensely pink—as if it's been soaked in Pepto Bismol. The front door is flanked by sculptured trees that are carved into the shapes of woodland creatures. There's a term for this. I believe the term I'm looking for is: GOD-AWFUL.

Worried I may get lost, I quickly turn back around and follow the rest of the directions. Within a few blocks, I'm on Highland Avenue, Lizzie's street. It winds up a hill and the houses get bigger and bigger the further up I drive. Then the houses disappear altogether because the properties are lined with high fences and security gates.

When I get to the address, all I see is a tall white stucco wall and a black iron gate closing off the entrance to the driveway. Her email didn't mention anything about a gate. What if this was all a joke? What if TMZ photographers are hiding in bushes waiting to shoot the picture of the girl breaking into Tom Cruise's house?

I guess I'm about to find out.

I pull my car up to the black box outside the gate. It looks similar to the one outside the car wash where you punch in the code from your gas station receipt. But this one is a little different because at the bottom is a large button labeled VISITOR.

I press the button and wait. And wait some more.

There's no response.

Punk'd—that's what this is. Cameras from MTV are about to appear. I yank the gearshift into reverse, but just before I back out, I hear a woman's voice, crackly, coming from the box.

"Yes?" She says.

I lean out of my window, feeling like I'm ordering a #2 combo at McDonald's. "Uh. Hi? I'd like—um, I mean, I'm here to—"

"Can't hear you over the engine."

Oops. Margaret's sputtery motor is about as lovely as a jackhammer. I turn the ignition off and try again. "Sorry…hi. I'm Tori. Here for the—" it feels weird to say it. "—job."

"Come on up!" Her voice suddenly sounds cheerier. The gate clicks and slides to the left allowing me to enter. I head up and by "up" I mean "UP."

The driveway is steep and I have to give a few dashboard pats to get Margaret up to the top. But then it levels out and I park next to a black Mercedes with tinted windows. Next to it is another Mercedes, completely identical. The people of Beverly Hills seem to love the concept of matchy-matchy. I can't believe I now know this—firsthand!

But the eeriness of this sets in...I am in Beverly Hills behind a private gate, about to enter the house of people who drive identical cars. I swallow hard, worried I may be in over my head.

Before I walk up to the door, I peek over the side fence and get a view of the backyard. Being quite the opposite of ours which consists of low maintenance bark in place of grass and oddly placed plastic chairs from Target, *this* yard consists of an infinity pool, chaise loungers, bubbling fountains, stone walls, and not one but *two* fire pits. This would fulfill Shannon's desire to burn photos of ex-boyfriends on the lawn, all while being super high-style about it.

I can't help but wish she were here with me. For one, I could show her this insane yard, and two, she could keep me from getting murdered because it's possible I'm in the middle of an indie Cohen brothers' movie.

But I'm wearing my favorite pointed boots, so at least I have a weapon should anyone come at me with a wood chipper and eerie music. I'm starting to sound like my mother.

I step up to the front door, which is enormous—wide enough to fit Margaret Thatcher through, maybe even with her doors open. I push the doorbell. (Yep, gold-plated.)

High heels click against the floor and quicken as they get closer to the door. A woman opens it slightly; her eyes scroll from my boots to the top of my head. Then she pulls the door open wide and smiles. She is beautiful.

She's in tight white pants and strappy platform heels with a fringed cape draped over her narrow shoulders, and she is literally dripping in jewelry. There are so many bangles on her arm, she could use them for musical instruments. She's tall and ultra slender, and her flat-ironed creamy blond hair is thin, too.

To be honest, I sort of want to feed her a rib eye.

"Tori? I'm Lizzie." She extends her hand, fingers covered in expensive-looking chunky rings.

I shake her hand, which is thin but well-moisturized. "Hi." Not too sure what to say now, but I take a stab at it. "So…you need an assistant or something?" I pop up on my toes a little and try to peer over her shoulder to get a look inside. The only thing I can see in the distance is a man working on a large computer.

"Yes, we desperately need an assistant. You need to meet Troy."

She motions for me to follow her as she zips through the living room. I immediately notice how quickly she jets around the room in those heels. Impressive.

The living room is super modern looking and simple, and the only furniture is a low L-shaped white leather couch and two matching chairs across from it that are lime green with white fuzzy cushions and look pretty similar to egg pods—whatever an egg pod might look like—but anyway, it's all very sci-fi.

There are stone sculptures of people's bodies slinking over each other and then sculptures that might just be body *parts*, I'm not sure, but I figure if it's so obscure you can't figure out what it is, it must be expensive.

"Troy—Tori's here!"

"Coming!" Troy says over his shoulder.

Lizzie holds up a container that seems to come from nowhere. "Coconut water?"

This doesn't sound appealing to me—I assume it would taste like drinkable suntan lotion. I wince and say, "Have any grape Fanta?"

She smiles and heads into the kitchen, which is completely visible since the house is one big open space.

Lizzie hunts through a stainless steel refrigerator the size of my bedroom. "Aha! Coconut water with pomegranate flavor." She pours some in a glass then cruises back across the room and gracefully hands it over to me. "You'll love it." Her voice is so reassuring and I can't help but smile. Even though I'm about to drink something that may have SPF.

I start to lower myself on the white leather couch, but before I can sit down, Troy enters the room, and I am overwhelmed with his fashion sense. Well-fitting striped pants, a crisp purple shirt, bow tie. His outfit isn't interesting, it's downright adorable. Plus his blond slicked back hair, thick-rimmed glasses and the huge smile on his face make me want to hug him because—and I can't quite explain why—he just looks like someone you'd want to hug.

"Tori, darling," he says. "Get comfortable—let's have a chat."

Oh wow, he has an English accent. Those always make everything feel cozy. Not sure why; there's just something about an English accent that turns me into a puddle of trustworthiness.

I do as he asks—sit down and get comfortable. Lizzie and Troy sit in the pod chairs, smile at each other, and wrinkle their noses.

So totally cute.

I take a deep breath—in and out—and sink into the lovely leather. Fortunately, I'm no longer feeling like I'm in the middle of a bizarre movie where I'm going to be chopped up. There's just something about Lizzie and Troy...their vibe. They're the type of people you want to put in your pocket and take home with you.

They lean forward, eyes bright, and energetic smiles spread across their faces.

I fiddle with the hem on my skirt and say, "So...do you have any questions for me? I have a resume out in my car. "

Lizzie laces her fingers together and gives me a serious look. "We don't need a resume, just answers to a few questions."

I grip my glass tighter and quickly take a swig of the pomegranate coconut water. It actually tastes pretty...no, wait. It's horrible. The coconut flavor comes at the end. Blech.

Lizzie clears her throat. "Let's suppose you needed to get fried chicken. Where would you go?"

That is the first question. *That*? Not "why do you want this job?" Not "do you have references or a criminal history?" Just... fried chicken locations. This makes me nervous. No clear-cut answer here. Did they mean *real* fried chicken or some gourmet vegan chicken that's faux-fried? Or maybe 'fried chicken' is code for some illegal substance and they're testing me on my street knowledge. Except I'm more of a suburban girl with extreme knowledge of drive-thrus and yogurt shops and Chili's locations.

I decide to take the literal approach to their chicken question, because it's all I know. "There's a KFC over on Glendale Boulevard—you can get a $20 family bucket deal right now. Or there's oven fried vegan chicken on the hot bar at Whole Foods—they're open till midnight."

Apparently Lizzie and Troy are pleased with my answer since they both smile and nod at each other.

Troy adjusts his glasses and scoots closer to the edge of his chair. He speaks slowly, making sure to articulate each word. "Do you know what a persimmon is?"

That accent—wow, I could listen to him say persimmon all day.

But, yet again, they've thrown me a bizarre question. Except I'm lucky with this one. Last year Mom had read an article in Better Homes & Garden Magazine about how to gourmet-tize your Thanksgiving meal. She decided baking a fresh persimmon pie would give our meal that touch of class that our meal normally never had. Maybe it was because we always ordered it from Vons and everything was smothered in gravy.

I'd tried to convince Mom that pumpkin pie would suffice because we could just buy it and it didn't even come with gravy, but she insisted that we have at least one dish that was worthy of talking about when people discussed how our Thanksgiving was. "Oh, the persimmon pie was to die for!" they could say. I didn't want to be rude and point out that our Thanksgiving dinner was only the two of us so *no one* would say that.

Mom didn't seem bothered we were the only ones eating, so she sent me to the store to get the persimmons. I had to hunt through the produce section of *three* stores before finally finding them. It was the best-tasting pie I'd ever eaten. Partly because of the extra cinnamon she used, but mostly because it was the first thing we'd baked together in years. I can still taste the sweetness of that pie.

I scooch back on the couch and the leather makes a squeaking noise as I settle in to answer their question. "Persimmons? It's a fruit that looks similar to a tomato. They ripen in the fall. But you can't find them at any Vons. You have to go to Natural Frontiers market. I go to the one near my house and Martin in produce is the guy who will point you right to them."

Lizzie looks over at Troy. "She's two for two, babe."

He leans in toward me, rubbing his palms together. "Just one more question, Tori. If you needed to get something from...let's say... a swanky restaurant but it was closed for a private party and the bouncer wouldn't let you in, what would you do?"

Huh. Maybe this is an ethics question. They want to know if I would be a good girl and walk away from a place I wasn't invited?

But it's Taylor who showed me and Shannon how to talk our way into Club Bump. NOTHING CAN KEEP ME FROM RETRO 80'S NIGHT, was pretty much Taylor's life motto. And he taught us well. So there's no way I would walk away from some ego-inflated bouncer. Taylor would be devastated if all his training went to waste.

I sit up straight. "I'd tell the bouncer that my brother is inside the party and he's proposing to his girlfriend. Except he left the ring in my car and I *had* to get in there to save that proposal!" I say this all dramatically and even set my coconut water down to add some critical hand gestures. "Not even a linebacker of a bouncer can handle the thought of stopping a wedding proposal—it's human nature."

Lizzie and Troy stare at me with blank faces. I've lost them. They're freaked out that I've just made up that story on the spot. They must think I'm ethically challenged.

Shoot.

Lizzie wiggles a bit in her seat. She leans over to him and whispers, "She's perfect."

He nods and folds his arms. "You might just be a natural, Tori."

CHAPTER NINE

Getting asked three ultra-bizarre questions and then me answering them perfectly was not how I figured this would all go down. I'm "a natural"…but at what? I'm still not sure exactly what this job is all about. "Are you guys telling me this job is to crash private parties?"

Troy sighs as he twirls his wedding ring around his finger. "At times, yes. But don't worry—there's nothing illegal, of course. It's just a case of you needing to be…crafty."

He's lucky his British accent is so enchanting. Because me and "illegal things" need to stay far, far away from each other. Given Mom's job as a night time news assistant, she'd more than likely know about any trouble I'd gotten into before they even had a chance to take my mug shot.

"Here's the thing," Lizzie chimes in. "We go to events. Charity balls, auctions, movie premiers, that sort of thing. We enjoy L.A. nightlife—the glamorous part. It's really the only way to enjoy living here. Otherwise, the price for real estate here isn't worth it. And the traffic…" She holds her palm up. "Don't get me started."

Troy nods. "And that's where you come in. We own a photography business and it gives us connections to some amazing people. So we need you to run errands for the photographers and help out with some favors."

Favors?

"What type of favors are we talking here?"

Lizzie giggles. "Oh, nothing bad, darling. It's easy stuff—gourmet food, theater tickets, that sort of thing."

"You can't get connected in this town just with money," Troy says. "Otherwise, there'd be *thousands* of people who could go to any movie premier or celebrity fundraiser ball they wanted. This *entire city* functions on favors. So that's what we do: trade, barter, do favors. And oftentimes people want...unusual things. Which is why we need you."

This was getting strange. And interesting.

Lizzie stands and grabs a piece of paper from the end table. "We'll give you a list of things to do or get. And we expect that you not ask questions—there are powerful people in Hollywood. We can't have it leaked that a certain gorgeous actress has an obsession with donuts, particularly the ones that come out warm from the oven at 10:15 at night. *No one* should know this. But *we* do, so we get the perfect treat into the hands of a certain important person and voila! Troy and I are at Elton John's party on Oscar Night. See what I'm saying?"

I do believe my instincts are correct: these people are crazy-awesome.

I've always wondered how regular people actually get into an Oscar party. Who knew all it takes are some warm donuts?

"We'd need you at least three nights a week," she says. "It pays $25 per hour and we cover all of your expenses."

Whoa. Twenty-five bucks an hour? That's almost as much as my mom makes. That's so many new pairs of boots, I can't even compute it! And then we could also use the extra money to upgrade Mom's blog to an actual website—something she's wanted to do for a while. *An actual website with a contact form*, she'd always say so wistfully. It's cute when she gets pumped up over a contact page.

"Plus, we'll give you this cell phone so we can be in touch at all times. You just drop it off back here at the end of each night."

"But I have my own cell phone." I start to reach for it in my purse. "You could always text me—"

"No need. The texts we send may have confidential information on there so we only use our cell phones." Lizzie then steps closer to me, looking down at me on the couch. "But most importantly, would your parents be supportive of you taking this job? We don't need problems."

Supportive is the key word here. Also the word *would*. And *this*. Okay, the whole sentence.

Because, yeah, Mom would be supportive of me getting a job. But *this* one? No way. The city driving, the weirdness of it all... she'd freak.

I figure if I'm home by 11:30, she'll never even know I was gone. "Don't worry. My mom is supportive," I lie.

"Then you'll take the job?" Troy asks.

I stand up and push my shoulders back. "Absolutely."

"Great!" Lizzie shoves the paper in her hand into mine. "Sign this—it's a confidentiality agreement. It says you promise not to leak any private celebrity information to the media."

Private celebrity information. She just said those words! This is too good to be true. I quickly sign the paper. "I just have one question though," I ask. "Why me?"

Lizzie raises an eyebrow. "Pretty simple, darling. You have time on your hands, you're familiar with take-out places, and you don't take crap from bouncers. Oh, and you're a girl."

"Why does being a girl matter?"

She rolls her eyes. "Our male assistant can't even get the grocery store clerk to talk to him. To get something done in this town, you need to be a girl." She shoots me a smirk—one of those Girl Power smirks that only females can recognize, like a dog whistle.

I'm really liking her.

Except this enjoyable thought is pushed aside because of the realization that the first part of her sentence included the words: our male assistant.

And that's when I hear the knock at the door.

"Adam—he'll be your co-worker. He's very sweet, not a problem." Lizzie hurries over to the door and peeks through the peephole. "He's here. Perfect timing."

She pulls the door open. "Adam…I want you to meet someone. Our new assistant, Tori."

He steps inside and we both look each other over. I assume he's quickly judging me because I'm totally sizing him up. His smile is kind enough—it's a no-teeth smile, but still pretty warm. Tall, a little on the lean side. He's wearing skinny jeans, skater shoes, dark rimmed glasses, and an arm full of multi-colored wristbands. A hipster. Throw in a well-groomed beard and this boy is Brooklyn ready.

Before I can get a chance to say hi, Lizzie kicks in with more instructions. "We need you to be safe, Tori, and you don't want to be in any sticky situations without help. Plus, the parking is ludicrous in this town so it works out better if Adam drops you off. He may only be seventeen, but he can navigate the streets of L.A. like no one's business."

I quickly glance him over again (because I like to be thorough) and instantly I know his story. His shaggy hair needed a trim a good two weeks ago, he's wearing a hoodie jacket one size too big, and his left skater shoe is untied. This is the official uniform of a boy with a broken heart.

I hold my hand out to shake his, but I notice I'm trembling a little. It's this moment, this touch. I know how big it is because this is how it's always worked for me. I meet a guy, he touches me, and whammo! Electricity pulses through my fibers and I'm hooked. It's almost as if my body knows how to select my next boyfriend just from a touch.

Adam steps closer to me, his smile has grown bigger—there's even a sliver of straight white teeth visible. And I notice the deep dimple in his right cheek and the velvety chocolate color of his eyes and…

"It's nice to meet you." Adam grabs my hand and there it is. This feeling...of nothingness.

No shock, no electricity. Just: nothing. It's sort of like shaking hands with a newspaper.

Oh, thank goodness. Adam and I are going to be co-workers, and that's it.

I tighten the grip on my handshake. "Looks like we're going to be partners," I say like this is some kind of buddy-cop movie.

"Partners." He dips his head and looks up at me. "I like the sound of that."

CHAPTER TEN

We stand in the driveway, and the security floodlight allows me to read the list Lizzie gave me. But I wonder if Lizzie and Troy are peeking through the blinds, watching us. So I look back, but no one is there.

It's just us.

And I suddenly feel nervous that I'm about to spend the rest of my evening with a total stranger. What am I doing?

Adam pulls his keys from his pocket and steps up next to me. "So, what's first on the list? Please tell me it's something with food. I'm starving." And then he laughs, like this is funny, even though it sort of isn't.

I glance at him and can't help but notice his mouth. Not in terms of kissability or anything, just its shape. The corners turn up slightly and not just when he's smiling—like it's a permanent state of being for his mouth. Which makes him look like a pleasantly content person at all times. That, or someone who drinks Prozac protein shakes for breakfast.

Hopefully it's just a matter of being born with an upturned mouth.

Because that's refreshing.

Now. I must point out that I am concerned about this situation I've found myself in: accepting a job in downtown LA while being driven around by a hoodie-wearing stranger who laughs at things that aren't actually funny. It's an odd move on my part—I get that.

But there is something about him. *All* of them actually... Lizzie, Troy, Adam...that feels safe.

I hold the list above my head to catch the light and read it out loud to him. "The first one says we're supposed to get a dozen Krispy Kremes, warm, straight from the oven, and deliver them to the back door of Blue Sky. Ask for Tatiana."

"Donuts." He sighs. "That'll work, I guess."

"Do you think we're delivering them to a movie star?" I actually just asked that. This is so surreal.

"A delivery to Blue Sky bar? Maybe. More than likely a TV star. Hop in." He opens the passenger door to his old, army green Jeep. There isn't a top, just a roll bar.

I hesitate. This doesn't look safe. One wrong bump and I'd be ejected out like candy in a pez dispenser.

He must sense my concern for remaining alive. "Don't worry. Wear your seatbelt tightly and you won't fall out."

But I don't respond and just stand frozen, staring at this death cube of a car.

"Orrrr...I could pull the top up. No problem." Adam unstraps the soft convertible top and takes a few moments to latch it on. While he works, I quietly repeat, "Thanks...thank you...thanks..."

With the last snap, he says, "Let's go, Miss Safety!" and jumps into the driver's seat.

I slide into my seat and secure the seat belt tightly around my waist. Then I turn to him as he fires up the engine. "You know, when people give each other pet names, the first one usually sticks. "Miss Safety" doesn't have much of a ring to it. Even though you do have one shoe untied and this Jeep is a stick shift and your foot could get snagged, so it's making me nervous...aaaand now that I think about it that name is probably accurate."

I sound like a freak. And the teen version of my mother. I need to get this under control.

He starts backing up but then stops the car. Without taking his eyes off the steering wheel, he quickly ties his shoe. When it's tied in a beautiful bow, he backs down the steep driveway without a word.

Once we get rolling down the street, he leans in to talk, which he has to do because his engine is loud and rumbly. "You're pretty observant. About the shoelace thing."

"Sort of in my nature."

"Why are shoelaces part of your nature?"

Does he really want to get into the details this soon? I've only known him for six minutes. But he asked, so I go with it. "I'm a Pisces, which means I'm the 'sensitive, observant type' so I notice everything and give it some sort of meaning. It's like my super power." I don't mention all the self-help love books I've read. No need to completely freak him out that I'm sixteen and practically ready for my own radio talk show.

We come to a red light and he turns to look at me. "So, my untied shoe...did you give that some sort of meaning?"

Well, here we go. I lay my hands in my lap. "You're going through a break-up. It's the oversized hoodie, the hair in need of a trim, the shoes you no longer pay any attention to. If you had a current girlfriend, all of these things would be of concern to you. But clearly you're distracted. So...when did she break up with you?"

The light turns green and he focuses on shifting gears. He's not saying anything, just glaring at the road as we roll along in silence. This worries me. Am I off in my assessment? Is that possible?

After a couple of turns, he finally clears his throat and says, "We're not broken up."

Aaah. Bingo. I turn my body to face him, but don't say a word. A tip I learned from The Idiot's Guide to Dating—just be silent and they'll fill in with more details than you could ever imagine.

Silence, more silence.

Oh my word, he's killing me.

Silence…

And then finally: "We haven't spoken in three weeks. She's not answering my texts and when I call her she says she'll call me right back but she doesn't. She waits—I think—to call when she knows I'm busy at school." He winces, as if those words hurt to say. "Then she says she has a bunch of stuff to do and she'll try again later when she has a chance." He shakes his head. "It's weird."

"So she hasn't actually broken up and you're wondering if she's trying to let you down nicely?"

"Yeah, it's like she wants me around but doesn't want to tell me it's over, and sometimes I think—" He stops mid-sentence and glances at me, cracking a slight smile. "Why am I telling you all this? We haven't even done any formal introductory stuff yet."

"We could do that," I say. "I'm Tori Wright. Sixteen. Lincoln High School. Head of yearbook staff. Recovering ballerina. Divorced parents, only child. Pisces. Now you."

He grips the steering wheel. "Adam Westcott. Seventeen. Senior at Beverly High. One sister. One father who is never impressed. Got to level fourteen on Streetfighter once when I was thirteen. Cancer."

I gasp. "You have—"

He laughs. "No, that's my sign."

I perk up to that. Our signs are pretty compatible. "July?"

He nods. "July the fourth."

"Aw, don't you love the fact that the entire country celebrates *your* birthday?"

"Hate it, actually. I've had a hotdog and barbecue potato chips on every single birthday of my life."

"I'll be sure to send over some spaghetti for your next birthday," I say.

"That would be appreciated."

I shrug. "Soooo, we've done the formal introductions…can we get back to your untied shoe?"

"We're here." He pulls into the parking lot of the Krispy Kreme and parks close to the door. The bright fluorescent lights shine into the Jeep and I can see him clearly. Just before I reach for my purse, he says, "I'm not sure if we're broken up, but I don't want to be. I just want things to be how they were."

Suddenly, it dawns on me that in all my time of giving out relationship advice, I'd never given it to a guy. My blog readers... the people at school...they're all girls. Helping Adam out could be a nice switch to see how the other side thinks. Plus, every girl deserves one good guy friend and I seem to be slowly losing Taylor.

I hop out then lean back in through the open window and raise a brow. "You want your girlfriend back?"

He nods as he picks at the leather on the stick shift.

"Don't worry about a thing. I can help you get her back—trust me."

Los Angeles County Juvenile Detention Intake Report

Name: Tori Wright   Age at booking: 16

Eyes: HAZ   Hair: BRN

Height: 5'5"   Weight: 124

Sex: F   Charges: Infraction 240; 594

Charging Officer: Ortega

Court date/time: To be determined

Intake Notes:

Suspect states she made friends with her co-worker, Adam. She says the pieces of the puzzle started to fill in when they met the photographer. Frank.

Suspect requests another Fanta. Accepts tap water instead.

CHAPTER ELEVEN

I hop out of the Jeep and glance down at my list.

* *A dozen Krispy Kreme donuts. (piping hot!)*

Adam rolls down his window and calls out, "Hey, could you—"

"I'll get an extra one for you," I say, remembering the poor guy is starving.

The line inside winds around the lobby, but it isn't moving. Well, it's *technically* moving because a lot of them were swaying, obviously drunk and lulled into a happy place by the glimmering neon lights and warmth from the ovens. Most are discussing sprinkles or plain. Not a hard decision, so what was the hold up?

Until a beeping sound goes off and the line surges forward. Oh, they aren't lagging around trying to figure out their order, they're waiting for 10:15 p.m., the precise moment when the warm donuts emerge from the ovens. I look around wondering if I am the only sober one waiting in line, much less the only one in there fetching donuts for a movie star. Or TV star.

The line suddenly moves crazy fast, people ordering boxes and boxes, the staff buzzing around filling orders.

In front of me is a girl who keeps getting texts. She sighs with each one. "Three boxes?" she mumbles to herself. "This girl, I swear."

"Ordering for someone else, too?" I asked over her shoulder.

She gives me up and down looks, not rudely, just figuring me out. She looks exhausted. "My "client" is very particular." She uses air quotes. "And she can't be seen in public." She taps at her nose, indicating a nose job is the reason. "So I endure endless texts with her donut requests. Don't get me started on her Slurpee obsession. What about you?"

"I have a 'client' too. She's partying at a bar right now. I'm not even sure who she is, actually."

"Which bar?"

"Blue Sky."

"Oh, could be one of the girls from that O.C. show. They always party there on Tuesdays. You're new at the celebrity assisting thing, huh?"

It's a hard question to answer because I'm not entirely sure that was what I was doing. Running bizarre errands for eccentric socialites? "Yeah, I'm new."

"Want my advice?"

I nod with enthusiasm.

She glances around, as if to make sure there aren't any eavesdroppers listening in on this information she's about to unload. "Don't ask questions. Don't be late. And stay away from Melrose Avenue after midnight."

The first two made sense but what exactly happens on Melrose after midnight? Would I turn into a gremlin? But her turn in line comes up and she stalks up to the counter before I can ask.

She gives me a thumbs-up after picking up her three boxes and hurries out the door. Knowing I should at least follow her second piece of advice—don't be late—I quickly buy my box of donuts (I ask for two extra, one for each of us), and rush out to the parking lot where Adam is waiting for me, the car already running and facing the exit.

I hop in and hand him one warm donut and snag one for myself. I glance down at the list. "It says we're supposed to take these to the back door and look for the yellow markings." I look up at him—he's already three-quarters done with his donut. "Do you know how to find that?"

He smirks as he gobbles down the last bite. "Uff course."

I take a bite. And then another. "Deez are good!"

He laughs as he turns onto the entrance for the freeway. "Another fresh batch comes out of the oven at 10:45. We should hit 'em up again."

"Totally."

The wind rattles the doors on his Jeep as we speed down the road. Part of me wants to keep talking about light topics, like donuts. But another part of me—a huge part—just wants to know more. I swallow hard and say, "If you want me to help you get your girlfriend back, you have to tell me about her."

He takes in a deep breath and lets it out. "There's a lot to say about Lana. Get comfortable."

Eeek! Thoughts on relationships from a *guy's* point of view... this is awesome research. I wiggle myself deep into my seat and it happens, I just can't help it—a huge, dorky grin fills my face.

CHAPTER TWELVE

We exit the highway, head down a back street, and that's when he starts in; all the juicy details I could hope for.

"We met at this writing thing, a weekend conference for teen writers—over at UCLA. I sat next to her and when the instructor asked a question, Lana raised her hand and answered 'in medias res' and she was right. But I had no idea what that meant so I purposefully sat next to her at our lunch break. She explained it all to me, about how she'd started her story from the middle of the action and then filled in with flashbacks...and I swear by the time she'd spoken her third sentence, I had fallen for her."

This is my favorite part—when people tell me how they met and fell in love.

"She gave me her number and said we should we should get together for a writing date, which sounded great to me because she used the word *date*. We met at the LA public library every Saturday morning for a month. Then I finally got up the nerve to ask her to do something *outside* of a library. The next day we met at the beach and that's where I first kissed her."

"Aww." I pull my legs in and snuggle deeper into the seat. I am a nerd.

"But we don't go to the same high school and she's the president of practically every club ever invented, so we only hang out on the weekends. But now there seems to be excuses for those too and I haven't seen her or talked to her in three weeks. We've played phone tag—that's it. So I don't know if that means we're broken up or just really bad at calling at the right time."

The traffic suddenly gets heavy, and he slows down almost to a complete stop. Then he looks over at me, and I'm a puddle of empathy—hearing someone unsure of where their relationship stands is my addiction. "What do you think is going on with her?" he asks.

I unwrap myself and sit up straight to increase blood flow. "Well, it's entirely possible she isn't calling when you'll be around because she knows you'll be around."

"So she's avoiding breaking up with me?"

"She's avoiding something—maybe just that she can't see you every weekend and she doesn't know how to fix it. But there is a short-term solution to this."

"Lay it on me."

"Don't be available at all. Don't return her calls or her texts—nothing."

"But then she'll just give up. Shouldn't I—"

"She won't give up. She'll *wonder*. That's the most addictive drug to a girl...wondering what you're thinking. Wondering where you stand, even if it's just for closure. If you stop returning her calls, I promise, she will call you at the right time."

Adam turns down a narrow alley behind a building—the Blue Sky Bar. The alley is lined with Hummers and Range Rovers and Mercedes, all with drivers waiting inside. A couple of them are gathered around the hood of a limo, smoking cigarettes, playing cards.

He pulls up parallel to a Hummer limo and one of the drivers taps on my window. "Hey, you can't park here."

But I hold up my box of Krispy Kremes, as if this will explain everything. And apparently, it does. "Oh, sorry," he says and steps back from the Jeep.

I look over at Adam, my saucer-like eyes probably giving away that I'm experiencing severe nervousness.

"You'll be fine," he says. "I'll be watching you from here the whole time."

Like I said before, something about him makes me feel safe. So I take a deep breath, open the door and step out—donuts in hand and shoulders back.

The guy who tapped on my window is several feet away, leaning on a black sedan. "You new?"

I nod.

He points to a gray door with an X on it made out of yellow duct tape. "Just knock. Tatiana will help you out," he says.

"Thanks."

I follow his direction and knock on the x-marked door. I glanced back at Adam, and he gives me a reassuring nod.

The gray door clicks open.

A short girl with round Harry Potter-like glasses and severe bangs pops her head out while smacking gum.

"Hi, are you Tatiana?"

She smacks several times before responding. "Got the donuts?"

I attempt to hand the box over to her, but she won't open it wide enough. She narrows her eyes at me. "That last girl sucked. She ate one *and* they were cold." Gum smack.

"Count 'em. They're all there." I shove the box through the opening. "Totally warm, too."

Over her shoulder I see Amber Latham, star of *The Girls of Orange County*. She has a drink in one hand, and her other hand is mounted on the wall to steady herself. "Those my donuts?" She's slurring, like she often does on her show. "Tatiaaaana...tell her she's five or ten or...no..." she counts her fingers. "FIVE minutes late!" Hiccup.

Tatiana lifts the top and counts them out loud then sticks her finger in the last one. "Twelve. And warm." She yanks the box inside and just before she slams the door shut, she says, "But don't be late. Ever."

"You're welcome!" I say to the closed door.

I fall into my seat, and Adam doesn't say a word, just glares at me, waiting for a report. "I think you should tell me why the last girl quit," I say.

"Bethany."

"Why'd she leave?" I'm a little scared to hear this answer.

He fires up the Jeep and backs out of the alley, a concerned look on his face, as if he wants to choose his words wisely. When we're heading down the street, he finally says, "She couldn't handle the people. We have to run errands for some pretty...um..."

Again with the choosing words wisely.

"...particular people. They never want us to be late and heaven forbid you give them something that isn't exactly to their liking."

I fold my hands in my lap and smirk at him. "By "particular," do you mean—"

"Rude."

"I was going to say bitchy, but I also like to swear."

"Where are we headed to next, Miss...wow, I guess I don't have a pet name for you now."

"I'm sure something perfect will come to you. For now, Tori will have to do."

He lets loose with a dimple.

"Where are we headed to next?"

I hold the list up high to catch the headlights of the car behind us. "It says we're supposed to take an egg salad sandwich to Frank near the corner of Beverly and Melrose."

"Extra pickles, right?"

I look it over again. "Yeah, you're right. It says extra pickles. How'd you know?"

"Trust me, the little details are important. Especially to Frank."

"You've done errands for him before?"

"All the time." He takes a sharp right turn.

"Where are we going anyway?"

"The deli on Glendale has the best egg salad sandwiches. They're open late." Another quick right. Lizzie was right—he knows this town like nobody's business.

"Also," I jab my finger at the list Lizzie gave me. "It says here that we're meeting him on Melrose."

He gives a little shrug. "Yeah?"

"Well, I met a celebrity assistant in line at the Krispy-Kreme and she said to never be on Melrose after midnight. Is that true?"

He laughs. "Don't worry about it. We'll never be over there that late anyway. Is there anyone in the lane next to me?" He cranes his neck, trying to get a better view. "My top is blocking my view."

The top I *made* him put on. I lean my head out and yell back, "Clear!"

We safely merge into the right lane. I have no idea where we are, it looks like a residential area. "Why don't we just take the highway?"

"Sometimes it's faster. But not right now. Diana Ross's come-back tour is at the Hollywood Bowl tonight. It lets out at 10:30 and there's no way cars are moving northbound for at least an hour."

"You know how to get *everywhere*, don't you? Are you some kind of traffic-predicting prodigy?"

He doesn't respond, just keeps laser-focused on the traffic ahead. We're now in a business area with lots of little shops around. But within moments we come to a complete halt—a total traffic jam.

"Oh, no. That girl in the Krispy-Kreme also told me to never be late."

He rubs at his temples. Then after a moment of being in deep thought, he yanks the car into a parking lot and turns around. "Forget it. Change of plans."

CHAPTER THIRTEEN

His change of plans involves a neighborhood a couple of blocks off Sunset Boulevard. Quaint cottage houses are lovingly wrapped by tiny lawns that are meticulously manicured and filled with blooming flowers and fruit trees. We come to a stop in front of a light gray house with a purple door.

"Why are we here?" I notice the gorgeous vine draped over the white picket fence. No joke—it's a white picket fence, as if we are in a fictional neighborhood.

"Janine, my sister—she lives here. There's no time to sit in that traffic and she can make the most amazing egg salad sandwiches. You'll see."

I follow him up the cobblestone path lit by hummingbird lanterns. "Is your sister going to be cool with making us an egg salad sandwich at 10:30 at night?" I ask to the back of his head.

He pulls on the doorknocker—a wooden woodpecker that pecks at the door when you tug on its feather tail. "She won't mind."

There is a large amount of certainty in his answer. I'm curious as to how this will go. And I have to admit: I am strangely excited to witness the scene that's about to happen. Adam is showing up at his sister's unannounced and asking her to drop everything, or wake up, and make a sandwich. I just love family dynamics. When you're an only child, observing people interact—especially siblings—is beyond fascinating. I'm more excited than I really should be. My dorky grin is back.

Janine opens the door; she's wearing a pink and black zebra-striped housecoat with jeweled flip-flops and her short pixie hair is dyed platinum blond. I'm guessing she's a few years older than him, probably in her early twenties.

"Bubs! What are you doing here, guy?" She throws her arms around him.

He hugs her tight then steps back and gives her a warm smile, like slippers-next-to-the-fire warm. "I need your help—it's for work," he says.

"Whatever you need," She extends her hand out to me. "I'm Janine."

"Tori."

She gives my hand a quick squeeze and then holds it for a moment, not in a weird way really, just more of an acknowledgment of your presence type of squeeze. It's kind of nice actually.

Adam is now standing at her fireplace. "We need an egg salad sandwich," he says as he straightens some miniature teacups on her mantle. "Extra pickles."

"Sure thing." Janine looks back and forth between me and Adam. "And how do you two know—"

"She's the new girl they hired," he quickly answers. "Tonight's her first night."

"They had to hire someone new already?" She turns on a lamp and a warm glow fills the room.

Adam has moved on to straightening an Audrey Hepburn picture over her faux fireplace—as if this were some routine for him. "This job's not easy. It's not for everyone."

Janine turns to me. "You must be a pretty daring chick."

I'm not very sure what I'm being so daring about. Running errands at night? Maybe that is sort of dangerous, but I've spent so much time doing things for myself, it doesn't occur to me that I need to be *anything*. I shrug. "I just needed a job."

Janine motions for us to follow her. "Come on into the kitchen. I've got some boiled eggs. This'll only take a few minutes."

Her kitchen is decked out in all '50s vintage furnishings. Butter cream-colored walls. Red appliances. Black and white checkered floor. Spinning soda-fountain bar stools. It's basically the kitchen of my dreams. Betty Boop would approve.

"Um, I don't know you yet, Janine, but you might be my hero." I walk around gawking at every perfect detail.

She pulls the eggs and mayonnaise out of her refrigerator and sets them on the counter. "Bubs helped me shop for most of this stuff at the Santa Monica flea market."

Just as she says this, Adam zips his jacket up as high as it Will go, and pulls his hood over his head. My best guess is he's trying to hide the fact that he's blushing. He sticks his face out momentarily to say, "Janine, don't let her think she can start calling me Bubs. We haven't established nicknames yet."

"Fine." She clears her throat. "Sir Adam Westcott is quite a remarkable thrift store shopper."

I smirk at him. "Sir Adam...now *that's* a pet name." But before he can sink any farther inside his hoodie, I turn to Janine and change the subject. No need to embarrass him any more. "Can I help you with the sandwich?"

"Nah, sweetheart. You guys help yourself to a snack though."

It dawns on me that their relationship is equal parts wonderful and odd. Janine doesn't act "big sisterly"—more like a mother. But it's nice that the vibe between them is so warm. And safe. They're Easy Bake Oven easy.

Whereas, the brief conversations I've had with my mom lately are difficult and require way too much effort. We are a soufflé.

Adam takes a seat on a stool and spins to face the counter, and I slide onto the stool next to him. He sticks his hands in a cherry-decorated porcelain jar, pulls out two oatmeal cookies, and places each one on a paper towel. One of them he starts to munch on, and the other he slides over to me without asking if I wanted one and without even looking at me.

We both munch quietly while Janine smashes eggs in a bowl and tells me about her job—which is a question I haven't asked but she seems to want to answer it.

"I work as an Obscurely-Themed Party Planner," she says.

Clearly, she is the definition of Los Angeles.

And the details do not disappoint. She explains how she hunts around the city in thrift shops and vintage stores to find one-of-a-kind party decorations, which is why her house is decked out so cute: leftover party decorations. Apparently all her clients only want parties that are unlike any other party. A James Dean theme. A Hello Kitty-with-devil-horns theme. Or one party she said she planned that was completely based on that old photograph of the sailor kissing a nurse in Times Square in the '40s. Everyone dressed up in sailor and nurses outfits and there was lots of kissing.

This is her *job*.

Thus sealing the deal on her being my hero.

"Voila!" she says. "One egg salad sandwich with extra pickles." She even wraps the sandwich in tissue paper that's decorated with drawings of cherries and pushes it into Adam's hand. "Better get going."

She leads us to the front door and the two of them hug. "Good luck out there," she says to me and shakes my hand. As he briskly walks down the path toward his Jeep, Adam turns back and says, "I'll call you later."

"No matter how late!" She yells out to him.

I start to head out to the car where Adam has already settled into his seat, but I want to linger on this hummingbird-lit pathway, because I am fascinated. And not just slightly...*profoundly*.

I guess I was under the impression that Shannon and Taylor were the only healthy brother/sister relationship in existence. But these two...they're almost too good to be true.

I hurry back to the Jeep, but before he pulls away, he unwraps the sandwich and pulls out a plain paper bag tucked behind his seat.

"Why are you stuffing the sandwich in a paper bag?"

"Trust me. This Frank guy—he isn't the kind of guy who wants his sandwich wrapped in cherry wrapping paper."

"Ah, gotcha."

We ramble down the street, and silence fills the space between us. I decide it's time to get some answers. The fascinated part of me wants to know more.

"So, your sister. If you don't mind me asking...why does she act more like your mother?"

He grips the steering wheel and stares straight ahead. "Because we don't have one."

CHAPTER FOURTEEN

"We lost her when I was nine," he says. " Pancreatic cancer. It happened quickly. Janine stepped up and pretty much took care of me. Helped me with homework, signed permission slips, made lunches, all that. Mr. Westcott—Dad—is an investment broker and he's rarely home for dinner. That's how Janine got to be a good cook, and why I knew she could make a mean egg salad sandwich."

I clutch my heart. "I'm so sorry. I shouldn't have brought it up." I can't help but hate myself for complaining about my mom—at least I have her.

"It's okay." He taps my knee. His mood seems to brighten, like he has a switch. "No worries, Tori. It was a long time ago, and Janine means the world to me. I learned to pull in the good people in my life as close as possible."

I smile, feeling relieved that I haven't completely weirded-out this moment.

"However," he says, pointing his finger at me like he's about to give a lecture. "You sorta weird me out."

Never mind.

"For someone I only met three hours ago, you sure have a way of getting information out of me. That last girl who took this job? It took days for us to move beyond the weather."

I fiddle with the hem of my skirt. "I just like to get to the heart of things, I guess—I'm kind of the queen of that."

"The Queen of Hearts…maybe *that* should be your pet name."
He laughs at himself, which—again—isn't all that funny, but the
sound of his laugh makes me giggle.

"Just Queen Tori, please." I joke.

"Queen Tori it is."

"Really?"

He glances my way. "It fits."

And so Queen Tori and Sir Adam continued on down the road in their
quest to complete the next demanding task. —it might say in a fairytale
book (a lame one)

It didn't seem fitting with our lovely and proper pet names that
we were on a journey to deliver an egg salad sandwich to some dude
named Frank over on Melrose.

My phone buzzes. Rather the phone that Lizzie and Troy *gave*
me buzzes. "It's a text from Lizzie," I hold up the phone for him
to see. "Frank's on the move. Head to the corner of Camden and
Wilshire."

"No problem. It's just a couple of exits."

When we pull off the highway, he takes us down several back
streets, and we're suddenly in an area with shops where the side-
walks sparkle and colorful pansies are planted at the base of each
and every palm tree that line the street. I guess these fine folks don't
actually want to see soil—that would be *so* Santa Monica.

We pull over on Wilshire and luckily there's an open spot to
park. Adam turns off the ignition and grabs the sandwich bag.
"We're doing this one together." He motions to a man across the
street, dressed in dark clothes, looking fidgety. "I need to introduce
you to Frank—he's not the trusting type."

This Frank guy paces in front of a ballerina slipper store, smoking a cigar. But I'll admit: I'm far more intrigued by the fact that
there is a store in Beverly Hills devoted solely to dance footwear. It's
fantastic. I can't believe even when I was into ballet, my mom never
took me here. So many things I've been missing.

Adam and I cross the street and I soon realize that Frank is not alone. To his left, a man and woman are gripping Evian water bottles and small digital cameras. Big grins are plastered across their faces and they're dressed like they came straight off the pages of a JC Penney catalog—the contempo casual section.

Frank scuffles toward us and holds his hand out, ready for the sandwich. His black hair is slicked back and he's wearing black pants that need to be lengthened an inch, and an un-tucked black button-down shirt. Frank, it appears, is a fan of The Black. His shirt, though nice, is not buttoned as high as girls typically prefer—poking out of the top is a big tuft of chest hair. Eww, just eww.

"Adam, my man." Frank snatches the sandwich from him. "Extra pickles. Right? You didn't let me down?"

"Home made this time. The best." Adam clamps down on his shoulder. "Trust." Then he gestures to me and says, "This is Tori. You'll see her a lot. She's very reliable, but if you don't watch yourself...." He glances over at me. "Soon you'll be telling her all your troubles."

There's something about the way Adam handles this guy that surprises me. Confident. Calm.

Adam pats Frank on the back and winks at me.

I crinkle my nose at him.

And it's as if we've been doing this routine for years.

Looking me over, Frank cocks his head and looks at me like I'm a bad smell. "Desperate for work, eh?" He takes a bite of the sandwich and talks with his mouth full. "Don't worry, we all need work, swee-hah."

Pretty sure he tried to say "sweetheart" but his mouth full of mashed eggs was not allowing for great enunciation.

After a couple of bites, Frank introduces us to the couple with him—Lisa and Bill Jenkins from Dayton, Ohio! They are very interested in a Brangelina sighting, and there'd been a sighting of them at Mr. Chow across the street. They're waiting for them to exit so they can snap a photo.

"I run a Hollywood tour company that specializes in late night celebrity stake-outs," Frank explains to me as he hands over a business card. "Tell everyone you know about me. Everyone—capiche?"

"Sure." I slide the card in my back pocket, then glance at the time, because I really need to get home on time, but I also wouldn't mind witnessing a Brangelina sighting.

Hanging from Frank's shoulder is a large Nikon camera—quite a nice one. He reaches into his pocket and pulls out a small digital card that holds photos, then he slyly hands it over to Adam. "Next time, tell your sister more salt and pepper."

As much as I want to stay for a celebrity sighting, I tap Adam on the shoulder because I need to get back home on time. He nods as if no explanation is needed and we head back to the car.

When we settle in our seats, Adam says, "Remember when that assistant told you not to be on Melrose after midnight?"

"Yeah."

"It's because the streets start to fill with paparazzi waiting for celebrities to come out of restaurants and bars. They memorize the faces of assistants and if they find out you've ever run an errand for one, they'll hound you for information. So we gotta get out of here."

We bomb down the highway and head back over to Lizzie and Troy's house. I roll down the window and breathe in the crisp air. Adam and I don't say anything to each other for a while, just take in the lights and the sound of the loud hum of his engine. It's awesome that we can be quiet like this, not say a word, and yet it feels comfortable. Joel and I would ramble on about anything—he always wanted to keep the conversation going.

And suddenly I realize I've gone the entire night without thinking about Joel. That is, until now. And my mind wanders to all the questions I want answers to: Does he feel bad? Is he thinking about me? Does he miss me?

We get back to the house and this time Troy answers the door, shushing us before he opens it all the way. "Lizzie's asleep." He quickly grabs the photo card from Adam's hands, thanks us, and suddenly we're back out in the driveway. Only this time, he's heading to his Jeep and I'm heading to Margaret Thatcher.

It's a little awkward because we're at that moment where we had a great time together and it's dark and a kiss or something usually happens. But there was no spark between us—when he touched me, I mean. It's like my body knows he has awesome potential as a friend. I hope he feels the same way.

Just before we split into opposite directions, he grabs my arm. "Tori, can I ask you something?"

Oh, no. He's interested. How do I tell him I only want to be friends?

"I have a boyfriend," I blurt out.

He laughs. "Good for you. But that wasn't my question."

My face reddens, but he doesn't seem to care about my face changing colors and instead grabs me by the shoulders and turns me to face him. "I have a favor to ask." He says it with the confidence and calmness he had while handling Frank. "I know we haven't known each other long, but for reasons I can't quite pin down, I'm going to ask a favor of you."

I look up at him, noting that his hands are still clamped down on my shoulder. "Sure, ask it."

He takes a deep breath then finally gets it out: "You told me I should leave Lana alone and not return her calls right away."

I nod.

He reaches into his pocket and pulls out his cell phone, holding it up for me to see. There's one voicemail from Lana. "I know how I get...I'm probably going to call her."

"Don't—"

"And that's where you come in—this favor. Whenever I'm tempted to call her...could I text you instead? Maybe you could be like my sponsor. Talk me down."

I break out with one of my big, dorky grins, even sway a little. "Like I said, we're partners."

He lets out a breath of air like he'd been holding it in this whole time. Poor guy—he's a bit of a wreck. But I need to keep my mind busy and off Joel.

So Adam Westcott is a project I will happily take on.

CHAPTER FIFTEEN

I'm home by 11:15. Mom's still at work, thankfully. I change clothes, wash up, and crawl into my bed. Just before I doze off, my phone buzzes. It's a text from Adam.

Him: *Tempted*

Me: *Think about something else. Krispy Kreme?*

Him: *Shoot! We forgot to stop by there again!*

Me: *Next time*

Him: *Definitely*

A few minutes pass by and I nod off. But the buzz of my phone startles me, as usual.

Him: *Lana just texted me. She wants to talk*

Me: *Don't reply tonight. WAIT. Tomorrow she'll be DYING to talk to you*

Him: *Dang, you're good.*

Me: *Believe me…I've had lots of practice*

Him: *And now I'm dying to know what that means…*

I reach out to put my phone on my nightstand, but he sends one more text.

I'm glad we met. I think I needed a new friend.

And I can't help but smile.

That's when I hear a click. Mom has opened the front door and a sliver of light shines under my door. I pull myself under my comforter so she can't see the glow of my phone. I'm not even sure why I do this—typical moms peek in to see if they're kid is still breathing or something. But my mom never does. Even as safety conscious as she is, she just...doesn't. If Margaret's in the driveway, she assumes I'm sound asleep so she goes about her routine and doesn't bother me. But honestly, I wish she would peek her head in—maybe I wouldn't feel so alone.

I send him one last text.

I think I needed a new friend, too.

CHAPTER SIXTEEN

The morning routine here at the Wright household normally consists of me rushing around to get ready for school—brushing out the tangles in my hair, gnawing on a bagel while getting dressed, frantically looking for accessories, blah, blah, blah, the regular stuff.

While this blur of activity happens, you can find my mom curled up on the sofa in her fuzzy peach robe, cuddling her cup of fresh coffee with such passion it's like she's worshipping it.

We usually don't talk about much other than basic survival items: what we need to get from the grocery store, reminders to take out the trash, relaying phone messages, discussing dates to set up a doctor appointment to get that spot checked out because she's worried I've come down with skin cancer, etc.

Except that today...something's different.

Mom doesn't cuddle up on the couch to worship the coffee gods. Instead she stands in the kitchen and leans against the counter, eyeing my every move.

Oh, no. She found out about the job.

She narrows her eyes and says, "Anything you want to talk about?"

Great. The open-ended question prodding you to fess up to all your sins. I nervously brush at my tangles even harder (ouch!) and stammer out some words. "T-talk about? Me? I uh...ouch!" I put the brush down and move on to shoving my books in my backpack.

She takes a couple of sips of coffee—long, exaggerated sips—that miraculously seem to cause time to slow down. It feels like she's been staring at me for hours. Torture—that's what this is.

Finally, she says, "I was just wondering when you were going to tell me about you and Joel breaking up."

Whew. She wants relationship details. That's refreshing.

"How did you know?"

"The education reporter's daughter goes to Lincoln High. The gossip flies fast." She shifts her weight. "I'm fine with you being out at night with a boyfriend, but if he's not in the picture, I don't want you going places at night by yourself. Even gas stations aren't safe. There was this article in—"

"Mom—don't worry. It might be a temporary thing. Shannon said he was asking about me at Wingers last night. I figure if I stay away from him, he'll realize how much he misses me. He'll come back begging. Then it will be safe for me to leave the house again." I roll my eyes but she doesn't notice.

Instead, she shoots me a wink and says, "Ah...sounds like you've been reading the rules from A Girlfriend's Guide to Heartbreak."

I nod and get back to packing up. "It's one of the better ones. And I especially love rule #8: If he calls, don't answer. Always call back the next day—make him wonder."

She cups my chin in her hand. "My girl's got a good head on her shoulders."

I look up at her and take a deep breath, wanting to hold on to this moment. We rush around each other like gnats, just bumping off each other, hardly ever taking the time to see how the other one is feeling, *really* feeling.

And here's the thing...the thing I haven't told you yet: as much as I wanted my parents to get divorced when I was twelve, now—the Tori who is sixteen—wishes they never had.

It's not that I necessarily want them back together like they were before because the two of them as a married couple was a disaster. So I don't know what the answer is, but I know there's an aching inside of me that I can't seem to fix.

She's obsessed over three things: blogging, watching The Bachelor, and Tori's safety.

None of those things involve Tori's *life*.

But the unselfish part of me is happy she has a "thing." Or several of them. I can relate because it's how I used to feel about ballet. I quit a few months after their split since getting me to practice on time *and* working was wearing her out—something I overheard her say on the phone to Dad when he claimed he couldn't get out there in time to take me to practice because of the traffic in the city. But I had heard enough of their arguments while they were married. I wasn't about to become the reason for their arguments when they divorced.

So I quit.

And even though I don't want to take up ballet again since that was the dream of twelve-year old me, Today Me wishes I also had a "thing." Something to obsess over. Something I can't stop thinking about.

Something other than a boy.

Mom leans against the kitchen counter and changes the subject. "Can you write up a blog post this week? Because if you can't, I'll try to cover yours—"

"I can do it—no problem."

She turns away from me to pour herself another cup of coffee. "Great. I'd love for you to write one about how to avoid being a Rebound Girl."

"But I wrote about that topic a few months ago."

"And it was the most hits I've ever gotten on the blog. But my numbers are starting to dip. I need something to get more exposure and people love that topic." She walks over to the table, sets her cup down, and helps me finish putting my books in my backpack. "Just try to take a fresh take on it. You'll do great."

A fresh take? It took me days of research to come up with my original post. But then I realize I have a new weapon in my arsenal of advice...Adam. Getting a boy's point of view—and not Taylor's this time—is precisely what I need to make this fresh.

"I'll do it." I grab my car keys and head for the door.

I hope this boy is ready to talk.

CHAPTER SEVENTEEN

"You didn't come to Wingers last night because you got a job?" Shannon pops a couple of Advil while she stands at my locker in between classes. "A *job*."

"I need to stay busy."

"Which you can do by checking out people's Instagram photos."

I grabbed her hands to get her attention. "Which I can do by running errands at night for a couple in L.A."

She folds her arms and glares at me. Concerned Face. "What is this job exactly?"

"I have to run errands for this ritzy couple. Last night I delivered warm donuts to the back door of Blue Sky Bar and got sandwiches for a dude who runs celebrity tours."

She's still maintaining Concerned Face.

"They pay $25 an hour," I add.

Her eyes almost pop out. "What? I want that job!"

"I already have a partner.

Except she isn't listening—she's adding numbers. "Wait, wait..." She holds her palm out like a stop sign and looks up at the ceiling. "That's only an hour and a half of work for that pair of DKNY knee-high boots."

"My partner is a guy—Adam. And don't stare up at the ceiling; you'll get asbestos in your eye."

"Or, oh! If you get boots on sale at Zappos that's only forty-five minutes of work!"

"Adam's in the middle of a break-up, so I'm going to help him—"

"Or that sweater we've been eyeing at Anthropologie, or some—whoa. You drive around the city at night with some 'guy?' Is he cute? Maybe that's the reason you're already getting over Joel."

I shake my head. "I'm not over him, I'm just..." I take a deep breath, considering my words carefully. "...I'm playing this right. There's no way I'm going to beg Joel to come back. The best thing I can do is make him think I'm not thinking about him at all. It's the only way to play the game—I have to be patient to get what I want. And it's not like that with this Adam guy. He's kind of dorky and funny. But there's not a spark. Trust me—I put him to the touch test."

"Well, if anyone knows how to play the game, it's you. I, on the other hand, ended up making out with Brent in the parking lot of Wingers last night and now he's not returning my texts again. He is awesome. And by awesome I mean awful. But watch out for the funny ones though." She winks at me. "They sneak up on you and steal your heart."

"Don't worry. My eyes are wide open now."

She loops arms with me and drags me down the hall. "We should make a spread sheet of all the boots you can afford now. You know how much I love charts."

"I already know what I'll do with the money. A pair of boots, yes, and then I'll help my mom..." I look around to make sure no one's listening, this ridiculous secret of mine—writing for my mom's blog. I wish I could just talk about it openly. But Mom is hoping to turn the posts into a book deal someday, her big break. And having a sixteen-year old daughter authoring some of those wouldn't work. But it makes her happy, so I try not to mind. "...I'm thinking I'll help Mom upgrade to a website. Don't you think she'll love that?"

She grins. "That's all the woman talks about—contact pages, home pages, search engines, and you not cutting yourself with a sharp knife." She bumps shoulders with me. "I'm sure she's excited that you're doing this for her."

I bite at my lip. "I haven't told her quite yet."

"You're keeping Nancy Wright—THE Nancy Wright—in the dark?"

"I have to. Otherwise, she'll never let me do this job, not with me having to drive into the city by myself. You know how she gets about L.A."

"The place where evil lurks."

"But once I have enough money to hire a web designer, I'll quit and dazzle her with flash sites and distract her from all these silly details about the job."

Shannon grips her books and turns the corner to head to homeroom. "Let's just hope she doesn't find out about it before you can dazzle her."

"Let's hope."

The rest of the school day goes exactly to plan: no interactions with Joel except for the one brief glance of the back of his head when he darted out of the cafeteria. But to be honest, part of me wanted to chase him down and ask him why he wanted to know if I'd be at Wingers last night. Did he want to talk? Why didn't he call me?

But I resisted—hallelujah!—and made it through the day by obsessing over the details of my blog post for Mom.

By the time I meet up with Adam that night, I'm feeling like I'm heading down the road to recovery. And apparently he is too.

We both arrive at the same time, and when he hops out of his Jeep, I notice that he's wearing a hoodie, but it's a different one and it looks like it's been washed. And the laces on his shoes are totally tied!

"You must be feeling better," I say as we both head up the sidewalk to Lizzie and Troy's front door.

He tilts his head, confused by this. "Better?"

"Your hoodie...it's clean. And look at your shoelaces—they're amazing, all tied and stuff."

He laughs as he stares down at his feet, looking like a proud parent.

"Next thing you know," I add. "You'll be wearing expensive button-down shirts and hair gel."

"Wow, my life is about to get exciting."

We walk up to the front door, Adam presses the doorbell, and as we stand next to each other staring at the door, I say quietly, "Did you call her back?"

"Nope."

"And?"

"And I'm not going to call her till tomorrow. You told me to wait a day, but I'm going to wait two."

A big smile fills my face. "You've made me proud, son."

Lizzie opens the door, looking happy to see us. "You're both here. And on time. I love it!" She grabs an envelope from a table in the foyer and hands it over along with our list of errands. "Follow the instructions precisely. Be safe and I'll see you later tonight."

When we settle in Adam's Jeep, I notice there's only one errand on the list. "This says we're supposed to drop off these Book of Mormon tickets to someone named Lanie at the Cobra Lounge."

He wrinkles his forehead. "They must have a lot of faith in you—giving you a big assignment right away."

I'm not sure what he's talking about because it sounds pretty easy to me. I just have to hand over an envelope. "I don't get it—why is this such a big assignment?"

"It's an over-21 club. And the bouncer there is impossible to deal with. It's hard to convince that guy of *anything*."

I shrug. "I'll give it my best shot."

He navigates back streets effortlessly, and I can't help but ask. "How do you know this town so well? Even the traffic patterns. It's like your superpower is Extreme Traffic Navigation."

"Here we go again—you finding out about all the details of my life sooner than I ever imagined." We pull to a stoplight and he faces me. "Figuring people out seems to be *your* superpower. What is *that* about?"

"The light's green."

We continue down the road not saying anything, because we are—it appears—at a stalemate. He wants to know why I am the way I am, and I want to know why he's the way *he* is. Curiosity gets me so I decide to give in. "I'll tell you about my superpower if you tell me about yours."

"This is starting to sound like something two kindergarteners would say—only without mentioning 'private parts.'"

I smirk at him. "There will be no showing of private parts; we're not that kind of friends. But I will tell you the truth about why I'm good at figuring out people."

He nods slowly. "Spill it."

Taking a deep breath in, I close my eyes briefly and realize that what I'm about to say is only known by my mother and Shannon. The fact that I'm going to share it with him baffles me a little. But it also feels right. "I secretly write a weekly post on my mom's blog. It's for divorced women and anyone going through a break-up. It's called I'M NOT DEAD, I'M DIVORCED."

"That's *you*?"

"You know about it?!"

He laughs. "Naw, just kidding."

I give him a quick punch on the arm. His humor is a little off and really displays his dorky side—but it makes him sort of endearing.

"I filled in for my mom once when she was sick. So I read relationship self-help books on a regular basis. Probably on an obsessive basis, actually. So I can spot a jerk from miles away, and I know exactly how to not end up the rebound girl."

"No offense," he says. "But all that sounds a little complicated. Why don't you just play on a soccer team and get hooked on drugs? It'd probably be easier."

I narrow my eyes at him. "Don't you ever put any thought into whether a girl is genuine? Study her gestures? Figure her out so you don't get your heart trampled?"

He shrugs. "Nope."

"Maybe you should do more of it."

"Maybe you should do less of it."

We both glance at each other and simultaneously break out into laughter. I don't even know why—other than the obvious fact that we do not see eye-to-eye on this subject. Something tells me I shouldn't even *try* to change his mind.

I pull myself together and place my hands in my lap. "Now. Your turn...why is getting around traffic your superpower?"

"I'm direction savvy, this is true." Then his face gets paler and the wrinkle on his forehead is back. "My dad—that man we call Mr. Westcott—he works six days a week, sometimes seven if the weather won't allow for golf meetings. It seems like the only time I see him is when we're in the car driving somewhere. Sometimes I will...and I can't believe I'm about to tell you this...but I pray for heavy traffic. That way I can use the app on my phone and navigate us around it and find the shortest route. He thinks I'm a genius, and it seems to be the only way I can get a compliment from Mr. Westcott." He grips the steering wheel tighter and shakes his head. "All that sounded so stupid."

"No, I get it. I cross paths with my mom so rarely that she hardly has time to give me a compliment."

His Jeep comes to a halt. "This is where you get out."

"What?"

"The Cobra Lounge. We're here."

Oh, that's right. We actually have a job to do.

"It's impossible to get in there." He cuts his eyes over at me and smirks. "You'd better bring your A-game."

CHAPTER EIGHTEEN

There's a line, a long one. I'm mesmerized by all the ladies in sky-high heels and metallic dresses short enough to be a blouse.

Adam peers through the windshield at the ever-growing line. His knees bounce nervously. "We gotta figure out a way to get you in there."

"So I'm doing this one solo?" I wince.

"The bouncer might be lenient with a pretty girl but not with some lanky guy in a hoodie."

The thought of him calling me pretty makes me blush a little. And all of a sudden, this moment—me blushing over something a guy says to me—makes me think of Joel. I haven't thought about him all day, but now here I am curious again. Why *did* Joel want to know if I was coming to Wingers?

But I shake this thought off because there's work to be done, and I need to concentrate on how to get myself into this club. I lean forward to get a better view of the bouncer. Broad shoulders, tight T-shirt, big biceps, buzz-cut, Nike cross-trainers.

I let out a satisfied sigh. Because I know *exactly* how to get in there.

Just before I jump out, I snatch the envelope with the theater tickets and turn to Adam. "Don't worry. I'll get in."

"We can always tell Lizzie we can't do this one. I hear it gets kind of wild in there—"

"Give me ten...I got this."

He crosses his arms and raises a brow. "Oh you *do*? Well then, let the games begin." Adam reaches across and yanks on the passenger door, closing it shut. I can hear him, muffled through the glass. "Good luck."

Luck. What I'm about to do has nothing to do with luck. Just sheer guts. I hope I have enough.

There is no way I'm going to wait in that long line, especially since it now snakes around the street corner. So I stand next to a group of giggling ladies (girls, actually—they don't look much older than me) who are only a few spots away from the bouncer. Then, whoops! I pretend to drop my lipgloss on the ground. As I pick it up, I nonchalantly step closer and manage to be absorbed by the line. No one even notices. I glance back at Adam parked down the street, and he gives me a double thumbs-up.

So far, so good.

The girls in front of me are fidgety and keep whispering to each other. When it's their turn, I overhear one of them explaining that their friend is inside and their I.D.'s are in her purse so if they could just go find her they *prooooooomise* they'll come right back!

Not surprisingly, the bouncer doesn't buy it, sends them away, and suddenly I am standing in front of him, face-to-face.

"I.D?" He holds out his ogre-sized hand to me.

"Sure." I say it in a tone as if I'm already bored with this conversation.

I reach into my purse, pretending to look for my wallet. "Where is it?" I pull out the envelope holding the theater tickets. "Well, at least I haven't lost these Lakers tickets."

And just as I had suspected—based on the size of his biceps and his choice in shoe wear—the bouncer gets a sparkle in his eye. "Are those play-off tickets?"

I have no idea if it's play-off season. "Yep." I don't look up and keep digging in my purse. "Darn. My driver has my wallet in the Town Car. I'm going to call him." I pull out my cell and hold my hand up to the people behind me. "Sorry to hold all of you up. He's probably only a few streets away."

The line groans and people throw their hands in the air.

I pretend to dial, pause, shift my weight, roll my eyes. "He's not answering." Another collective groan comes from the line. Luckily, the bouncer is still interested in the contents of my hand.

"How'd you get those tickets? They're impossible to find."

"These?" I wave them around like they're grocery receipts, stalling for time until I come up with a whopper of an excuse. "My guy is obsessed. Always center court. But Leo says this one is important so I need to make sure I get these to him. That's why I'm here, to give these to Leo. Did you see him go in yet?"

"Leo. *DiCaprio?*"

Wow, I'm really going for it here. I nod slightly, as if it's up to interpretation whether I'm *actually* nodding. I lower my voice and say, "Don't tell him I was waving these tickets around. He'd just die."

More impatient groans and sighs come from the people behind me—time to seal the deal before these party-goers kick me to the curb. "Leo probably used the private entrance. Maybe I should..." I motion to the back of the club, as if *I* should be using that entrance. Truthfully, I have no idea if there even *is* such a private entrance, but faking it with confidence is all I have right now.

Fortunately, bouncers love to be the decision-maker—good or bad—and in this case the decision is luckily good. "Just go in." He waves me on. "Enjoy yourself. And don't lose those tickets."

With a dinky wave to him, I enter the bar, relieved and rather proud of myself. I'm in. I'm here. I'm actually good at this job!

My eyes drift up and I take in my surroundings. This club. Wow. I'm floored by the decadence. Blood red walls and uncomfortable-but-hip couches surround tables full of candles, while ornate black iron chandeliers hang from the ceiling. Waiters and waitresses dance through the room with trays held high full of brightly colored cocktails. It feels like being immersed in dangerously rich red velvet cake, but with more alcohol.

Gorgeously dressed people fill the room, and I turn and twist my way through the crowd, attempting to approach the bar. I study the bartenders trying to figure out which one is a girl named Lanie, except that is clearly the problem…they are all guys. (Sidenote: and also very hot.) (Additional sidenote: I love my job!)

So I tap the shoulder of a waitress hurrying by with a tray of empty drink glasses. "Hi, I'm trying to find Lanie."

She tilts her head, looking confused. "Lanie? Is that a type of drink? How about a dirty Martini, you'll like that—" She jams a napkin in my hand.

"No, Lanie, the *bartender*." I say it louder this time and snag an empty glass just before it falls off her tray because she seems to be uninformed about space requirement, too.

"Don't know her." She spins away from me, and someone else grabs a glass that falls off her tray as she whisks through the crowd.

I ask a couple of more waiters but *no one* has heard of Lanie. I keep looking and asking, and next thing I know, fifteen minutes have gone by. What am I going to do? Surely there is someone in here who can help me. I pull my cell out to call Adam.

But before I can finish dialing, I feel a hand on my waist. From behind, a guy whispers into my ear, "You need a dance partner."

I whirl around to find a guy smiling at me—a complete stranger—swaying, sweaty, and completely drunk. He's wearing a woven rope necklace, making an *attempt* at bohemian, but it's not a good one because I can tell the fabric has hardly been worn so it was newly purchased—*just for tonight!*—I'm sure. Gross.

I start scanning the room. "No. I'm looking for someone, thanks."

But Sweaty Guy ignores my answer and starts moving his hips around without any touch of rhythm, and he doesn't seem to be embarrassed, even though he *should*. "Come on, gorgeous." He puts his hand on my hip.

All right, that's it. This jerk deserves a swift kick in a vulnerable part. My foot wiggles with excitement, but I just can't go through with it. This isn't a place where I should draw attention to myself.

The smell of stale alcohol on his breath makes me gag, so I firmly slide his hand off my hip and start to turn away. Except he puts his hand back on and grips a little tighter.

I then feel a hand on the small of my back. Oh, please...not another drunk guy. I whip around. "What the—"

But it's Adam.

"Back. Off." Adam practically growls at Sweaty Guy. I'm glad he's here, but getting into a bar brawl would not be ideal at this moment.

"She came on to *me*, bro." Sweaty Guy grins like a jerk. "But I'll dance with her..." He takes a swig of his drink and some of it dribbles out of his mouth and lands on his shirt. He starts to reach out for my hip again. And that's when Adam steps in between us.

"Hey, scumbag. Don't touch her like that."

"Just bein' friendly, bro."

"Back. OFF," Adam says through clenched teeth. He then turns around and whispers to me, "If he doesn't leave, I swear I'll deck this guy."

This is nice and all, but I've seen far too many episodes of Gossip Girl to know that this will only lead to some big scene and we'll be the ones who end up getting kicked out.

Sweaty Guy sees Adam turn away and decides this is his opportunity to make his move. "Les dance, girl!" But before he can get any closer to me, I jam the heel of my boot on the top of his foot.

Fortunately, Adam lets me balance my hand on his shoulder while I do it. "I'm going to dance all right..." I say with a smirk. "...but you aren't." And I press my heel in a little deeper.

Sweaty Guy bends over, groaning in pain. Adam looks like he's shocked, but he also has a satisfied smile on his face. "Come on!" He grabs my arm and we rush back through the crowd, zig-zagging in between couples and we finally spot an opening next to a wall where we stop to catch our breath. My face is flushed with warmth and my toes wiggle with excitement. "Ohmygosh...that felt great!"

Adam shakes his head, laughing at this. "You certainly didn't need my help."

I wave him off like it's no big deal, like I do this all the time (this is my first time). "Heels are sometimes a girl's only weapon. But you have to go for their toes or shins or man-parts. It's the only way a jerk will listen." (p. 59 of Girlfriends Guide to Dating)

Adam lifts a brow. "I guess that's a good reminder for me to never be a jerk."

"Consider it my public service announcement."

As my head starts to clear, it dawns on me that Adam is here, in this club—just a lanky guy with a hoodie. "How did you get in here?" I poke him on the shoulder. "And why did you come?"

"I double-checked the paper. Lizzie's handwriting is pretty bad. It didn't say Lanie, it said Lance. He's one of their top informants. Whatever Lance wants, Lizzie and Troy make sure he gets it... immediately."

The uncoordinated waitress with the tray of glasses walks by again, and I tap her shoulder. "It's Lance I'm looking for. Which one is he?"

"Oh, Lance! Behind the bar, at the end. Red head, dimples, Matt Damon jaw line." She then flutters away, sloshing drinks around as she moves on.

Quickly studying the bartenders, I spot Lance immediately. That jaw.

"There's our guy." I turn to Adam before I head over there. "But wait. How did you get past the bouncer?"

He shrugs, but looks as if he's pretty proud of himself. "When this jacket's zipped up it pretty much looks like a driver's uniform."

"But how'd you get past the door?"

"I told him my client left her epi-pen in the limo and she was severely allergic to citrus. If she got too close to a pomegranate martini her throat would swell shut."

"Throat swelling. Nice touch. You may even be better than *me*."

"Except then he asked me to show him the epi-pen."

"And?"

"Who knew all I'd have to do was show him a regular ballpoint." Adam holds the pen up and clicks the end letting the pen slide out. He lifts my arm and carefully writes on the back of my hand: *hi*

It tickles my skin.

I flick my eyes up to meet his. "Hi," I say. Then we let our hands drop.

He clears his throat as he scans the room. "We'd better get those tickets to Lance. That meathead bouncer is at the entrance looking around. Maybe for us."

Without thinking, I grab his hand and pull him along as we weave in and out of partygoers, moving through wafts of what I determine to be at least four different smells of designer men's cologne. One was Abercrombie & Fitch—*way* too much of it and I gag a little.

But the thick cologne forces me to move even quicker, and we slide right up to the bar in front of the red head with the Matt Damon jawline.

I slap the envelope on the counter. "I have tickets for you. Book of Mormon—orchestra section."

"Yes!" He gives a fist pump.

Adam leans into me and says in a low voice, "Don't look now, but there are two bouncers by the door—they're studying a ballpoint pen and looking around the room."

"You two want a drink?" The bartender asks as he snatches the envelope.

Adam grabs my hand and pulls me away from the bar. "No, thanks!" I yell back.

"Good luck with the Sienna Hart thing!" The bartender calls out as we disappear into the crowd.

Sienna Hart. *My* Sienna Hart? What is he talking about?

Adam tugs on me and we duck behind a group of girls, all wearing almost the *exact* same outfit. They are pretty much the reason that quote "birds of a feather" was created. We follow behind them, trying to blend in, until they suddenly stop. It's some sort of emergency—one of the girl's feather hair extensions has gotten stuck in another girl's earring. Such dangerous accessories!

We spot a well-dressed man pulling out his keys. So we stick close to him with our hands still gripped together, and Adam and I manage to dart out the exit without the bouncers spotting us.

But when we spill out onto the sidewalk, we stop just short of two large feet planted on the cement and in our way. My eyes drift up to see a large policeman in front of us.

"Excuse me," the cop says.

Oh, no. Is he going to bust us for being under age? I didn't take the drink the bartender offered. I shouldn't be arrested—I should be congratulated.

"You dropped your pen." The cop picks it up off the sidewalk and hands it back to Adam.

A big smile fills his face. "Thank you, sir. Have a fabulous evening."

And we take off. For two blocks Adam and I run, laughing the whole way. We finally slow up when we glance back and realize we're free. We did it.

Still laughing a little, we catch our breath with our hands on our knees. "You told a cop to have a fabulous evening."

"And you stomped on that guy's foot with your boot. That was so redneck. And awesome!"

We both break into hysterics again.

It feels good to laugh this hard.

I take a moment to catch my breath and look around. Then I realize…this street, the building up ahead…I know this place! We're only a few blocks from my dad's loft. And up the stairs in the building adjacent to us, is my spot.

My favorite spot.

I grab Adam's arm and drag him along with me. "Come on. I want to show you something."

Los Angeles County Juvenile Detention Intake Report

Name: Tori Wright   Age at booking: 16
Eyes: HAZ   Hair: BRN
Height: 5'5"   Weight: 124
Sex: F   Charges: Infraction 240; 594
Charging Officer: Ortega
Court date/time: To be determined

Intake Notes:
Suspect states she never imagined things would turn in such a drastic way with Adam—all right there in a public bathroom.
Suspect is very fidgety.

Requests ice for her water.

CHAPTER NINETEEN

"Where are you taking me? My Jeep is back there—" He tries to squirm out of my grip, but he doesn't try hard enough. I clamp down tighter and drag him across the street, like he's a toddler.

We step up to the sidewalk and I spin around to face him. "I want to show you my spot. I only know a few places in this city, but this one is my favorite."

He surveys our surroundings. "The 24-hour Laundromat? You watch clothes on spin cycle?"

"Not there." I whirl him around to face the tall building next to it and point. "Up there."

He scratches his ear. "Your favorite spot in the city is in the L.A. County Water & Public Utilities building. That's not weird."

"You'll see." I take off up the empty stairwell attached to the outside of the building. There is a small fluorescent light on each floor, giving us some visibility, but not much.

Adam follows behind me closely, but by the time we get to the second floor he stops.

"Hold up." He's slightly out of breath. "Are we climbing all the way to the top?"

"Not all the way." I glance down at his feet. "But you're going to have to tie that shoe. That broken heart uniform won't cut it here."

He bends over to tie his shoe and tilts his head up at me. "There. I'm ready to take on the world."

"Good. But right now you need to take on these stairs—we're running the next four flights."

"What?!"

I don't answer. I take off up the stairs in an all-out sprint. To me, it's just more fun to haul it.

On each floor there's a window facing the street, but only the even ones for some reason. I reach the sixth floor, slightly breathless, but completely energized.

This window on the sixth floor is something I discovered one night when Taylor tried to drag me to the roof for a spectacular city view—but I never made it there because it was *this* window that ended up having the view I loved most...a view of the sixth floor across the street. Not so glamorous sounding, I know. But stick with me—I have my reasons.

Without warning, Adam rounds the corner, except he doesn't realize I've stopped. He runs right into me. I'm not talking *bumped* into me. He RUNS INTO ME.

Not wanting to *completely* plow me over, he holds his hands out to stop himself. So picture this: I'm facing him and his hands have *no* control over where they land. Yep, it happens: one hand lands on my ribcage and the other cops a feel.

"Dude!" I yelp.

"Sorry. I'm sorry!" he fumbles with my shirt, trying to straighten it out, then quickly stuffs his hands in his pockets. "Sorry."

My face flushes and I stand there in silence, my mouth gaping—shocked that we just got to second base without ever rounding first.

But at least I can say, without a doubt, that we are just friends. His unsolicited breast smoosh didn't send *any* electrical charge through me at all. In fact, I may be lightly bruised. And I suddenly find all of this incredibly funny. I clutch my chest and let out a hearty laugh.

His face fills with relief. "Whew, I'm glad you're not mad. I don't normally go straight for the breast with my other friends. Consider yourself lucky, I guess."

I punch him lightly on the shoulder. One of those awkward buddy-punches like we're fourth graders. Sometimes I'm not super-graceful.

So I point out the window to move on to the real reason why we're here. "Look across the street."

The view is of the window in the building directly across from us. And only at night—when it's lit from inside—can you see him.

Adam squints, focusing on the man in the window. "I just see a guy sitting at a table with a microphone, wearing headphones."

"Not *any* guy. That's Jo-Jo Lopez." I scramble around in my purse and pull out my phone. Luckily SLY 107.5 broadcasts live over the internet. "This spot right here is the only place in the city where you can listen to him *and* watch him at the same time."

I turn the volume up and we watch Jo-Jo, his hands flailing, as he rambles on about ridiculous celebrity gossip. But Jo-Jo is different from the other celebrity gossipers—his angle is to share the gossip, but then question its source, analyze it, break it down and determine whether it's real or not. He makes a prediction, then later goes back to see if he was right. That rumor about Jennifer Aniston being pregnant? It was Jo-Jo who correctly guessed it was a burrito she had for lunch. Crazily, the guy is right 9 times out of 10.

Adam folds his arms, looking like he's solved a mystery. "So *this* is where the it is. My dad owns stock in the radio station—he's always trying to get me to work there. Along with every other company he owns stock in."

"Why'd your dad let you work for Lizzie and Troy?"

"They met once at a Vanity Fair Oscar party. He owns stock in the magazine, too." He rolls his eyes. "So Lizzie told him about her photography business and Dad feels that if I'm not pounding out the great American novel, then I should be working. So next thing I know, I'm working for them as a 'photographer's assistant.' But he has no idea what I really do." He shoots me a sneaky grin. "Now you. You haven't told me why *you* took the job."

Aw, man. This subject makes me queasy. "Just needed a job. No reason."

He takes a step closer. "Yes. There is."

I bite at my lip as I focus on his eyes. From his intense gaze, I can tell he's not going to let me squirm away from this question. One deep breath and I lay it on him. "My boyfriend, Joel, broke up with me a couple of days ago. I've done enough blog research to know the best way to cope with a heartbreak is to stay busy. And also stay away from dairy." I fold my arms and look out the window. "If he thinks I've moved on, then without a doubt, he'll—"

"Want you back," he finishes my sentence. But for some reason, hearing the words come from his mouth sounds...strange.

I shrug and keep focused on Jo-Jo.

Adam steps up next to me bumps shoulders with me. "You come here to *watch* a radio announcer?"

"It's a one-man show in there—an art form," I explain. "The guy's a genius."

The thing is, I've been obsessed over radio DJs ever since I was little. I would hold a pretend microphone to introduce the world's next biggest pop star sensation, also known as my best friend Shannon. She'd dance around my living room, do some cartwheels, then sing a Hannah Montana song out-of-tune. In between I'd make up fake commercials because we needed sponsors—somebody had to pay for this show! But I could never do it as well as Jo-Jo Lopez. In my eyes, he was a legend.

Holding my phone out, I turn the volume up as high as it will go. Jo-Jo is now on a tirade about Sienna Hart.

SIENNA HART!

Jo-Jo's hands fly around wildly. Even more than usual. "Her rep says she took some time off because of exhaustion?" he says in his brilliant, raspy voice. "No, I'll tell you *exactly* what it was. Jake Jeffers dumped her for his new co-star on Vampire School 3. Clearly the girl went on a depression-drinking binge. Do the math. Mark my words, this one will be true, folks."

No, surely not. I'd heard she went to a resort to relax, but I had no idea Jake Jeffers broke up with her—I didn't see that coming at all. And I'm the expert on this stuff! Or I used to be. This sudden break-up with Joel has me guessing whether I still have the touch.

Adam rubs his temples. "Let me get this straight. You love coming here because radio is...an *art form?*"

I nod with strange amounts of pep. "And you can take it with you—everywhere. It's like having a personal soundtrack for your life. All your daily movements...set to music. And gossip. Such a trip, right?"

He turns to face me—the light is dim, but I can see a glint in his eye. "If anyone's a trip, it's you, Tori."

This causes a big, stupid grin to fill my face.

Then his phone buzzes. He pulls it out from his pocket. It's a text.

I search his face as he reads it. He looks happy. No...shocked. Wait, frustration? Shoot, I don't know. "Who's it from?"

"Lana. She wants to see me." His voice softens. "Now."

I take a deep breath, relieved that my advice worked for him. All he had to do was stay away, and she came running. Maybe I *do* still have the touch.

But to be honest, on top of that relief is a dash of resentment. Partly because Lana is pulling him away from me at this moment when I'm trying to explain to him why this spot means so much to me. And partly—if not mostly—because I'm not the one getting a text from my ex wanting to see me. Joel hasn't tried to get hold of me for two whole days.

"That's great," I say through slightly (very) clenched teeth. "This is just what you wanted."

"Yeah, but she wants to meet at Gordon's Coffee Shop."

"What's wrong with that?"

"I'll tell you along the way." He takes me by the elbow and pulls me back down the stairs. "You're coming with me."

CHAPTER TWENTY

Gordon's Coffee Shop is only a few minutes away. His knees bounce nervously and sweat beads appear on his forehead. This boy is in serious need of a pep talk.

"Take some deep breaths. Roll your shoulders. Get it together—you can do this."

He nods, breathes, rolls and makes an attempt to get it together. We pull into the parking lot and he searches for her car. "She's not here yet."

"Good. This gives you time for you to explain why you're so freaked out. What's so special about this place?"

He cuts the engine and turns to me, his face softly lit by the warm glow coming from inside the coffee shop. "This is where we went on our first date. And second. And third. The majority of them, actually."

I glance inside the window and notice almost all of the people are sipping coffee while typing away on their computers. No talking, just writing. I don't see the appeal, quite honestly. "Why did you come here?"

"I was writing a novel, but I was stuck. That's how I met Lana at that writer's conference. She is brilliant and prolific, already has a novel submitted to agents. But I couldn't make it past the first chapter of mine. I wrote and re-wrote, but nothing was working."

"So you want to be a writer. She thought she could help you find your groove, and you met here to write together. Correct?"

He nods.

"It's symbolic. So it makes perfect sense for her to ask you to meet her here. What's the problem?"

"I never told her how much I freaking hate this place. Coming here with her, watching her pound out page after page, and then leaving without a single word added to mine...it was crushing. Lana thought she could cure my writer's block. But all I got was a large latte bill."

"If you love doing it, why are you stuck?"

He presses his head hard against the seat. "I used to fill notebook after notebook years ago, but once I mentioned the idea of writing a novel, it was all my dad could talk about. 'How's the novel coming? When can I send it on to people? I know this agent...' His pressure was non-stop." He clenches his jaw. "The problem is this city—there are too many freaking prodigies in this town, and they all seem to have parents who know my dad so he sees all these teenagers who own their own business or play classical cello or write screenplays on spec for Ron Howard. It's like he expects me to have the great American novel penned before graduation. That's the other reason I learned so much about streets and traffic in L.A....it gave us something else to talk about other than my writing." He shakes his head. "That's weird isn't it? Most guys probably go through this crap with their dads over baseball or soccer or whatever. Not me— my dad just wants to know about daily word count."

I lean over and catch his eye. "Do *you* want to write a novel?"

"I want to write...something. And maybe someday I'll get inspired and start putting some words down. And if I do, I'll come here and sit at that front table and pound out the pages." He taps my knee. "So don't disturb me, got it?"

I laugh. "Got it."

Headlights blind us briefly, and a car pulls in two spots away. "There she is," he says.

Looking over, I see a girl with long, dark hair sitting in a yellow Volkswagen Beetle, brand new. Unbelievable. We have the *same exact car*. Except for the thirty-five year age difference. And Margaret's character-defining rust spots.

Adam catches her eye, and they wave at each other. She steps out of the car and onto the sidewalk, waiting for him. Lana glances back and forth between Adam and me, probably wondering who the hell I am.

She's wearing dark-rimmed hipster eyeglasses practically identical to his, a tight-fitting flannel shirt, tiny cut-off jean shorts, and a scowl on her face. But I have to be honest here...she's totally gorgeous. The smartest girl in the class wearing Daisy Dukes—a lethal combination.

Adam pushes his head back into the headrest again, looking paralyzed. He whispers, "What do I say to her?" He's asking me the question, but his eyes are on her.

For some reason, my typical pieces of advice are just...gone. No tip, no trick—nothing. This girl isn't just a name anymore, but a living, breathing person and she's standing in front of us, glaring at Adam as he hesitates to go to her. She may have been toying with him earlier, but I can tell from the determined look on her face, she is ready to talk. "Go tell her how you feel," I say. "Be honest."

He looks at me, crinkling his forehead. "Really? I thought you'd have some trick or list of do's and don'ts. A line graph? Pie chart? Anything?!"

I shrug. "At some point you just have to say what you're thinking."

"Fine. But this better work." He hops out of the Jeep and slams the door shut, all while keeping his eyes on Lana. It's pretty obvious how he feels. He may not have to say anything at all.

But I'm certainly not going to sit here in this stuffy car while he does...whatever he's about to do. So I quietly roll down my window.

Yes, it allows better airflow. And yes, it allows me to hear every word they say. This moment is totally a win-win.

Him: *Hey*

Her: *What have you been up to?*

Him: *Work. You?*

Her: (she sighs deeply, then subtly motions to me) *Who's that?*

I immediately stare down at the screen on my phone as if it's full of wonder. Oh, a clock—wow!

Him: *I work with her. She's just a friend.*

Her: (fidgeting with her long hair, scowl on her face) *Why didn't you call me back?*

Him: *I've just been busy, and I think maybe—*

Just then, my phone buzzed. It's a text. From Joel.

JOEL!

I fumble the phone and drop it as if it's coated in butter. *Calm down, Tori.*

His text is short, but to the point.

Where r u? I want to talk.

Oh, good grief. He wants to talk now? I was just about to hear the good part of this conversation. Bad timing!

I ignore the text, and lean over a little farther to hear every word.

Him: *...and that's how I feel.*

How he feels? What?! I missed it! My phone buzzes again—*another* text from Joel.

It's Tuesday. You out dancing? Can you call me pleeeeez?

Wow. I can't believe Joel actually remembers my social schedule. And he's trying to contact me. He wants to see me! I just wish he'd picked a better time. I hit the power button and turn my phone off. I'll call him later...when I'm ready.

Him: *Bye, Lana*

Her: (She says nothing. Storms away, gets in her car and squeals out of the parking lot)

Dang it! I've missed it the entire conversation!

Adam scuffles back to the Jeep, head hanging, then slides into his seat. He drops his keys in his lap and stares down at them. "You heard everything, didn't you?"

"I tried to, believe me. But my phone kept buzzing and I got distracted." I don't tell him it was buzzing because of Joel. "What did you say to her? She left in a hurry."

"I asked her why she wanted to see me and she said she couldn't stand not hearing from me. So I said that means if I *had* called her back, we wouldn't be having this conversation right now, and she said yeah, it's weird, but thinking she can't have me makes her want me more or something like that and then she asked me to kiss her and that's when I told her bye."

I'm confused. "I'm confused."

"Why?"

"You said you wanted to get back together, I gave you advice on making her wait before you called her back...it worked, she wants you. Why did you walk away?"

"I thought your trick would work, but it actually didn't. I want to be with someone who *wants* me to call. Someone who will text with me late at night. Someone who wants to go places together, like the movies or hiking or dancing..." He pauses, looking off at the street where Lana just blazed off.

I realize this is bad timing, but I can't help but ask. "You dance?"

He puts the car in gear and pulls out of the parking lot. "Nah, it's just something I've never done with a girl, certainly not Lana, and I've spent so much of my time going to writing conferences and doing things to pretend that I'm writing, or just simply sitting in traffic with my dad, that I haven't even done...stuff. FUN STUFF. When am I going to stop *planning* to do things and just DO THEM?"

Wow, he's yelling, but not in an angry way—so I can't stop staring at him. It's a frustrated yelling, like he's finally letting it all out.

I totally love this.

"This is good," I say. "Get it out. I really wish I had some popcorn—but go ahead."

"And I can't even write because I'm too busy working so that I don't have to write!"

He takes in a long breath, calming himself down.

I didn't know he had this side to him. There are probably more sides to him, and honestly, I'd like to find them all. This boy is bit of an Easter egg hunt.

But I don't like seeing him with a wrinkled forehead. Even his naturally upturned mouth is stuck in neutral. In moments like this, I always ask myself 'What would Taylor do?' And it's usually the same answer: time to have some fun.

"Hey, head to Wilshire and take a left," I say.

"Don't we have to get back to Lizzie's?"

"We have over an hour left. Just…trust."

Within a few turns, we're there, parked on the curb in front of the building. A crowd is growing outside, but I'm not worried because *this* time, I know the bouncer very well.

"Where are we?"

"Club Bump." I raise an eyebrow. "Come on, guy. I'm taking you dancing."

CHAPTER TWENTY-ONE

I'm in need of some ear popping music, we don't have any more errands to run, and this boy needs to let loose. So this is a no-brainer. "Let's go."

He pulls back a little. "In there?"

There are groups of teenagers in line, hugging, dancing, twirling. One even just did a cartwheel right there on the sidewalk. It's Brittany, one of the regulars here. Everyone is pumped—as usual.

I tug at his arm. "Just one dance. Or three."

"But what if—"

"And Taylor might be in there—he's one of my best friends. You *have* to meet him."

"But—"

Ignoring his protests, I hop out of the Jeep and glare at him through the windshield. He hesitates so I yell out, "Move it. LET'S DO THIS!" like a drill sergeant.

He smirks and gets out slowly, every movement like a dramatic rebellion. He finally joins me on the sidewalk two weeks later.

"Lord. Come on," I say as I drag him up to the bouncer. It's Dustin, as usual. He is what you would call an actual *nice* bouncer, which may be a contradiction of terms, but he always asks how you're doing and compliments you on what you're wearing. Love him. And he also has a crush on Taylor—a severe one. Which explains how I'm always able to cut to the front of the line. "Lady!" he hops up off his stool and hugs me.

"Is he in there?" I ask.

Dustin nods and busts out a huge smile. "Boy's looking fine tonight." He unhooks the latch on the rope— not velvet, just normal rope, post-office rope.

I wish Taylor would give Dustin a chance, but he's always outside the club working the door when he needs to be *inside,* dancing with my Taylor. They only have a door entrance relationship. Two ships, those boys.

We step inside the club. The darkened room is thick with bodies and the smell of Axe body spray. We are enveloped by swirling fake fog, and when my eyes adjust, I see flickers of glowing necklaces and bracelets moving on people's bodies as they dance wildly. This place, the way it makes you want to move your body, has become my replacement for my ballet dreams. Two very opposite things, I know, but anywhere I can throw my limbs around while it's set to music is a place I want to be.

Adam and I hover near the wall and take it all in. The thumping bass vibrates through my bones—a feeling that always makes me tingly and happy, like my batteries are getting charged.

Not surprisingly, it doesn't take him long to spot me. "Puppy! What are you *doing* here?!" Taylor clobbers me with a hug and kisses me on the cheek. He's wearing a collared polo shirt, as always, but this one is electric blue. Which matches the blue eyeliner ringing his eyes along with the blue streaks in his hair. Dustin is right... boy's looking fine tonight.

Taylor gently squeezes the back of my neck. "And who is this?" But he doesn't wait for an answer, just reaches across me to shake Adam's hand. "I'm Taylor. Are you Puppy's date?"

Adam looks a little confused. "I'm Puppy's...co-worker."

I lean into Adam so he can hear me. "He calls me Puppy."

"Figured."

"Because she's so damned cute!" Taylor yells and throws his hands in the air as a Cyndi Lauper song comes on. Yep, it's definitely '80s night.

Adam says, "Nice to meet you, Taylor," then he turns to me, fidgeting nervously with his zipper and says, "I'm going to...I'll be...I think I'll sit down for a minute."

I nod and he quickly walks over to the bar, which is only selling Icee's and nachos, and he slides onto a barstool.

"All right." Taylor bumps shoulders with me. "Who's the adorable stray?"

"You think he's cute?"

Taylor casually looks him over, sizing him up. "Good bone structure. It's possible something interesting is going on beneath that hoodie. I tend to be right about these things."

"We're just friends."

"Oh really?" He doesn't look convinced.

I glance back at Adam to make sure he isn't watching me while I unload all this on Taylor—luckily he's intrigued by the disco ball on the ceiling.

But when I turn back, Taylor is eyeing me like I just got caught with my hand in the cookie jar. "Why are you looking at me like that?"

"You are *not* just friends."

"Yes. We are." I cross my arms defiantly. "And Joel keeps texting me, wanting to talk." I pull my phone out and turn the power on to show him proof. When the screen lights up, I see I have four missed calls...all from Joel. "Whoa."

Taylor peers over, checking out my phone. "Interesting development. Joel is back in the picture, huh?"

"He can wait. I have to follow my own advice...if I call him tomorrow, he'll be putty in my hand."

"True." He winks. "But are you telling me you haven't gotten *any* sort of hint that there's some magic between you and this Adam, King of Hipsterville?"

"No, in fact, I took him to my spot—"

"The sixth floor?!"

"Yeah, and when we—"

"You love him."

"—got there I ran ahead of him, and when we made it to the sixth floor, he—"

"You LOVE him."

"Stop." I grab his hand. "He ran straight into my boob. But he gripped onto it like it was a truck door handle."

"Oh. Not sexy."

"Right? But even with him accidentally going to second base with me, I didn't feel any electricity. Nothing." I shrug. "If a guy's touch doesn't turn me to Love Pudding, it's not going to happen. You know that."

He squints at me. "Are you sure you're not missing something?"

"What are you talking about?!"

Taylor grabs my hands and turns me toward him so that we're facing each other. He can now get a full view of Adam by looking over my head. "I'm watching the way he looks at you."

"*How* is he looking at me?" I ask into his shoulder.

Taylor watches for a few more seconds. "Huh. He's trying *not* to look at you, but…he can't help himself." He adds under his breath, "God, that's cute."

I grip his arm. "What do you mean?!"

"Go ask him a question—any question. You'll see it, I promise." He kisses me on the forehead then shoves me away as he takes off to the dance floor.

Suddenly I am there by the wall all alone. I adjust my shirt, fluff my hair, then strut over to Adam. I decide to start with an easy one.

"Want an Icee?"

"Nah."

"Nachos?"

"I'm not hungry."

"Can I ask you a question?"

"You just asked two."

"There's a third. Are you glad you broke things off with Lana?"

He folds his arms and looks around the room, taking his time with this answer. "Yeah. Very glad."

But something in me wants to get to the bottom of this. Especially before I talk to Joel. Because maybe Taylor has a point. Maybe I *am* missing something. "Why? I thought you were convinced you wanted to get back together with her."

"Did you see the scowl on her face as she walked off?"

"She looked like a serious ass kicker, honestly."

"That's not an unusual look for her. She looks serious like that all the time. For whatever reason, she thinks she has to play this role of "tormented writer" like it makes her deep or something. Hemingway-chic, you know? And I thought it was something missing in me, so I was drawn to her. But when I saw that look on her face again tonight, all I could think about was wanting to just have some fun. I kept thinking about me and you running out of the Cobra Lounge and laughing hysterically." He looks away toward the bar, but then with a quick flick of his eyes, glances back at me again. The flick, the look. That. *That's* what Taylor is talking about! Wow, he's right...*God that's cute.*

I suppose I could keep questioning him and dig deeper. But instead I go with the first thing that pops to mind. "Let's dance."

"Now?"

I grab his hand and pull him off the stool. "Yes."

"I don't dance."

"Everyone dances."

"Not me."

"You have a heartbeat. The universe gave you a way to keep the beat. We were all born wanting to shake booty. It's biology."

"No, really. I just. Don't."

I sigh. Even if a person can't dance, they should be able to sway. You can walk, you can sway. What does he mean he *doesn't* dance?

An old Duran Duran song comes on, and the crowd goes absolutely wild. Taylor has joined a group of people who, my word, *really* know how to dance. I can understand Adam's intimidation, but no need to not enjoy the music.

I sway in front of him. "Come on. You're a tree. Sway."

He stands firm. He is a skyscraper.

The guy needs help. I've witnessed enough people getting "lessoned" here at this club before so I know *exactly* what to do. Not sure why it always has to happen in the bathroom, but it does.

"Let's go. Time for a lesson."

I drag him straight to the ladies room. He protests for a moment but then we pass through the door, and a group of girls are fixing their hair in the mirror. "Emergency dance lesson, ladies!" I announce.

They giggle and quickly exit—one of them even stands guard at the door to make sure no one comes in. This club: beyond awesome.

I drag him into the large handicapped stall, pull the door closed and lock it.

The music is thumping through the walls. He has a smirk on his face. "You're going to *teach* me?"

"I'll start slow. Just follow my movements."

While I sway my hips back and forth, slowly, he says, "Wait." Then he takes off his hoodie and carefully drapes it over the railing, making sure it doesn't wrinkle. When he turns back, I decide Taylor is a genius. Because there is definitely something interesting going on beneath that jacket.

He may be lanky. But he's more than that. Boy. Is. *Ripped.*

Lord.

He sways a little, then sticks his hands into the front pockets of his jeans. "This is dumb. Or I am. You're not. You're a fantastic dancer. I just don't—"

I need to take a different approach. "Close your eyes." I gently brush my hands over his face, forcing him to close them. "Do *not* look at me."

Turning away from him, I back in a little closer, take his hands and let his body relax into mine, letting him follow my every move. He's a little rigid at first, but I keep silent, keep moving, and within moments we're moving together in a completely fluid way.

The music is hypnotic and we don't say a word. He moves in closer and the way he is draped over me, our bodies suddenly match up perfectly like two puzzle pieces. Adam releases one hand and gently wraps his arm around my waist, pulling me into him. And then suddenly, a rush of adrenaline fills every cell in my body. The touch of his hand sends a bolt of energy through me, and I feel lightheaded, hardly able to catch my breath. I spin around to face him, and a gorgeous smile fills his face.

"See? You can...dance." My voice quivers. *Get your act together, Tori.* I grip at the fabric on my shirt to force my breathing back down to a normal pace. But it isn't happening.

His hand is still on my waist and he grips tighter. Our lips are close, and our eyes lock in.

He leans in, his mouth brushing my cheek and whispers in my ear, "I want to dance. With you."

I step back, taking in his sweet face. "Follow me." I'm barely able to get the words out.

He stays close behind me, his hand on my back as we rush out of the bathroom and toward the pounding, electric dance floor. But just before we step onto it to dance, I hear a voice.

"Tori!"

I turn and my eyes drift up. Standing in front of me, is Joel.

CHAPTER TWENTY-TWO

I freeze. I can't move. Can't talk, think, breathe. Nothing.

Joel is here—in front of me—with a smile on his face and hands that aren't stuffed in his pockets, but outstretched ready to pull me into a hug.

Adam is behind me, his hand still lightly touching my back.

I can't believe this—of all times for Joel to show up...*now*?

"Why are you here, Joel?" I fold my arms to punctuate my disbelief.

"I figured you'd be here tonight. I need to talk to you." He smiles at me as if this is good news or something. Honestly, twenty-four hours ago, this would have been the best news. But now, after that moment with Adam. Dancing in the bathroom, his touch. How could I—

"I'll wait by the bar," Adam whispers in my ear. And before I can respond, he's gone.

Joel steps closer to me—close enough that I can tell he's chewing spearmint gum. He's wearing a worn T-shirt, cut off cargo pants, and the flip-flops I bought him for his birthday. He is totally aware of my love of boys in sandals, so it's clear this look was not put together by mistake.

"Who's that guy?" He motions to Adam who is facing the bar, sipping on a blue Icee. Taylor has joined him and is chatting him up. Trying to find out the scoop between us, I'm sure.

"That's Adam. He's my co-worker."

"Yeah, Shannon told me something about you getting a job. Why'd you go and do a drastic thing like that?"

"So I could keep my mind off of things, like, oh I don't know... YOU." Wow, look at me being all straight forward. I'm not sure where that came from. But I like it.

He puts an arm around me. "But I *do* want you thinking about me—that's why I came to find you." He leans into me, nuzzles my neck, then whispers. "I want you back, Tor."

Lord. These are the words I was hoping to hear from him. My plan of staying away and keeping busy has worked to perfection. But now I'm not sure it was the right plan.

There's no way I can talk to Joel with Adam sitting only twenty yards away. "Let's talk outside," I say.

Joel follows closely behind me and I glance at the bar as we pass by. Adam is facing the other direction, not looking my way. But Taylor stands up and we connect looks. I mouth to him, "What do I do?"

But he just shrugs as if he feels sorry for me.

We step outside to the sidewalk just beyond the long line of people waiting to get inside. My phone buzzes and I glance at it—a text from Shannon. I ignore it, because I'm planning to call her tonight anyway to give her a rundown on this event that's unfolding right at this very moment.

"Listen, Joel. I'm not sure—"

My phone buzzes again. And again. Two more texts from Shannon. What is going on with her?

Joel gently pulls the phone from my hand and slides it into my back pocket, his breath on my neck.

"We're back on, Tori," he says in a soft voice. Then he lifts my chin and leans in to kiss me. My head is telling me to stop, but my body isn't letting me.

But then he steps back. "Wait." He blushes, looking embarrassed. "Let me throw this gum away first." He winks at me then heads down the sidewalk to the trashcan on the corner.

I glance over at the long line of people waiting to get in. They are noticeably quiet and all eyes are on me. Oh, sheesh. They've all been watching this make-up scene. Gabby, another Tuesday night regular here, has an arm full of bangles and white lacey gloves (an attempt at '80s Madonna). She and her friends give me a thumbs-up.

We're their sidewalk entertainment. Great.

Joel starts to head back toward me, so I quickly grab my phone to see what Shannon is wigging out about.

I went to find Brent last night. I know, breaking the rules. He was at Sam Clark's party.

It's interesting how Shannon and I have boy issues at the same exact time. Maybe we regulate with relationships, not periods.

The party wasn't just for the guys. Joel was there. With HER. They were all over each other. So gross.

Oh my god—I know exactly who the "HER" is. Carly, his ex.

Glad you're getting over him. He's such a douche-basket. LOL! xoxo

My stomach drops. He hooked up with Carly again. He hasn't gotten over her. I am just his…oh, lord. Even the thought of the word makes me nauseous.

Just as I stuff my phone back in my pocket, Joel runs up to me and wraps his arms around me. "Kiss me." He says it loud enough for our audience to hear.

But I pull back, not wanting to feel his touch. Not now—not ever.

"Kiss him!" Gabby yells out from the line.

"If you don't, I will!" one of her friends adds and starts cracking up.

I square my shoulders up to Joel, staring him down. "But who were you kissing last night?"

"What?"

"The party, last night."

He holds his hands up, like he's the innocent bystander. "Look, Carly wanted to get back together with me."

An "ooooooo" comes from the audience.

"Get back together at Sam Clark's?" I stick a hand on my hip. Throwing out a little attitude feels good. "The party that you told me was just for the guys—*that* one?"

He takes a deep breath and lowers his voice. "Can we talk about this in private? I'll explain everything." He points to his Toyota parked down the street. "I know how much you like the front seat of my truck." He grabs my hand and gently starts to pull me along.

"No, Joel." I yank my arm back and decide to end this right here in front of our 80's dressed fans. "You don't have to explain a thing to me—I got it all figured out. Carly broke up with that last guy, and suddenly she was free. *That's* why you broke it off with me, not because of all your Ultimate Frisbee practices. And you knew Sam's party was a date thing and you took *her*. I'm guessing she broke it off with you— yet again—and *that's* why you're here. Because I'm available."

He dips his chin, trying to look sorry. "I want us to try again, Tor. Does it matter why?"

"Yeah. It does." My bottom lip quivers. "I can't believe I'm about to admit this. It's finally dawned on me that I am your Rebound Girl. We met in that yogurt shop right after she broke up with you. And now here I am again—just a fill-in while you wait for her."

"Kick him in the balls!" someone in line yells out.

He ignores them and gives it one last shot. "Please, I want us to be together. Can't we try—"

I shake my head. "I won't be the girl to pass the time with while you wait around for something better. I'm done."

A few more of Gabby's friends—tough-looking girls wearing headbands with spiky hair (Pat Benatar look-alikes)—start clapping.

But just beyond them, I see Adam leaving the club and walking briskly toward his Jeep. "Adam! Wait!" I call out to him.

The line gives me assistance. "Wait, Adam! We love you!" they yell out.

Without giving an explanation, I run away from Joel and chase Adam down, catching him just before he opens his door. I throw my hands on the hood. "Don't leave. Please."

He zips his hoodie. "You need to talk to him—I get it."

"But it's not—"

"Taylor said he'd take you to your car. That guy's a good friend to you." Adam looks away from me as he opens his door. "I'll see you tomorrow, Tori."

He fires up the Jeep and pulls away without even looking my way.

I shuffle back to Joel, my head hanging. As much as I want to finish telling him off, I'm emotionally drained. I walk up to him slowly but I don't say a word.

He's the one who does the talking.

"Looks like you've already found your rebound guy. I wonder if he knows it." He pulls his keys out and raises a brow. "Good luck with that." There's venom in his voice.

He turns and walks away, leaving me there on the sidewalk not knowing what to say or do.

Even my Pat Benetar cheer section is frozen in stunned silence.

CHAPTER TWENTY-THREE

"Thank God for you," I say with my forehead pressed against the passenger window of Taylor's car. "Turn right."

He taps the beat of the song on his steering wheel. "I'm glad you ended it with Joel. Such a tool."

"I wish I'd figured him out earlier. I'm the one who feels like a tool."

"Stop." He pats my knee. "Did you ever have fun with the boy?"

"Yeah. It was fun sometimes, sure."

"Then it was worth it. You gave love a shot. I'm pretty sure that's why we're put on this planet, don't you think? Stop worrying about the rest."

I smirk. "Me? Not worry about a relationship?"

"True. Which way do I go?"

"The house on the left there, the one with the black gate."

He pulls into the driveway, punches in the code, and pulls up the steep driveway next to my car. The house is darkened. It's late. I check the time: 11:25. Shoot! Mom will be home soon!

I quickly push the door open, but he grabs my arm before I can leave. "What are you going to do about Adam?"

"Nothing."

"NOTHING? You both have the hots for each other. Kissing that boy needs to be in your near future. That's an order."

I love it when Taylor tells me what to do, and he's usually correct. But this time, I'm not so sure. "It's the last words that Joel said to me—they're still lingering. He said Adam is just my Rebound Guy...and he doesn't know it. What if I only want Adam because I need a quick fill-in? A substitute? I can't do that to him."

Taylor lets go of my arm. In a soft voice, he says, "Darling, I love you. But your brain is wrapped up tightly in precious little bows. Let loose, Puppy."

I sigh and blow him a kiss goodnight.

When I reach my street, it's nearly a quarter till midnight. Pulling into the driveway, I see her car. And my heart stops. Oh, no. Oh, no.

A litany of lies run through my head, but I just can't do it. Mom deserves the truth. It's possible—*possible*—that she will understand. That it will be alright.

But it's also possible she'll force me to quit, and I won't see Adam every night.

There are no good choices here.

Deep breath in...here I go.

The front door creaks signaling my arrival. But she's not sitting at the kitchen table, or pacing the floor, or calling the police. She isn't anywhere. The house is dark except for the light over the stove that we always leave on.

This is weird. And scary.

Carefully, I tip-toe to her bedroom and push her door open just slightly. Immediately I hear the snoring. She's sleeping.

SLEEPING!

I stagger to my room and fall onto my bed, staring up at my ceiling in disbelief. My own mother came home and didn't even notice my car wasn't here. She didn't check in on me because she never does.

I roll over and clobber my pillow, crying deep sobs. I'm not hurt because we don't talk...I'm hurt because she doesn't even notice me.

Finally, the only thought that pulls me out of my cry fest is of Adam. I didn't have to confess to Mom about my night job, so at least I'll get to see him tomorrow night. My bright spot.

If we give each other the space to get over our breakups, we might just have a chance. But until then, we can be friends. Good friends. Dancing friends.

And I can't wait to see him. I wipe away the tears, snuggle deep under my comforter and fall asleep with only one thought in my head: tomorrow can't get here soon enough.

The day of my unfortunate incarceration

CHAPTER TWENTY-FOUR

We both arrive at Lizzie's at about the same time. Just as I'm getting out of my car, he pulls up next to me. The first thing I notice is the pleasant look on his face. Technically he was born with that look, but at least he doesn't look like he's upset with me for walking off with Joel last night.

Or he's doing a good job of hiding it.

"Hey, you." His voice is upbeat. And I can't help but focus on what he's wearing...or *not* wearing. No hoodie, just a tight black T-shirt. And his skater shoes are tied. His Boy With A Broken Heart Uniform is starting to vanish. Already. (Though his hair is still a little shaggy.)

It is a warm night, so that might explain the lack of a hoodie. Or maybe he's actually getting over Lana in the span of 22 hours? Or maybe his father tied his shoe for him before he left the house? Or MAYBE I'm over-thinking this?

"Ready for another exciting night of running errands?" He asks, interrupting the tornado of thoughts whirling around in my brain, thankfully, because I'm starting to annoy myself.

"Ready, captain," I say, sounding dumb.

We start to head up the sidewalk, but Lizzie is already standing there, list in hand. She's wearing slippers, yoga pants, and a baggy sweater. She takes a large gulp from a steaming cup of coffee. "I'm glad you're both here on time. There's so much going on today, I haven't even had time to get dressed." She winces as she looks down at her slippered feet. "I'm so sorry."

I wave her off. "No need to apologize. You look great." She does. Her disheveled look is actually quite adorable.

"Go ahead and get started with this." She hands me the list while taking another gulp. "I'll call you later with more updates for tonight. We're still working out the details."

If I'm not mistaken, I believe there is a glint in her eye. "Something big going on?" I ask.

She grips her coffee cup tighter. "VERY. I'll call you later. Get going, you two!" She happily shoos us off the sidewalk then shuffles back up to the house in her fuchsia slippers.

Once Adam and I are headed down the road, I unfold the list and read it out loud to him. There are only two items listed:

1. Deliver a six-pack of Red Bulls, a box of Nutty Bars and two packs of Bubblicious Watermelon Splash to Frank over on Sunset Blvd, across from Chateau Marmont.

2. Wait for my call with further instructions

"She doesn't say how long we're supposed to wait?" he asks.

"Nope."

We stop by a Rite-Aid to pick up the items, then head over to Sunset to drop them off to Frank. His clients tonight are Doug and Darcy Miller from Wichita! They're wearing matching Twilight T-shirts and fake fangs, hoping for a Rob Pattinson sighting.

"Rob will be exiting through the side entrance around 8:30," Frank explains to me while he chews on a toothpick.

"How do you know?" I am genuinely curious.

"Gave the dishwasher two tickets to Josh Groban at the Hollywood Bowl."

"Ah." Lizzie is right—this town runs on favors.

Frank snatches the bag from me and immediately cracks open a Red Bull then tosses the rest into an ice cooler.

"That sure is a lot of caffeine you're storing." My attempt at small-talk.

He takes a long swig. "Gonna be a long night. Lizzie got you on stand-by?"

"Yeah, we're supposed to wait for her call. But I don't know why—she didn't tell us."

He nods. "Probably better you don't know until we find out if our lead from Lance works out."

"Lance…the bartender from the Cobra Lounge?"

"Movie star jaw line?"

I nod.

"Hopefully those theater tickets were good enough seats, and he pulls through for us."

Suddenly Doug-and-Darcy-from-Wichita get very yippy and fumble around, practically dropping their drugstore bought cameras. They snap pictures of a guy exiting Chateau Marmont.

"Settle down, settle down," Frank waves his hands around at the giddy couple. "False alarm. It's just a look-a-like, folks. Lots of brooding handsome fellas in this town."

"Good luck!" I say and head back to Adam's Jeep where he's waiting for me.

Frank calls out to me. "See you later tonight. Hopefully."

I give him a thumbs-up but I don't know why. I'm curious about what in the world this lead is that has everyone all excited and cranked up on caffeine. But truthfully, I'm more curious about what Adam and I are going to do with our time while we wait for Lizzie to call.

Chit-chat about politics?

I flop down in the passenger's seat and look over at Adam who is busy scrolling through his phone.

"Frank told me we're waiting on a lead from Lance with the jaw."

He nods and sets his phone down on his lap. I take note of that gesture...that he stopped what he was doing to respond to me. It seems like a simple courtesy, but there were so many times when Joel would find SO MUCH wonder in his phone, and always when I was talking about something. Now that I think about it, he did that sort of crap quite a bit. And I *stayed* with him?! Why is it that I'm only seeing it now?

"It could be a while," Adam says. "How about we head to Krispy Kreme?"

"Sure. That's work-related."

He smirks. "We should make sure the warm ones are suitable for our clients."

"Quality control."

"Because we're awesome at our jobs."

"We are awesome." I face out the window, my stomach churning. I clutch at my shirt—the hem, the sleeve, back to the hem. An overwhelming feeling has come over me to grab him and tell him that I'm done with Joel. I'm ready to move on. Tell him we aren't just awesome at our jobs...we're pretty much awesome together.

But he hasn't asked me any questions about last night and he's acting like absolutely nothing happened. Not a trace of angst or weirdness. I'm the only one who seems to be resorting to fidgeting for comfort.

And it's possible I'm the only one who's overanalyzing all of this.

Just act normal, Tori. Stop yanking on your shirt—you're going to rip a button off or something.

We park at the Krispy Kreme, and he hops out. "I'll grab us a box. Be right back."

I watch him as he crosses the parking lot, unable to get my mind off his sweet smiles and his hands that were wrapped around my waist last night.

Stop. Get it together!

I nervously tug on my shirt to straighten out the wrinkles when—POP! My top button pulls right off. It's a very important one, too! It's the one that keeps you from showing borderline inappropriate cleavage. Oh my God.

Frantically, I pull the fabric together trying to get the material to cover all the necessary parts without a button, but no luck.

Dang. DANG! Now Adam's going to think I'm trying to seduce him with my chest that's busting out.

He strolls back to the Jeep with a warm box of donuts and I instinctively pull the fabric tight with one hand, covering virtually everything up to my neck.

He slides into his seat. "You okay?"

"Fine," I squeak.

He tilts his head looking confused, but he doesn't question any further. Thankfully.

He lifts the box up and opens it. "Gaze at our fine selection of donuts—each one truly unique." They're all the same, but he's waving his hand over them as if he's selling me knives on QVC.

I snatch one with my free hand. "Wow. I'd pay $19.95 for those. Plus shipping!"

"But wait...there's more." He reaches into his pocket and pulls out a wad of napkins. "For a limited time only—this sanitation cloth. Perfect for garment protection."

I want to grab one but I'm out of hands. "Um..."

Our infomercial routine now comes to a complete halt.

He narrows his eyes and places a napkin on my knee. Then he sits back and stares up at the roof. After taking a deep breath, he says, "Are you going to tell me what happened last night? I'm dying to know. You don't have to tell me, but I just..."

He's dying to know. HE'S DYING TO KNOW!

I swallow my bit of donut and blurt out, "I broke it off with him."

He cuts his eyes at me. "You did?"

"He just wanted me around until Carly wanted him back. Carly is his ex," I explain. "I was his rebound girl."

"Rebound girl—that's a bad thing?"

My eyes grow big. "The worst. The rebound person is just the fill-in. A substitute." I let out a deep sigh. "I mean, I wrote a whole blog post on the topic, did research, the whole bit. It got the most hits of any post. So me finding myself in a place where *I'm* the rebound girl...it just feels..."

"Ironic?"

"Pathetic."

He smiles a little. "You're hardly pathetic."

"I wasn't the one he actually wanted. But the strange thing is," I take another bite of my donut and settle into my seat, making sure I'm clutching my shirt to hide my cleavage. "...now that I think about my relationship with him, I realize he wasn't right for me. How did I not see that? I mean, we always went to parties together and hung out at the beach and watched movies at his house—"

"Sounds awful."

"But those are all the things *he* wanted to do. Eat food. Go to horror movies. Fool around. That's it."

"Maybe he was—"

Yeah, yeah, back and forth conversation would be nice, but at this moment I just need to get this *out*. "And he's always talking about himself, texting on his phone, doing whatever he wants to do. He wouldn't even compromise on his munchies. Like the time I took him to Crepe Café because there is *nothing* better than a brie cheese crepe, but he wouldn't even get out of the car, and I ended up eating a 3,000 calorie limp-ass salad at Jack-in-the-Box and I gained weight just so he could have a Bacon Sourdough Jack."

"Maybe you—"

"And *then* there was the time I drove past this fortune teller's place and told him I'd always wanted to have a psychic reading because maybe it'd help me figure out my future, because hell if I know what my future is going to be, but nooo, he wanted to see the midnight showing of Rocky Horror Picture Show because there was a group of stoners he was going to meet in bubblegum alley before the show. And, get this, one time we—" I look over at Adam but he's just staring at me. Not at my eyes, my chest.

Glancing down, I realize that with all this "getting it out" I forgot about my blouse malfunction and was waving my hands around to make my point.

"The top button popped off." I bite at my lip.

"I'm not complaining." He whips his head around and stares at the steering wheel. "Unless you *want* me to complain. Otherwise, no complaints."

I laugh. "But how am I going to work tonight looking like this?"

"It's just some cleavage. There's nothing to worry about."

He's now looking at me—my eyes. We stare at each other for what feels like a month. Then he says in a low voice, "Like I said, I'm not complaining."

Stomach flip.

I look out my window because all this eye contact is making me woozy. "I got a ride back to my car from Taylor last night," I say. "But I wish you had stayed."

I turn back to him, but he's scrolling through his phone again. Really?

"Hey!" I poke him on the shoulder. "I'm trying to talk to you but you aren't listening."

"Just a sec," he says.

Oh, come on. He's acting just as self-absorbed as Joel.

"Here." He flips his phone to show me the screen—it's an address. "It's on Sepulveda Boulevard. Stellar Insights Psychic reader. Five minutes and we're there." He cranks up the Jeep and backs out of the parking lot—a heart-melting smile on his face.

I breathe him in and try to focus. Adam isn't self-absorbed—he's downright awesome. "You're taking me to a psychic reader... *now?*"

He raises a brow. "I, for one, can't *wait* to find out what's going to happen in your future."

CHAPTER TWENTY-FIVE

It's a cream-colored building—very crisp, very clean. The French doors are flanked by two ornate bushes, sculpted and shaped into perfectly round spheres. Like green bushy planets. A sign outside says: YOUR FUTURE IS AN OPEN BOOK. READINGS: $10.

My future. And all it takes is a ten-spot? Cool.

"I'll wait here for you." Adam says.

"No way—you're coming with me, son!" I start yanking his keys out of the ignition.

He fights me off as he laughs. "What if they get into personal stuff? I don't want to intrude. Give me my keys back!"

I wiggle them out of his grasp. Victory!

I dangle the keys in the air, teasing him. My insides fill with warmth, not just because the lovely smirk on his face is becoming addictive. But because he wants to give me space if I need it.

Which makes me wonder if I should go in there alone. Maybe the psychic would talk about my love life, tell me what to do. Will the magic ball foresee Adam in my future?

I don't want to do something like this alone. I need a friend, a good friend—and strangely he is becoming just that. Well, one of those friends who sometimes touches you and makes your skin tingle and your insides turn to mush.

"Come inside with me." I crinkle my nose to ensure he'll agree. "Please? I'll even give you your keys back."

"Fine."

Nose crinkle, for the win! (Or maybe it was the keys.)

We step up to the door and I try to open it, but it's locked. Just to the left of the door is a handwritten note that says RING BELL and an arrow points down to a doorbell inside a metal plaque engraved with unicorns. Weird. Or *not* weird. I mean, I'm going to a walk-in psychic at 9:30 at night. What do I expect?

I ring the bell.

As we wait—looking at each other, then the ground, then at people as they pass by—I suddenly get nervous. What am I about to find out? What if I don't want to hear this? I fidget with my shirt (the very revealing one) and nervously wiggle my toes in my shoes, hoping someone will show up at the door soon.

Finally, the door creaks open and a waft of lemon smell over-whelms me. A woman peers out. "Yes?"

"I'd like a reading," I whisper. Why am I whispering?

"Both?" she points at Adam.

"Just me, not him," I say in a regular voice.

She opens it wide and glances us over not looking all that impressed. "Come in then."

She is older, maybe in her 50s, and she's dressed in a crisp, white tracksuit with red stripes down the arms and legs. Her shoes are the opposite—red running shoes with white stripes. Very yin & yang.

I guess I thought she'd be a bit more bohemian—flowy skirt, sandals, more jewelry than necessary. But she looks like she's ready to run a half-marathon.

The room is like a waiting area in a doctor's office. Simple, stark, complete with outdated magazines: People magazine from five years ago.

The only difference is the carpeting; it's thick, plush and purple. Vibrant purple, like the kind you find in a Skittles bag.

Four white leather chairs surround a glass coffee table and in the middle is a ceramic carving of two hands reaching up out of a base of marble, cradling something. Probably something important. The sorcerer's stone? I lean over and peer down. No magic stone, just business cards.

The psychic—and sponsor of Adidas—pumps lemon-smelling hand sanitizer in her palm. "What would you like? Palm? Tarot? Psychic reading?"

"I…um…"

"A combo?" She asks.

Sounds like something that comes with fries. But I didn't know what else to order. "Sure. I'll take the combo."

I hand over a ten-dollar bill. She folds it neatly and tucks it into her tracksuit pocket, then points to a room in the back corner. "Get comfortable."

I glance back at Adam. He gives me a shoo-ing motion. "Go," he mouths as he settles into a white leather chair in the corner and starts reading an article about the very recent break up of Brad Pitt and Jennifer Aniston.

I give him a quick finger wave with just my pointer finger, like a puppet.

Really? I did the finger puppet move? So dorky.

But he mimicks me, with his pointer finger and everything. Oh my gosh, that's sort of cute. This is us now? We do dorky cute things with each other?

I can't believe this. I've just ended things with Joel and now within twenty-four hours, I'm falling for someone else. Deep in side I know it's too soon. I'm supposed to go through a grieving stage first. A marathon movie stage. A non-fat pretzel stage. A smug I'm-only-eating-vegan-now stage. *Something.*

But it also feels like something I have no control over.

Or do I?

The room is small and there isn't a door but a scalloped entrance with a beaded curtain. It's lit with only one lamp—another hand sculpture, but this time the hands are holding a dim light bulb.

As I slide into a wicker chair with a worn padded seat, she gracefully sits across from me. She doesn't look at me, doesn't say a word. Just takes a stack of tarot cards, shuffles and re-shuffles all while staring down at the plush Skittle carpet.

Am I supposed to talk to her? Ask her name? Explain my life story?

"Think of a wish. Something you want to have happen to you. Your dream for your future. Don't say it out loud—keep it to yourself," she instructs.

My mind whirls. What do I want to have happen to me? I search but can't come up with an answer. She isn't even asking me to say it out loud, a totally reasonable request. But I'm a complete blank. I remind myself to fake it, make something up, whatever it takes to not sit here with a contorted painful look on my face.

Think, think.

I flick my eyes up at her. I'm still a blank. I need more time. Am I *ever* going to come up with an answer to this question? Is it possible to *fail* a psychic reading? Hi, panic.

"Ready?" she asks.

No. No I am *not*. She's going to kick me out or something. Oh, come on, how hard can this possibly be? Since I can't come up with something specific and I can't even *fake it*, for crap's sake, I decide the question itself will be my wish—my dream for myself is to figure out what I'm dreaming. I'm a complex case.

"Ready," I say with fake confidence.

She nods. "Cut the stack in three then put them back together in any order you wish."

I follow her directions, separating the stacks as equally as possible, hoping I've done it right. Then I realize this must be some insight into my soul—how I stack and re-stack. Everyone does it differently. We are all snowflakes when it comes to cutting a deck of cards.

She takes my newly created stack and flips the cards over, placing them carefully on the table to create a diamond shape.

When she's finished with her art project, she says in a sharp voice, "Hold your palms out. Keep them still."

I do. Also, she scares me a little.

With her fingers interlaced, she sits back in her chair and glares back and forth between the cards and my hands. And she says nothing—not a word.

Is she thinking? Having a motionless seizure? Totally dying? The woman just stares, silently, no emotion on her face *at all*.

She finally takes a deep gulp of air and sighs deeply. And that's when she completely unloads on me.

"You're a loyal person. When someone new comes in your life you take the time to get to know them, all about them, almost study them. But you tend to keep yourself a secret. It's not because you're a private person, though. It's because there are a lot of things you don't know about yourself. Not yet. But I sense you will."

"So how do I—"

"Palms *still*," she barks. She's is a psychic with an attitude.

"Yes...Mrs....ma'am...psychic." What am I supposed to call her?

"And I sense there is a boy in your life. A new one. A good one."

I smile, feeling the rush of warmth in my cheeks. Can Adam hear us?

She wags her finger at me. "But you need to be by yourself for a while. Don't date anyone. You need to figure out what you're dreaming for yourself, or else you won't find your match."

I don't understand. Isn't that why I came to her? So *she* can tell me my future? She's telling me I now have to figure this out before I can *date*. Doesn't she understand how high school works?!

I sit up straighter and try my best to be calm about this. "By 'not date' do you mean not...*date*?"

"There is a guy." She breaks the slightest smile. "He'll show up. Later than you'd like, but you should wait for him."

He'll show up...but later than I'd like? Is she talking about Adam? How could she...he's already in my life.

"You, my girl, are a Pisces. You're a diehard romantic. You cherish relationships—flings don't work for you." She reaches out and squeezes my hand. "Be a Pisces—it's who you are."

She stacks her cards and neatly places them in a drawer behind her, signaling the session is over. She stands and says, "Figure out what you want. Don't date for a while. And call your mother."

I snap my head up at her, glaring like she truly might be psychic. She knows I'm keeping things from my mother? She must be able to at least read my expression because she adds, "It's something I always say at the end of sessions. It's just good advice." She shoots me a wink and hands over a coupon. "Bring a friend on Tuesdays. Two for one."

Huh. Not a bad deal, really.

I trudge back out to the lobby, dazed. And dreading telling Adam what she said.

He joins me, walking beside me all the way out to the parking lot and doesn't say a word until we're both in the car. "So? What's your future like?"

I bite my lip and stammered. "My future...it's..."

"Bright? Full of riches? Over soon?"

I have to tell him what she said—*he* was the one who convinced me to come. He deserves an explanation. "She said I have to figure out what I want for my future."

"Your psychic was my father?"

I cut right to the point, the one I don't really want to cut to. "We talked about my love life."

"Oh." He stares at his fingernails.

"She said I need to be on my own a while."

"You mean—"

"Don't date."

We're silent for a minute, just breathing—in and out—as we sit in the dimly lit parking lot, not able to look at each other.

I feel my eyes sting with tears on the verge of falling. What should I say to him? What do I *want* to say to him?

He starts the car up. "Are you going to take her advice?"

"Should I?"

We both turn at the same moment and our eyes meet. His face softens and a slight smile forms on his face. He gives a shrug as if he has no answer.

Tell me no. Tell me to date whenever I want. Tell me to kiss you.

My phone buzzes. It's a text from Lizzie. I read it out loud to him.

Good news! Come to the house now. I need to give you instructions.

We stare at each other, as if we're searching for answers. As if we're wondering how to finish our conversation. Or if we should.

He sighs. "I guess we should get going."

We drive through the back streets of L.A, and I glance at his silhouette as we pass the glow of blurring streetlights. As much as I want to reach out to him, kiss his perfectly upturned mouth, tell him we are awesome together...I also know that I want to do this right. Getting together with Joel when he'd just broken up with Carly was a mistake. One I don't want to repeat.

I know what it will take—just like it says on my blog post... thirty days.

I just hope when the psychic said the guy would show up, even if it was later than I wanted, that she meant Adam.

CHAPTER TWENTY-SIX

Lizzie and Troy are full of nervous energy—you can feel it. They buzz around the living room gathering papers, checking and re-checking their phones while Adam and I sit patiently on the white leather couch.

Lizzie and Troy finally take a seat across from us. "Okay. Here's the deal," Lizzie takes a deep breath to calm herself down. "Our tip from Lance didn't come through. But you did a great job getting those tickets to him, Tori."

"Was there a problem with the tickets?" I ask.

"Obstructed view. Some seats are far to the side and there are parts of the play you can't see."

"But not to worry," Troy chimes in with adorable British-ness. "Frank got the tip on the whereabouts of Sienna Hart, so now we can go forward with getting a photo of her."

I swallow hard. "You're going to get a photo of Sienna Hart. *The* Sienna Hart?"

He nods. "We didn't think we'd get the lead since Lance wouldn't help us out." He leans forward and lowers his voice as if he's telling a secret. "Lance's roommate is Sienna's massage therapist, so we thought this would be a rock solid lead. But Ticketmaster is a bloody beast."

Lizzie interrupts. "But thankfully, the tip came through. Rather unexpectedly."

"How?" Adam asks.

From down the hall we hear a toilet flush. Franks steps out of the bathroom and enters the room as he attempts to tuck his black shirt into his pants. He's unsuccessful.

"I was the one who got the lead. Sienna will be at the X-Bar tonight—celebrating her birthday, I'm told." Frank passes right by us, no eye contact, and heads to the kitchen. "I need a friggin' snack."

Lizzie leans forward to catch my eye. "Here's where you come in, Tori. We need you to get in the X-Bar. Find Sienna and watch her. When she starts to leave, call Adam on the cell and tell him which exit she's using." She turns to Adam. "Then you inform Frank and help him get set-up in position."

Lizzie then jumps up out of her chair and paces the room. "But here's the most important part: you cannot talk to her. You can't even let her see you, Tori. Just blend in. Sienna's assistant is extremely protective—if she senses you're a plant watching her moves, then it's over. She'll find a way to sneak Sienna out of there. She always does."

Adam tilts his head. "You guys seem pretty amped up over this one photo. What's the big deal?"

Frank calls out from the kitchen where he's hunting through the refrigerator. "I've taken pictures of hundreds of celebrities. But that Sienna Hart girl..." He turns around and places a jar of pickles on the counter. "No one has shot her picture in public in over a year. That assistant of hers..." Frank fishes a pickle out of the jar. *Crunch.* "She's done a good job of protecting her. So this photo could be huge." *Crunch.* Pickle juice spills down his shirt but he doesn't seem to mind.

Lizzie checks her phone. "It's getting late, let's get going." She walks us to the door. Before we step out she reaches for my hand. "If we get this photo, it'll be an exclusive. That means a big pay-out...like six-figure big." She gives my hand a warm squeeze. "You haven't let us down yet. You can do this."

I squeeze her hand back and smile. "Of course I can."

I'll do whatever it takes to make this work. Because I'm about to see Sienna Hart…in person! This might turn out to be the best night of my life.

And all I have to do is stay away from her and not get caught.

Easy.

Los Angeles County Juvenile Detention Intake Report

Name: Tori Wright   Age at booking: 16
Eyes: HAZ   Hair: BRN
Height: 5'5"   Weight: 124
Sex: F   Charges: Infraction 240; 594
Charging Officer: Ortega
Court date/time: To be determined

Intake Notes:

Suspect states her job to watch Sienna Hart was not as easy as it seemed. Claims the incident was not her fault and no maliciousness was involved. Suspect states she thought she was helping, but she was wrong. She does not want any more to drink; requests a quick bathroom break.

CHAPTER TWENTY–SEVEN

"You sure you can get in there?" Adam leans up to get a better view of the X-Bar half a block away. There isn't a line, just crowds of people milling around, probably trying to figure out a way to get in there. Or maybe they're hoping to get a celebrity sighting.

"With this cleavage?" I yank on my shirt so it's giving the illusion I'm a fully formed twenty-one-year old. "Be sure your phone is on. I'll track her down and let you know which exit."

I jump out of the Jeep and slam my door shut without even waiting for his response. Because inside that bar is Sienna Hart: flesh and blood, hair and feet—all of her. I was about to set foot in the same room as Sienna, for real. Shannon will *not* believe this.

I practically skip to the front entrance, but my scrumptious feelings immediately turn to dread when I see the bouncer. He is your basic nightmare. Thin and waif-like. Wire-rimmed glasses way too big for his face. Pants far too short to have been purchased within the last several years. More than likely a tech school student learning gaming software.

A gamer.

And gamers do *not* fall for the helpless-rich-girl-with-a-driver act. Or the my-client-needs-her-epi-pen act. Or even the brother-needs-this-ring-to-propose act. They don't fall for *anything*. They believe in rules of logic.

They are nightmares.

To make this one work, I'm going to have to dig deep. But I've watched some movies on the Independent Film channel, so I know what it'll take: excessive amounts of feminist movement behavior. Gamers dig ethics. If I mix that with some of Taylor's no-fail methods to 'getting your way' it might actually work.

"Invitation?" His voice is nasally. He doesn't give me eye contact, just does the one-finger scroll on his phone looking for something clearly more interesting than my presence.

"Jack's inside. He said he'd leave my name with you at the door. It's Tori." I shift my purse on my shoulder and cross my arms, pretending this is as equally uninteresting to me. (Step one of Taylor's method.) And saying a name like Jack without giving any last name is how you make someone sound like a very important person. (That's step two.)

Game Boy takes a moment to look away from his phone to check a small piece of paper he pulls from his pocket. "Nope. Not on here." More phone scrolling. But he keeps the paper in his hand and I tilt my head to get a quick peek. It's a short list—I catch only two names: Daniel. Peter.

Bingo.

"I'm one of Jack's assistants. He said he put all three of us on there. Me, Peter, Danny."

He looks me up and down, unsure. "Uh, it's just Daniel and Peter."

"You have GOT to be kidding me. He put the *dudes* on there and not me? What the hell? He did this with the X-Men premier too, just so they could troll for girls." I stick my hand on my hip like I'm not going *anywhere*. "I'm starting to think women can't get a fair shot in this town, you know?"

He shakes his head, looking disgusted. "That is just. Lame."

Score. There is nothing better than witnessing a gamer experience empathy.

"But I can't let you in. Amy, my boss, is a total bitch."

Okay, not cool. When girls call other girls bitches, it's simply descriptive, but when *guys* call girls bitches it feels like a violation of our constitutional rights. Maybe he had *some* empathy, but he didn't need to go and disappoint our Founding Fathers!

"Sorry." He folds his arms showing his nails, which have been chewed relentlessly. Maybe Amy *was* a sort of a bitch.

But what am I going to do? Walk away? Give up?

As I stand there, mouth gaping, thinking, thinking...a group of women approach Game Boy and flash their invitations at him.

One of them, decked out in a '50's style black dress with a large cherry pendant leaves her group and rushes up to me. "Tori!"

Looking her over carefully, I recognize her. It's Janine, Adam's sister.

I almost start bouncing on my toes. "So glad to see you!" I say because I really am glad to see her—she might be my only way in. I guess the universe *does* have good timing when it wants to.

"You headed in?" Janine puts her hand under my elbow and starts to guide me toward the door. I search her face not sure what to say.

She leans in and whispers, "Don't say a word. Just nod." Then she turns back to Game Boy who is gnawing on his thumbnail. She must frequent this place often because she knows him by name. "Ethan, I'm taking Tori in with me. Cool?"

"But she's not—"

"I'm putting together your girlfriend's Minecraft party. You know I want to make it perfect for her..." She wags her finger at him, tsk-ing.

It's convincing because he nods and motions us inside. Thank you, Universe. And Janine. And gamers who want to make their girlfriends happy.

We make our way through the entrance, and Janine leads me to the bar. "This place is amazing, right?"

"Yeah." I'm suddenly aware my jaw has hit the floor. Because this place *is* amazing. The room is ringed with circular high-backed booths covered in black leather. A twinkly chandelier hangs above each table surrounded by gorgeous people drinking champagne and martinis.

"Where's Adam?" she asks. "You two hunting down something tonight?"

"He's waiting for me in the car." I don't want to tell her it's not a "something" we're hunting down, but a "someone." I need to be careful so I don't blow this.

"I'm just tracking down some of those little paper umbrellas they put in drinks," I lie.

Janine nods cheerfully. "Yep. I once planned a party all themed with paper umbrellas. Don't worry—I'll order some cocktails and get a couple to you." She winks and waves at the bartender.

Pressing my back against the cold bar, I scan the room for her, looking over the groups of people in each booth. But no Sienna.

In the far corner I spot an opening to another room. I need to get a peek. "I'm going to use the restroom," I tell Janine. She gives me a thumbs-up with one hand while flagging down a bartender with the other.

I slink across the dance floor and when I near the opening, I see a small, intimate room filled with people dancing, drinking, laughing.

In the middle of them all, I see her. Sienna Hart. Wow, it is completely strange to see a real star right in front of you only a few car lengths away just...just...sitting there like a human or something.

She's smaller than I had imagined. All her features are cute and compact, like a kitten.

She sips on a large drink with at least four umbrellas stuffed in it—which would be helpful if I *actually* needed them. Surrounding her is a bunch of girls, other actresses probably, who are moving to the loud thumping music and throwing their hands in the air. One of them steps up on a chair and immediately falls back down, breaking into hysterics. Another girl pulls her back up by her bra strap. They are completely drunk.

This is entertaining.

Admittedly, I want to sneak in there and grab Sienna by the shoulders—tell her how much I loved her in American Party Girl, the pep rally scene in episode two in particular. And tell her that she shouldn't take the role she's up for in Werewolf Angel because she is truly fantastic as a regular girl with regular problems, and no actress can make me tear up, but *she* can, and oh-my-god she is fantastic.

I want to tell her all of this. And she's right here, so close I could toss a peanut in her mouth. How can I pass up this opportunity?

Calm down, calm down. Keep cool.

I can't jeopardize what I'm here to do. Plus the last thing she wants to deal with is some annoying fan crashing her birthday party.

Pushing my back against the wall, I peer in and get a better view. Sienna is dancing next to her table, not doing a very good job of it. She's having a hard time staying vertical in her platform gladiator wedge heels. Which are GORGEOUS.

A waitress emerges from the room carrying a tray full of empty drink glasses. The partiers yell out more drink orders. "Of course, right away!" She replies as she rushes past me mumbling something about "being entitled" and "bunch-a-brats." Plus a couple of expletives I won't repeat.

Sienna's partying is clearly going to take some time, so I decide to take a quick bathroom break. This may be my only chance for a while.

Further down the hall in the far back corner, I find an open bathroom door. Inside is a single bathroom, no stalls. It is totally modern with a marble sink and a beautiful wood hutch covered with lotions and soaps, along with feminine products displayed tastefully in wicker baskets. There's even a chandelier hanging from the high ceiling to match the ones in the bar room. Clearly this bathroom is made for people with expensive taste.

I squat over the toilet, trying to be graceful about it since this room is overwhelmingly elegant.

But within moments, I realize I've forgotten to do one important thing: lock the door. Without warning, someone rushes through the door.

And suddenly, wavering only a few feet from my face in gladiator wedge heels...is Sienna Hart.

Hiking up her skirt.

CHAPTER TWENTY-EIGHT

"Whoa! Don't back that up!" I hold my hand up, trying to block my view from things I do *not* need to see.

Sienna spins around clumsily and faces me. "Oh, crap! I didn't know anyone was in here!"

"Yep. Just me. Peeing right here...in front of you."

So this is how I meet Sienna Hart. Hovering over a toilet. Awesome.

"Go 'head." She gives me a hand wave and takes a sip on her drink. "I'll close my eyes." But this causes her to sway, almost falling over. She reaches out to the sink to balance herself while I finish.

I can't believe this is happening. I'm not even supposed to let her see me and now here I am having girl time in the bathroom.

As I wash my hands, she stands behind me and studies my face in the mirror. "Don't I know you?"

Well, this is an odd moment. I'm not sure how to answer because I'm not supposed to talk to her. But she's asking me a question, a direct one. I can't just ignore her.

"Wait." She wags her finger at me in the mirror. "You were in Vampire School 2, right? The sister?"

"No, I don't act."

She tilts her head, like she's in deep thought. "Oh! American Party Girl—the nosy neighbor. Am I right?!"

"Um. I'm more...behind the scenes."

"Cool." She stumbles over to the toilet and pulls up her skirt. Wow, drunk Sienna is not modest, that's for sure.

"I'll be outside," I say.

"Naw. Help me?" She reaches out with her hand and I grab it instinctively. Sienna uses my entire forearm to steady herself as she sits down, not taking the time to put down any protective tissue. Ick.

I have to continue steadying her because she tips even when she's planted firmly on the seat. I squat down, inches from her face, and stare straight up at the ceiling while she pees. True Hollywood Glamour, this moment.

Sienna must have had *a lot* of cocktails because I have to hold her up for quite some time. So long, in fact, that she settles in and gets totally comfortable, like this is her living room. With her arm perched on her knee, she rests her chin in her hand and looks me over with a sweet smile. "Thanks for helping me. No one else would stop dancing long enough to walk me to the bathroom." Then she sighs and all of a sudden her face looks sad. "I really don't wanna go back out there."

"To the party? Why not?"

"I don't know if you noticed but...I'm just a lot drunk." Hiccup.

I pat the top of her hand. "You're just a little tipsy. That's all."

"But my friends won't let me talk about him. All they want to do is party and they won't even let me bring up his name."

"Whose name?"

"Jake. You know...Jake Jeffers—my ex." She looks slightly irritated. "Didn't you see the cover of last month's In Touch? They did a two-page spread on our breakup. He looked so amazing."

"I saw the cover of Star—you were about to walk in the front door of rehab. Exhaustion rehab." I can't help but bring it up—it's my chance to see how accurate Jo-Jo Lopez was about his celebrity predictions.

She laughs and clamps down tighter as she lifts herself off the toilet. Aaand she's a drip-drier. These are things I do *not* need to know.

While she washes her hands (I am shocked by her sudden sense of hygiene), she talks at me in the mirror. "Jake broke up with me— in a text. And I tried to get over it, I really did. Did mani/pedis with the girls, ate ice cream—"

I know exactly what she means. "Movie marathons, too?"

"Of course. I have a strange fascination with *really* old movies."

"Like James Dean? Rebel Without a Cause?"

She wrinkles her nose. "No, silly. Sixteen Candles."

I hand over a paper towel and she keeps talking like we know each other—as if we're friends.

Like all this is normal.

Deep breath—in, out, in, out. I'm about to come down with a happiness migraine.

"Anyway, even after the movie marathons and all that, I realized all I wanted was for him to call. But he didn't." She piles on the lip gloss while still chatting away—it's totally impressive. "It was like he had no idea how much I was hurting." Pucker, smack. "And *that's* how I ended up on a gin & tonic binge—it was his favorite drink. I figured I'd be all symbolic about it, you know. Except gin & tonic sort of tastes like ass. Why can't he love strawberry daiquiris?"

She went on a drinking binge…because of *him*? And not even a tasty binge? Surely she knows how sad she sounds.

I help dry her hands because she's not doing a very good job. She's patting down her forearms. "So you drank yourself silly on something that tastes like crap because *he* liked it?"

Her eyes light up, but not in the way I'm hoping. "And it was worth it! When he heard I was drinking non-stop, he finally called me. I wish I could remember the conversation though—I sorta blacked-out."

She tries to pull her fingers through her hair to get out some of the tangles, but she's making it worse. Drunk Sienna is completely unable to get through the rigors of life without assistance.

"I got this." I run my fingers through her hair, gently pulling out the tangles and *wow*, her hair is pure silk. This girl is using some seriously high-quality conditioner.

She closes her eyes while I fix her hair and her shoulders relax. "My assistant acts like she's my mother, and she forced me into rehab. *She* was the one who told the tabloids it was exhaustion. But it wasn't." She shuts her eyes tighter. "It was a broken heart."

Wow. I can't believe she's sharing all this with me. Sienna isn't some untouchable movie star, *clearly* because here I am...*touching her*.

I hold her by the shoulders and spin her around to face the mirror. "There. Open your eyes. You're beautiful."

She smiles as she realizes I'm right, but then her smile falls and she presses her lips together, trying to hold back tears. "When I leave here tonight the paparazzi will find me and my drunk picture is going to end up on the front of tomorrow's tabloid. The studio will probably fire me from Werewolf Angel."

Oh, no. This poor girl. "But Sienna—"

"It's inevitable." She shrugs. "At least Jake will see the picture and maybe he'll call me. Silver lining, right?"

Oh my god, here she is just trying to get over a guy, something I have plenty of experience with, and now her pain is going to be splattered all over the newspapers.

And my job tonight—the whole reason why I'm here—is to make sure it happens.

No. No way. I can't do this. I know I have a job to do for Lizzie and Troy, but I'm also a girl who won't let another girl suffer. Not if I can help it.

"Listen, I know a way out of here—I saw a back exit at the end of this hall. The paparazzi won't find you. I'll make sure of it."

"It's okay." She pats her face with her palms to dry her tears. "It comes with the territory—I have to play along, I guess."

I grab Sienna by her hands. "Listen to me. I can help. Jake Jeffers is *not* going to see you on the cover of any magazine tomorrow. Got it?"

She taps me on the nose. "Aw, you're so sweet. What's your name?"

I break out with my big, goofy grin. "I'm Tori."

"What do you do, anyway? Sound? Craft services?"

Apparently I'm coordinating a plot to smear her reputation—not something she really needs to know right now. "I...I do personal...assisting...and stuff."

She studies me like I'm saying something completely cryptic. Then: "Oh. OH! No worries. I know so many girls who do the escort thing. Total shush from me." She silently zips her lips.

Okay, maybe she's quick to assume things, but there's something about her I like—not just Sienna Hart the movie star, but *her*, this sweet drunk girl in a bathroom with a broken heart.

The problem is, if I help her out, Lizzie and Troy won't get their photo they so desperately want, and I'll get fired. The firing isn't the worst part, it's that I won't be able to see Adam for our nightly adventures.

But this girl isn't just any girl—she's Sienna Hart. She's the reason I willingly chopped my hair and dyed it platinum blond in eighth grade. I can't just let her walk out that door and ruin her career, her reputation, and never get the guy. The first rule in Girlfriend's Guide to Exes is to never let him see you pathetic. And a drunk photo on the front of every tabloid with her holding a gin & tonic—his favorite drink—is beyond pathetic.

This girl needs me.

CHAPTER TWENTY-NINE

I lead her out to the hall. "Go get your purse. I'll wait here and get you out back without anyone seeing."

She takes a long sip on her drink and salutes me. "Yes, sir. Mrs. Captain. Of. A'merca."

Sienna laughs then staggers back into the private party room and I quickly dial Adam's cell. What I'm about to do makes my insides twist, but it's for his own good. I can't have him involved and get fired, too.

Adam answers after the first ring. "Hey!" His voice is sweet and luscious. He is cake.

I blurt it out before I change my mind. "Sienna's coming out the front entrance."

"Really? Celebrities rarely use that exit."

I bite at my lip. "Yeah, I guess she doesn't mind having her picture taken tonight."

"That makes it easy. I'll tell Frank."

"I'll find you soon." My voice wavers, so I quickly hang up before he asks me what's going on.

Sienna emerges from the party room, but she's not alone—she's flanked by her group of friends. I motion for her to follow me. "Hold on a sec," she tells her friends.

Sienna wobbles over to me and I whisper into her ear, "I can get you out this back exit. Follow me."

"You're soooo awesome." She's slurring even more than before. She must've had more to drink back into that room. She can hardly stand up straight.

Grabbing her by the elbow, I let her lean on me and we head toward the back exit. But that's when I hear a loud voice from behind. "HEY! What are you doing?!"

A girl in a short mini skirt, sky-high heels, and a see-through white blouse storms up to me. "What's going on here, Sienna?"

Sienna clamps down on her shoulder. "Maddie, shh. 'Sokay."

Maddie glares at me. "Who are you? Get your hands off her!"

Sienna answers before I can respond. "This is Tori! My new friend! She's an ESCORT! Isn't she adooooorable?" Hiccup.

"Go over with the other girls, Sienna."

"But—"

"Now!"

Sienna waves and blows me a kiss.

Maddie isn't done with me though. "I'm Sienna's assistant. *No one* gets in this party without my approval. How did you get in here? Are you some freaky stalker?"

"No, no! I'm uh..." Really, there's no good explanation I can come up with at this point. Besides, my attention is on what's happening over Maddie's shoulder. Sienna gets sucked back into her group of friends and they loop arms, staying in formation as they round the corner—all together like a pelican migration—and headed for the exit. The *front* exit. What is she doing?!

Maddie pulls her phone out to make a call, which is weird timing since she's in the middle of railing on me.

"Got your umbrellas." Suddenly Janine is in front of me. "Had to drink three of 'em though."

Universe, seriously, your timing is back to sucking! "Thanks, but I can't talk right now—"

Janine cups my chin and sticks an umbrella behind each of my ears. "Pretty!"

"Gotta get back to work!" I yell as I push past Janine, sprinting toward the door where Sienna's group is about to exit. I yell out behind her, "Sienna! No!"

But it's too late. They burst through the doors and within an instant, Sienna Hart is surrounded by cameras and flashing bulbs. And right there, front and center, is Frank. Getting exactly what he came here for.

Sienna tries to cover her face, but has a hard time because she's also reaching out for the railing to steady herself down the stairs.

And then: Step, tumble, wham! She busts it right there on the sidewalk.

Flashes spark in the darkness, documenting her public humiliation.

Oh, no. This can't be happening! Please, no crotch shots!!

I sprint down the stairs, kneel by her side and hold my hand out to help her. "I'm so sorry. I didn't mean for this to happen to you—"

"Get back, you freak!" Maddie snarls at me. She yanks my arm back and pushes me away from Sienna.

But I ignore her and turn to Frank. "Please, stop," I beg.

"What do you mean? It's all going as planned." He adjusts his flash then leans in closer to Sienna and lays on the motor drive. Every twitch and blink and fabric movement is now captured on Frank's camera.

As I back away from the scene, Maddie pulls Sienna back to her feet and guides her down the sidewalk toward their limo. Sienna looks back at me, "Don't worry—I'm going to be fine." She shoots me a sweet wink and climbs/falls into the backseat of the limo, while Frank documents every unfortunate shift of her skirt.

Within seconds, the sidewalk is cleared, Sienna's limo pulls away and Frank disappears into the night, like a bat.

And there I am, alone on the sidewalk, knowing that girl's life has just been wrecked. I plop down on the stairs and drop my head in my hands. If only she'd listened to me. I know exactly how to play the game and showing your pathetic side will never get the guy back.

A pair of black skater shoes appear next to my feet. Adam.

I lift my head and study his face. It does not say: I want to kiss you deeply. Not at all. "What were you doing? Did you try to sneak her out?"

Tears sting my eyes. "It was for a good reason. She's trying to get over this guy. She thought her drunk photo plastered everywhere would make him come back to her. Please don't be mad."

He lifts me to my feet. "You're a hard person to be mad at."

Oh my word, I want to kiss this boy. But I can't. I CAN'T. The truth is, I'm terrified. Terrified of not being the girl he wants, just the fill-in for another.

He gently cups my chin and turns my face toward his. "Talk to me."

I shake my head then shut my eyes tight and a tear drops. He wipes it from my cheek. "You know how to play the game, I get it. But that night when I took you with me to see Lana, the only advice you gave me was to tell her how I was really feeling. And I did." He steps closer and leans in, his breath tickling my neck. "Tell me what you're feeling, Tori."

I pull back, searching his face—his eyes, that dimple, those lips. I want to smother him with kisses...*that's* what I'm thinking.

His phone buzzes with a text. He lifts it up and I'm able to get a glimpse. It's from Lana.

CALL ME.

I back away from him. "I need space and so do you. We shouldn't be doing this."

He stuffs the phone in his back pocket. "Tori, please—"

"I'll talk to you later." I turn and head down the sidewalk.

"When?" he calls out.

I shake my head.

"How are you going to get home?" he yells.

I turn back to him. "I'm calling Taylor. And tell Lizzie I quit."
I spin on my heel and storm down the sidewalk. Lana wants him
back. I won't be a substitute. I won't.

I pull my phone out of my pocket, but before I dial Taylor I
glance back. Adam is hurrying toward his Jeep, his jacket hood
pulled tightly over his head.

Tears fill my eyes as I search for Taylor's phone number. Before
I can dial, I hear footsteps charging up behind me.

"That's her!"

I whip around to see Maddie pointing at me, and standing next
to her is a police officer.

"She's the stalker who was trying to hurt Sienna Hart."

"What?! I was not! I was trying to help—"

The officer clearly doesn't want to hear my side. "You'll need to
turn around," he orders. "You're under arrest."

CHAPTER THIRTY

The guy fastens handcuffs on me. I repeat: he HANDCUFFS me. Then he gives some spiel about my rights and silence and attorneys and courts and appointing things and oh-my-god my life has suddenly turned into a Law & Order episode. Minus that leggy brunette cop. *My* cop is rail thin with high-waisted pants.

He dips my head as he guides me into the back seat of his squad car. Through my dirty window I see Maddie, arms folded with a smug look on her face. I realize now what her phone call was about while we were "getting to know each other" outside the bathroom. She was calling the police.

I have gone from Head of the Yearbook Staff at Lincoln High to the stalker of Sienna Hart.

As we pull away from the scene of my crime, tears well up in my eyes. I've decided that crying is the only solution I have to solve this problem. But it's going to require lots of tears. At the moment, I have many problems:

1. I am headed to jail for stalking my idol.
2. Mom will hear about this on her scanner.
3. She will flip.
4. I may be grounded until I'm of legal drinking age.
5. Or longer.
6. I just told Adam we need time apart.
7. I'm not sure that was the right move.

8. Fortunately, there is no number eight.

8b. Oh, wait—there is! My arresting officer won't stop chit-chatting while I'm organizing this numbered list of problems in my head.

"So you're a stalker of Sienna Hart, eh? You aren't the first. That assistant of hers is very diligent. The last guy I hauled in *swore* he was just the pizza delivery guy. Likely story."

He stuffs a piece of gum in his mouth and talks at me in the rearview mirror. "Your license says you're sixteen, so I'm taking you to juvenile hall. Lucky you're not eighteen, or you'd be in for a rough night at county."

He squints, glancing back and forth between me and the road. "But most stalkers just want to get an up-close picture or steal underwear. Why in the world were you trying to hurt Sienna Hart? Didn't you see her on the cover of In Touch? The poor girl's been suffering from exhaustion."

"Hurt her?" I awkwardly wipe my tears away on my shoulder. "You have *got* to be kidding me! I was helping her!"

"Settle down—"

"Look, no offense Mr. Officer, but you got it all wrong. I was protecting her from the paparazzi. And she wasn't in rehab for exhaustion." I add under my breath. "She was there because of a guy."

"What's that?" He perks up at this tidbit of gossip.

Time to change the subject. "Aren't you supposed to have a partner? I figured there'd be some kind of bad cop/good cop thing going on."

"I *should* have a partner, but the department's been completely restructured. Budget cuts. So for situations like this with the juveniles, I'm it, all the way through processing." He rolls his eyes as he glances at me in the mirror. "The psychologists—some Harvard types—think it's less traumatizing for the kids. And saves money. I shouldn't even be talking to you about this."

I guess he figures *saying* he shouldn't talk about it makes it okay to talk about. "And we shouldn't be talking about Sienna's visit to rehab. It's a medical issue," he adds.

"But her ending up in rehab is the reason I had to help her."

He raises a brow and eyes me in the mirror. "Are you aware of HIPAA, young lady?"

"Hippa. He's a rap star, right?"

Officer No-Humor finds no humor in that and, truthfully, I'm not even sure why I said it. "The Health Insurance Portability and Accountability Act. HIPAA," he says.

"That was my next guess."

"In the state of California it's a serious offense to share someone's medical records without their consent."

"The tabloids don't seem to mind sharing."

He taps at his chin, like he's thinking. "Huh. Hadn't thought about that."

We are quiet for a moment and we drive along with only the sounds of his scanner spouting generic descriptions and addresses and codes that I can't decipher.

Wait. Is this all Mom hears at the paper? "Excuse me, officer? Do they announce the person's name over the scanner when they've been arrested?"

"Nope, just whether the person is a juvenile or an adult."

I let out a long happy sigh. Even if Mom heard about my arrest, she won't know it was me, just some juvenile.

"Plus the violation code," He continues. "You had two codes: 240 and 594."

"What do those mean?"

"The first one's battery and you're lucky I didn't book you on assault. And a 594 is malicious mischief."

"I don't even know what malicious mischief means."

"It's sort of a catch-all code. We give it to most stalkers."

I drop my head, unable to process everything that's going on. I've been given a violation code. Two of them!

This can't be happening. This can't be happening.

He turns the volume down on the scanner and glances back at me with a curious smirk on his face. "Did you see Sienna in American Party Girl? She took that Jenny part and made it her own. No one could make me cry, but that scene—"

I nod. "The pep rally scene. I know. Gets me every time, too."

Well, at least we share an obsession with Sienna Hart's movie career. He must start to feel comfortable because as he cruises down the highway, he babbles on and on about how much he loves working as a cop in Hollywood—the best beat out there!—and how he's only been on the force for a few months and he's a rookie from Sacramento but it's lame because *no* stars ever go to that town, except for governors, and blah, blah, blah, I just want out of this car.

He exits off the highway and I notice that the twinkling skyscrapers have become neon-lit strip clubs, bail bonds stores, and deserted lots. We must be close. Strangely I'm relieved because the sooner I'm out of this car, the sooner I can talk to a manager or something. There has to be some way to get out of this mess.

"But in Hollywood, if you're darned lucky, you might get the opportunity to arrest a movie star," he continues, now chewing on two pieces of gum. "And the drunk ones are the best...I'm told they talk a lot. A buddy of mine on the force said he once got a star to autograph his speed detector. I can't say who it was, but she *may* or may *not* have been on that Bachelorette show. Anyway, she signed it on the side with a sharpie, but it was a black one and, like I said, she was drunk, so it looks more like a smudge. I was supposed to take a left back there."

My arresting officer is completely celebrity-obsessed and bad with directions.

Lovely.

He turns the car around and heads in the right direction, I'm hoping, then continues his chat fest. "But this one time I pulled over a Mercedes for rolling through a stop sign without coming to a complete stop." He grins while smacking his gum wildly. "It was Jack Nicholson!"

"Congratulations," I say with an even tone.

"Exactly. Except it turns out it was just a guy with the same name. *This* Jack Nicholson owns a bunch of Jiffy Lubes in San Bernardino. But, man...I got close to arresting a real celebrity. Actually, now that I think about it, having you in my squad car—Sienna Hart's attacker—is the closest I've gotten to a celeb encounter. Crap, missed my turn."

We turn around three more times before he finally finds the L.A. County Juvenile Detention Center. Officer Starstruck escorts me inside the building and into a small waiting room. It smells like urine and bleach and cat litter. The room is stark and gray with only a metal table, two worn plastic chairs and a clock. It's 11:00.

Oh, no. I'm supposed to be home in thirty minutes. What if Mom gets home first and, surprisingly, happens to notice I'm missing. She'll freak.

When Mom finds out what happened, the odds of her ever letting me come into the city are zero-point-zero. I just wish she knew about the cool, beautiful parts of L.A. Though this waiting room at juvie is not one of them, I'll admit that.

The officer steps back into the room. "I tried calling your mom, no answer. I'll try again later. Or how about your dad?"

I dip my head. "Out of town. Like usual."

He clicks his ballpoint pen. "I need to write up an incident report so they have all the background on your case." He squares up his paper, carefully sips his coffee, then flashes an energetic smile at me like he's actually excited about this. "Start at the beginning. Tell me everything—like I said, this is the closest I've gotten to a celebrity arrest so don't spare a *single* detail. Now, how did you—oh, wait! I should offer you something to drink. Water? Coffee?"

"Grape Fanta?" I ask, because why not.

He shakes his head. "Sorry."

"I'm fine," I say. Except I'm not. The reality of where I am hits me—the grayness of the walls and the metal-ness of the furniture—and I flop my head on the table. "I...I can't do this."

He thinks I'm talking about soda. "You really like Fanta, I get it. Okay, don't cry." He leans in and lowers his voice. "They'll think I intimidated you or something. I'm...I'm pretty new. Just hold on, all right?" He disappears for a minute then reappears with a Fanta in hand. "We have vending machines in the officer's lounge. That was the last one. Grape's pretty popular." He takes the cuffs off my hands and slides the can over to me.

Slight relief fills me as I drink the soda with my own free hands. Once we are settled with beverages and his papers are all lined up perfectly, he starts again. "Please tell me why you were found on Melrose Avenue accosting Sienna Hart. Again, I love details."

I can't remember if I'm supposed to wait for a lawyer or something because I've never actually watched a cop show, just commercials for re-runs. But I didn't do anything wrong and I was in possession of a grape Fanta for strength, so I tell him. I tell him every little detail from the moment Shannon was blowing her nose on my favorite t-shirt on my shag rug all the way up to this moment where he is currently arresting me.

Officer Starstruck writes all this up for some "intake report" because the psychologists won't let them call it an arrest report—something about not damaging our fragile emotional state. But no matter what he calls it, I doubt the report includes all the facts because most of the time he just listens with his head propped up in his hands. I have to tap on the metal table from time to time so he'll get back to work. Graciously though, he does get me water with ice when the Fanta runs out. And he allows me a quick bathroom break at one point. He's pretty cool.

Once I'm finished, he tucks his pen inside his notebook and stands up, looking rather satisfied with his own *amazing* investigative work. "Everything looks good. I'll hand the paperwork over to receiving and they'll take care of you over there. I have one more round tonight and then my shift is over."

Everything looks good? Whew. As far as arrests go, this is pretty easy. Maybe I can even get home in time to head off Mom.

I guess if it had to be anyone, I'm glad I was arrested by Officer Starstruck. He has a lot of room for growth, that's for sure, but he seems like a nice enough guy. "Hey, maybe you'll get lucky," I say. "The *real* Jack Nicholson could run a red light tonight. There's still hope for you."

His face fills with a warm smile. "If it makes you feel any better, I believe you."

Oh, thank God. This nightmare is over.

"But your mother will have to come to the hearing and we'll see what the judge rules."

"Wait. A judge?"

"8 a.m. tomorrow." He points at a dry erase board hanging in the hallway. "Let's see..." He goes down the list until his finger lands on my name. "Oh, you got Montrose for a judge. Sorry, she's brutal."

"You're saying I'm not going to see a judge until the *morning*?!"

My heart pumps double time, and I wipe my sweaty hands on my skirt.

But he doesn't seem too concerned with my on-coming panic attack and escorts me down the hall toward the receiving area. This is where I am to wait—yet again. Officer Depressing-The-Hell-Out-Of-Me explains this is where they'll record all my belongings and figure out which room to assign me. Except this is not the Hilton

Hotel and I remind myself that when he says "room" what he really means is "jail cell."

My stomach drops.

He pushes open the door to the receiving area, but before he turns me over he leans in and says, "Get comfortable. This part takes a while. Good luck."

When the door slams shut behind me, I face the room and realize this is where they take *all* the girls who've been arrested tonight.

I am not alone.

CHAPTER THIRTY-ONE

The receiving area looks like a waiting room—there are rows and rows of benches and a guard stands behind a glass window watching the room. Several girls are curled up on chairs, some sleeping. In the far corner is a group of three girls, two are sitting down, but one of them is standing, feet planted firmly, and she's totally staring me down. Blond dreadlocks with beads woven in them hang all the way down to her waist, and her arms are covered in butterfly tattoos. She motions for me to come over.

She's either going to murder me or hug me. This is fun.

As I make my way over to them, the two girls sitting behind her don't look in my direction, seemingly uninterested. One of them has a shaved head with super long feather earrings. She's wearing baggy overalls with only a lace bra underneath, and she's pretty gorgeous actually. Another girl is curled up asleep in her chair with her head in Feather Girl's lap, but she's sucking on a lollipop ring so she can't be *that* asleep.

I approach the dreadlocked girl cautiously.

"You waiting for them to assign you a cell?" she asks.

Something tells me she frequents this establishment on a regular basis. "Yeah," I respond and glance down noticing that I am still showing daring amounts of cleavage. Nice.

"That officer said they can't put three of us together. So one of us is going to get stuck with a stranger. Maybe we could be cellmates. I'm Piper." She sticks her hand out, which is covered in chunky silver rings, one of them a large peace symbol. I notice she also has hearts and smiley faces and unicorns drawn all over her hands.

She'd certainly make for an interesting cellmate. I shake her hand. "I'm Tori."

She stuffs her hands in the pockets of her army green cargo pants, which are rolled up to the knees and her bare feet are covered in sand. She begins to pace as she talks. "Man, we've only been in here an hour and I'm already going stir-crazy. The lighting is harsh. No food, just water." I don't dare tell her my arresting officer loaded me up with grape Fanta. "Why'd you get arrested?" she asks.

"Battery. And malicious mischief."

"Ah, stalking. Yeah, that's a tough one to talk your way out of. I'll give you some advice. The 'I swear, I didn't do it' defense won't get you anywhere. Right girls?" She turns back to her friends for confirmation.

The "sleeping" one nods and continues sucking on her ring. Feather Girl rolls her eyes and replies, "As long as there's no video tape. Video tape, you're screwed."

Piper whirls back to me and raises a brow. "Video tape?"

"No, I don't think so."

"See, no worries for you."

I can't help but wonder how these three ended up in here. "Why'd you get arrested?"

Piper closes her eyes and draws in her breath. Before she answers, Sleeping Girl pulls the ring out of her mouth and mumbles, "The trip was not my idea."

Feather Girl nods in agreement. "And at least *I* can read a calendar."

It is clear there are some blame issues going on with these three.

Piper leads me by the elbow to an open corner of the room. I guess she wants to explain this without them hearing, but the room isn't nearly as big as she probably needs.

She glares at me with great intensity. "We were on our way to the Coachella Festival. And I had to find Randy."

Feather Girl clearly can hear all this because she calls out, "Raaaaandy!" with her hands clasped in the air in fake adoration.

"Stop." Piper says to her like she's mad, but she has a smirk on her face. "I'm going to tell our new friend here about Randy or else she won't understand."

She turns back to me to continue, but then sleeping girl yells out, "Oh, Randy, you're my soul mate! My prince in another lifetime!" And the two of them break into giggles.

Piper places a hand on my shoulder. "Forget them. They don't understand this thing I have with Randy. But I can't blame them really...I mean—" she pushes me further in the corner and lowers her voice. "I mean we all have our issues, you know? And Ellie over there—the one with the feathers—she falls in love weekly. She gets more boyfriends than periods. And then Gina, the one sucking on her ring? She was born with this problem where she's only hot for boys who like other boys. So she's *constantly* disappointed. Poor thing."

Gosh, lots of details flying around in here. I try to get her back on track. "So this Randy guy?"

"Right, Randy. So we first met when I spotted him in a yellow beam of light at the Electric Daisy Carnival. It was—"

"Raaaaaandy!"

"Would. You. Stop?!" She growls at them lovingly then continues. "Anyway things moved fast with him and he told me to meet him at Coachella and I knew he was dyslexic going into this relationship, but I thought it was only with letters, not numbers, and he totally got the date switched around. And man, I feel really bad about the whole thing, but anyway we drove halfway from L.A. to the desert when I stopped for gas and the cashier asked us where we were going and I told him and he laughed and said that's not for *months*. So we headed back to L.A. and they were so disappointed that I pulled over at an exit. We ran around in the dirt singing and yelling with our lighters in the air so we could have our own festival, you know?"

"That's how you ended up getting arrested?"

"That's how we ended up barefoot. We got arrested because we stopped off at the KOA in Riverside and stole a bottle of Sunny D off this dude's picnic table, and we got totally jacked-up on sugar and tried to climb the Hollywood sign. Apparently, you aren't supposed to climb the Hollywood sign. Also, you're not supposed to resist arrest." She sighs as if she's thinking it over. "But in hindsight, I don't regret it because it was a blast, and we had a killer view of the city for a few brief glorious minutes, but really, deep down...between you and me..." She leans in closer and whispers, "I just wish Randy would get some freaking tutoring. I love that boy."

She's a little hard to follow but there is something about her that makes this "getting arrested thing" easier to take.

"What about you?" she asks. "Boyfriend? Girlfriend?"

"Neither. Not anymore."

She twists her dreads around her finger. "Spill it, girl. It'll help."

It may be the gorgeous butterflies covering her arms that are lulling me into some therapeutic state, but I strangely feel comfortable with telling Piper all about my love life. Or maybe it's just that she asked.

So I explain about Joel and how I realized I was just his rebound girl. And then I tell her about Adam and us dancing in the bathroom and going to the psychic and me wanting to kiss him madly, except we both just broke-up with someone so I told him we need our space.

"Space? I don't get it." Piper twirls her dread even tighter around her finger.

"I've done a lot of research on this and you should give yourself a month before starting a new relationship so you can formally get the person out of your system and move on," I explain, sort of lecture-y.

She holds her hand up. "Wait. You and Adam dig each other but you aren't going to date him for a month because of a book? Are you suffering from bad PMS?"

"No." I fold my arms looking a little defensive. "But I've seen what happens when a girl follows her heart and not the rules—she ends up drunk and in rehab. And it's the reason I was arrested."

"This is getting goooood." She rubs her palms together in excitement. "Tell me what happened."

"We were doing this job—long story—but we had to get a photo of Sienna Hart, that movie star, coming out of the X-Bar."

She nods. "On Thursday nights they have two for one Long Island Iced Teas. I've heard of that place." Piper seems far more interested in good drink deals than movie stars.

"So anyway, I got inside and I managed to talk to her—and I mean *really* talk. She was just trying to get over her breakup with Jake Jeffers. The guy broke up with her in a text, something I'm completely familiar with."

"Me, too." Piper admits.

"Hear, hear." Ellie Feather Girl, raises an invisible glass.

"I tried to help her get out of there without being spotted and that's when Maddie, her assistant, saw me with my hand on Sienna's arm, and she thought I was trying to assault her. So she called the cops."

"The nerve!"

"Right? And then Sienna did end up getting her picture taken, just moments after taking a nasty fall down the stairs. The poor thing, I feel so guilty."

Piper waves her hand. "Forget that Sienna girl. Tell me what happened with Adam!"

Quickly scanning the room, I notice all eyes are on me and they're waiting for me to finish the story. Even the guard has slipped out from behind the window glass to listen.

I answer in a loud voice so everyone can hear. "I told Adam I was trying to help Sienna get over this guy, and it reminded me that we both need time to get over our exes before we start dating each other. And, then, while I was telling him all this...his ex called."

Piper narrows her eyes. "But did he answer it?"

"Well, no. But still. We need to wait thirty days before we date—that's the rule."

The room breaks out into hysterics. Even the guard doubles over from laughing so hard.

"What??" I throw my hands up. "I'm trying to do this the right way."

Piper finally stops laughing long enough to stand up and clamp down on my shoulder. "When you like someone, you go for it. *That's* the rule. Forget your timelines."

I nervously grab at the hem of my shirt, unsure of what to say.

The door clicks open and Officer Starstruck pokes his head in the door. "Ladies? I've finished up my shift, but I made one more arrest tonight." He winks at me and flashes a giddy smile. Why is he so happy? "Play nice," he says with a smirk.

And in scuffles a rumpled blond, wobbling in her Gladiator wedge heels—the source of Officer Starstruck's giddiness. His first celebrity arrest.

Sienna Hart.

CHAPTER THIRTY-TWO

"Tori!" Sienna rushes over and hugs me. Then she does her best to sit down next to Sleeping Girl Gina. But she has to hold her hand out to steady herself, and there's really no grace involved.

Poor Sienna is an absolute mess—tangled hair, stained clothes. I slide into the seat next to her and tug at a knot in her hair, smoothing it out. "Thanks," she says in a gravelly voice.

"What happened, Sienna? You got *arrested?*"

She looks down at her feet, turning her toes inward like a little girl. "We tried to steal a Rodeo Drive street sign."

Piper leans in and sticks her hand out to give her a fist bump. "Right on, lady."

Sienna flicks her eyes up at her and wrinkles her nose as she takes in the massiveness of dreadlocks and tattoos now in her presence.

"This is Piper," I say.

"I'm Piper. I've never seen any of your movies because I don't watch movies, but your shoes are wicked cool." She's still holding her hand out for a return bump.

"Thanks," Sienna reaches out and shakes Piper's balled up fist, resulting in the world's most awkward handshake.

"So that nice officer out there arrested us," Sienna explains. "And then the paparazzi found us again."

"No, way!" My fists clench and I immediately want to throttle Frank.

"The photos of my arrest will be in papers tomorrow, I'm sure. The weird thing was—and maybe I'm being paranoid—but when the paparazzi showed up, I glanced back at that officer, and I *swear* he was smiling while they took pictures."

I laugh. "You were his first celebrity arrest."

Her face brightens. "Really? Aw! Now I'm sort of honored."

I can't believe she's handling this so well. Her life is about to become a public relations nightmare. She's going to have to deal with the humiliation of having her ex see her like that and probably lose her role on Werewolf Angel. And yet she feels glad she could help out a poor starstruck cop.

I try to console her. "Maybe Jake won't see the paper tomorrow."

"Ha! He'd better!" She snorts.

"What do you mean?" I tugged at another tangle.

"I worked too hard at this for it to not work. He'll call. I know it."

I yank my hands away from her. "What do you mean? You worked too *hard* at it. At what?"

"The photo of me drunk? It was all planned. *I* was the one who tipped off the photographer—Frank. There just wasn't any other way to get Jake's attention. Once he sees how out of control things have gotten he'll call, I know it."

Whoa. Whoa! This can *not* be happening. "Are you saying you *wanted* them to take your picture drunk and getting arrested?!" Bending over, I try to get some air because this plane is clearly going down. *Breathe slowly. Surely she isn't saying what she's actually saying.*

She calmly crosses her legs. "It was all planned out—I made sure Frank was outside the X-Bar. He told me he would send some girl in there to watch me so he'd know which door to stand by. So weird, right? Someone was watching me the entire time, and I never figured out who it was. That girl must be good at her job."

Hyperventilate—I'm going to hyperventilate!

She punches me lightly on the arm, not noticing that I'm turning blue from lack of air. "I couldn't call Jake because he'd never answer and then I'd end up leaving a message and sounding all pathetic. So I *had* to do it this way. I even had my friend call the police on us when we were stealing the sign. Then I made sure Frank was in ready position when the officer showed up. Such perfection."

This girl is my idol?! Shoot me now.

I sit up straight and glare at her. "And staging your own drunken arrest photo just so he'd feel sorry for you isn't PATHETIC?!"

She folds her arms. "What are you getting all upset for? Haven't you ever noticed those "candid" shots of celebrities strolling through farmer's markets all dressed adorably? That's not by accident."

"I tried to protect you. I got arrested for you! I dyed my hair in eighth grade for you!!" I really want to punch her gorgeous face right. Oh, what the heck—I'm already in jail. Punching out a movie star while I'm here will only add a month or two to my sentence.

Totally. Freaking. Worth it.

Sienna pats me on the knee like this is all no big deal. "But I don't understand how *you* got arrested? How does it have anything to do with me?"

I clench my jaw. "Because the girl in the club watching your every move…was me."

Piper bounces up closer, rubbing her hands together. "This is getting really interesting, y'all."

We ignore her and stare at each other with blank faces as if we're seeing each other for the first time.

Sienna shakes her head. "This doesn't make sense—you said you were an escort."

"*You* said that. I told you I was an assistant. I was supposed to watch you so I could let Frank know which door you'd be coming out. But instead you almost peed on me and then told me all about your breakup with Jake and I just couldn't let them take your picture and ruin your life. Why didn't you tell me you *wanted* them to take your picture?!"

"I thought you were an escort! I wasn't about to tell my biggest secret to a hooker!"

Piper leans in with a beaming smile. "Okay, seriously, this is the most interesting story ever in all of *ever*."

"I'm not a hooker. And I just wanted to help you—after I *met* you, that is." I take a deep breath trying to get my heart rate down to irate rather than ballistic. "Look, I know what it's like to deal with a breakup. You'd do anything to get him back. That's why I took this job—to stay busy so Joel would miss me and come running back. I get it. So that's why I couldn't go through with my job. I didn't want you to lose your dignity. But then your assistant thought I was stalking you, not *helping* you, and next thing I know I'm paying an overnight visit to L.A. Central Juvenile Detention Center."

Piper sticks her hands in her pockets and paces. "Hold up, people. Let me get this straight." She turns to Sienna. "*You* are in jail because you wanted arrest photos to show up in the paper to make your ex feel sorry for you." She spins on her heel and faces me. "And *you* are in jail for helping to get those photos all because you wanted a job that would make your ex feel sorry for you."

That about sums it up.

We both nod and stare at invisible items on the tile floor.

Hearing it put that way, I start to wonder if I'm as pathetic as Sienna.

"We have this thing—" Piper says.

"Tell them about the thing." Feather Girl Ellie points a finger at her.

"I'm *trying*," Piper is half annoyed/half giggling. "See, we have this *thing*, it's like a pact I guess, and here it is: do your own thing."

"Your *own* thing," Ellie repeats, like it's some sort of mantra with them.

Piper nods and continues. "Because a boy—"

"Or a girl," Ellie adds.

"Isn't worth *not* having a thing over. That's our pact."

Sienna winces as she tries to cover her yawn. I look over at Piper plainly. "You realize this isn't actually making sense yet, right?"

She sighs and chews on her thumbnail for a moment. "Okay, so let's say God or whatever you want to say is head honcho of the universe—"

Sleeping Girl Gina dislodges the lollipop ring from her mouth to say, "She-Wolfstress."

Piper cups the side of her mouth and whispers to us, "She believes in this half wolf, half goddess thing. She basically worships that singer Shakira. Anyway, let's say *your* God was up there working away, creating people to put in his—"

"Or her."

"Or her world. She or she would make musicians or writers or sculptors or dancers or scientists or mathematicians or hairstylists, right?"

I nod like this is making sense. It isn't making sense.

"So then the he/she/wolf/god/goddess/whatever *wouldn't* create someone whose purpose on earth was to spend their precious time getting someone *else's* attention. I mean, come on. What is *that?*"

"So you're saying..." Sienna makes an attempt to summarize, but her voice trails off and she doesn't finish her sentence. She's still confused. Or still drunk.

Piper drops to her knees and grabs our hands. "No dude is worth becoming a pitiful human being. Have your own thing. Because we are children of God the She-Wolf."

Sienna laughs a little, and I kind of want to, too. But I'll be honest—I still want to throttle her. I got arrested because of her.

A woman guard opens the door. "Tori Wright?"

"Yes?"

"Your cell is ready."

CHAPTER THIRTY-THREE

An orange jumpsuit hangs from the guard's arm. "Come with me," she bellows.

Gulp.

I'm not sure if I'll see these girls again, even though I figure I'll have to share a cell with someone in here. I wave bye to Piper and her friends. Sienna stares down at her gorgeous sandals. We don't say another word to each other.

I step out into the hallway and look up at the guard who seems to be twice my height. "Can I request Piper as a cell mate?"

"Oh, sure. We take requests. You want HBO, too?" She laughs at herself.

She hates me already. Great.

Walking down the dim hall, I'm reminded of what it's like to walk down the English hall in my high school—musty, long and leading to a room where time will move very slowly.

But I would give anything to be sitting in Mr. Madison's English class right now instead of heading to my jail cell, even if it was Beowulf week.

"You can get undressed in there." She points to a small room— more closet-like—with only a curtain for privacy. "And put all your belongings in the plastic bag." She hands over the carrot-colored jumpsuit and a pair of black slip-on shoes that look like creepy old man loafers. I shudder.

She sticks a hand on her hip. "They're not Nike's but believe me, you'll want them on your feet for the walk to your cell."

The words "your cell" make me shudder as much as the shoes.

I shuffle into the closet, change into the oh-so-heinous jumpsuit and hand my bag of belongings over to the guard. She then escorts me down a different poorly lit hallway with the only shot of color coming from the posters taped to the walls with words like: RESPECT! RESPONSIBILITY! HONOR!

Because, of course, it is *POSTERS* that will turn you into a better person. Especially ones you read while being escorted to your jail cell.

Note to jail: Too late, perhaps?

The guard suddenly becomes chatty and as we walk. We talk about the weather, where we're from, our families, all that. But then she puts two and two together. "Wait, does your mom write that I'M DIVORCED, NOT DEAD blog?"

I nod.

"Oh, honey. That blog got me through some tough times."

I can't help but ask. "Did you happen to read the one on how to not be the rebound girl?"

"For sure. It was strangely written though—different tone, lots of exclamation points. In the end I wish I hadn't read that one though. Don't tell your Mom."

I don't understand. "Why do you wish you hadn't read it?"

"Right after my break-up, my best friend in the world— Stanley—admitted he has feelings for me. But I told him to stay away for thirty days, just like your mom told me. Only, when I called him after a month, he was dating someone new. I figured it wouldn't last but here I am, reading Facebook posts of all their plans for their upcoming wedding." She shakes her head and sighs. "I can't help but wonder if that could've been me. But I was too much of a rule-follower, I guess."

I stare down at my feet as we shuffle down the hall. The tears start to gather and I see the drops skitter down the front of my orange suit. What am I doing? I'm making Adam wait for thirty days...because of a book?

We stop in front of a door and she pushes a button. We're buzzed through several security doors until eventually we're outside. Outside? "Where's the cell?"

"D building. Over there." She points to a two- story building beyond a yard with a couple of basketball goals. "And there's no need to cry, hon. They'll treat you right over there."

A mangy black cat joins us for our walk—it has patches of fur missing and possibly an eye missing, unless the little guy is giving me one *very* long wink.

"Don't touch the cats, hon. They live...somewhere. Not really sure where." She leads me up an outdoor cement stairwell covered in fencing, like a cage. My stomach twists in knots. This is scary.

But when she opens the door, I'm almost impressed. It's a large room with high ceilings and looks like a nicer version of our school cafeteria. There are tables with benches, just like at school, and the room still has a lingering smell of cafeteria spaghetti—which is not like the restaurant kind, and has its own distinct smell...like ketchup and meat and metal.

Along the outside walls are doors, each with a small window and I can see girls inside, sleeping or pacing or glaring at me.

She takes me over to my room and slips the handcuffs off. "Leave your shoes by the door." Just before the door closes, she winks and says, "And welcome to Central."

I am the star of a horror movie.

Muffled sounds come through the walls—crying? Yelling? Murdering?!

I sit on one of the two beds and cover my ears, wishing this was a bad dream.

All of this—the entire mess—happened because of that stupid break-up text! I *knew* break-up texts were unforgivable.

After a few minutes, the door clicks open and the guard pokes her head in. "We're doubling up. Here's your roommate. It'll be just like having HBO. She says she's an *actress!*" She laughs at herself and motions for Sienna to sit down on the bed across from me.

The door slams shut, and we stare at each other.

"You couldn't get your own room?" I turn away from her. "I thought stars got special privileges."

Sienna huffs. "Oh, I tried. Apparently, that guard has never heard of Werewolf Angel. Or even American Party Girl. Can you believe that?"

"Such a travesty."

And then we both sit in silence, not moving—just two angry orange pumpkins.

Glancing her up and down, I realize there's something comforting about seeing her without her designer clothes and wearing a color that does *not* work with her skin tone. I decide to break the silence. "Let me show you around at least."

I give her a tour of our new home: two lovely cement slabs topped with a spongy mattress and dingy mauve sheets. One gleaming metal toilet. And one tiny window in the door in which we can gaze out of during our free time.

The tour doesn't take all that long, despite my use of adjectives. After a while, I get bored and start asking questions. "When did you move to L.A?"

"I was twelve." Her voice is late-night raspy. "I begged my parents to let me audition for that Kidz Bop show. I was totally obsessed with becoming an actress. And to be honest, I was pretty much friendless. Acting was all I had."

We both flip over on our stomachs and lay our heads on our hands. Suddenly I feel like we're in junior high together, having a slumber party and sharing secrets way later than our parents would allow.

"So my mom and dad decided we would drive out to L.A. for a week, I could audition, and if I got the part, we'd stay. I don't think they actually thought I'd get it. But I beat out 206 other girls." Her face is beaming.

Wow. I can't think of *anything* I can do better than 200 girls.

And then it hits me—all that bizarre stuff Piper was saying...I get it now. She has the answer to getting over heartbreak and it certainly isn't my ridiculous set of rules.

I pop up onto my elbows. "Piper finally makes sense to me now!"

"She does?"

"Yeah! Acting—that's your thing. The thing that you can do better than hundreds of other girls. The thing you dreamed about all your life. You have talent, Sienna. And that's why I dyed my hair in eighth grade...to be like you: Sienna Hart: the incredible actress. And my guess is that's the girl Jake fell in love with—not some drunk on the front of a tabloid magazine who stages her own arrest. Who *does* that?!"

She buries her head in her hands. Then I hear her crying. Deep, long sobs. She's starting to ugly-cry so I go over and sit down next to her, running my fingers through her hair. I didn't mean to make her sad.

After a moment, she wipes her nose with the back of her hand and blurts out, "I want in the damned pact."

"You mean *the thing*? What Piper was talking about?" I wiggle my toes.

"Yeah. The thing." She sniffles like a toddler—messy and animal-like. "I just want to be an actress. That's it. Don't ever let me do anything otherwise. Got it?"

"That's right, girl. And you can do the same for me."

She sits up, seeming calmer now, and puts her arm around me. "Tori—I went on a gin & tonic drinking binge for a guy. It's crap, in liquid form. What the hell was I thinking?!"

I laugh. "And when Boy Who Drinks Liquid Crap calls you tomorrow after he sees your picture plastered everywhere, what are you going to do?"

She takes in a deep breath as if she's thinking this through. (Hallelujah!) "I'll let it go to voicemail. *He's* the one who can leave a pathetic message."

We giggle and let our legs dangle off the side of the bed, like we're twelve. After a minute she bumps shoulders with me. "So what's *your* thing?"

The question sends a chill through me. "I don't know. I don't have one."

She pushes the cuticles back on her nails. "Then we'll start at the beginning. What did you like doing when you were a little kid?"

"Ballet, but I stopped." I don't tell her why. "But there's this other thing..." My voice trails off because I'm embarrassed to admit this.

She leans in and catches my eye. "What other thing?"

"I used to grab a hairbrush and pretend I was a radio announcer. I'd introduce my best friend, Shannon, who would butcher a song into the bristles of my brush. Then I'd make up commercials, you know...sponsors and stuff. One time I pretended to run a telethon to raise money for hurricane victims. I even pretended to raise millions of dollars for research on how to stop hiccups."

Her eyes grow big. "My dear, Tori. I do believe we've found your thing. Hair brush announcer."

We laugh. She twists around toward me, folding her legs crisscross applesauce. "Now. What about this Joel guy?"

I press my lips together tightly. "I was just his Rebound Girl. And I'm terrified it will happen again. So when I met Adam, I told him to wait. Thirty days. Like an idiot. What if I call him in a month and he's seeing someone else, planning a wedding?!"

"Thirty days? That's slightly irrational. But I get it. I can tell you this: sometimes love comes and finds you when you're not expecting it. Jake found me when I was backstage in a bathroom practicing my big monologue for the show. He stood outside the door because he had to meet the girl who could deliver a speech about vampire love with so much flair." She smiles sweetly. "That's how it works sometimes. You just look up and BAM! It's there. No warning."

Suddenly a flash of Adam's face fills my thoughts and my eyes start to sting. "The night I met him, I told him we were going to be partners. And he said: 'Partners. I like the sound of that.' He squeezed my hand and held it for a second."

She lifts a brow. "He felt it. The moment he first met you, he felt it. And now you do, too. You're lucky, really. It's all about timing."

I drop my head. "What am I going to do, Sienna?"

"Sounds like you need to get out of here and go talk to the boy."

My whip my head up. "You mean break out?"

"No, silly. I just mean getting past that judge tomorrow morning."

"But didn't Officer Starstruck tell you how tough she is?"

"I know." She looks away, chewing on her thumbnail. "We might be totally screwed, sweetheart."

CHAPTER THIRTY-FOUR

I must have fallen asleep because when I open my eyes, the room is empty—Sienna is already gone.

Gone? She didn't even say goodbye or wish me luck with the judge who will undoubtedly keep me here *forever*?

The door clicks open.

"Tori Wright?" A woman guard, a new one, steps inside but has her eyes down at a clipboard.

"Yes?"

"You're up. Judge Montrose. Courtroom C. Follow me."

Turns out, the morning guard is not nearly as chatty as the evening guard. We walk in silence aside from an occasional "Hold on" while she buzzes me through one of several doors I have to pass through to get to the courtroom.

Leading me through one more door—the final one, she promises—I step into a room that doesn't look like a courtroom at all. No witness stand, no jury box, no excessive use of mahogany. Just a regular room with several desks, a couple of swivel chairs, cheap wood paneling.

And my mother.

Her eyes are red. I can tell she's been crying.

My stomach drops.

We connect looks, but she immediately looks away and stares down at the tissue crumpled in her hand. It hurts, but I can't blame her for not wanting to even look at me right now.

The guard shows me to my chair, and Judge Montrose enters the room from a back door. No robe, but a power suit along with four inch heels but even with those she's still not much taller than the top of her chair.

"Miss Wright," the judge bellows at me. "You were detained for battery and malicious mischief against Sienna Hart."

Mom lets out a giant sob.

This is breaking her heart; I *have* to find a way out of this.

Judge Montrose clears her throat. "At this time, you do not need to respond to these charges—"

"But I will, your honor-ness." I sit up straight take a deep breath. Before I jump head-high into an apology, I remind myself what Piper told me: judges don't like the 'I swear I didn't do it' thing. So I take a different approach. "I am guilty."

Mom gasps and covers her mouth in disbelief.

"But there's an explanation." I turn my chair slightly and face Mom—she's the one who really needs to hear this. "I've been working a night job running errands for a couple in L.A. But I did it for the wrong reasons—I wanted Joel to feel sorry for me. I've been giving all this relationship advice, the rules and guidelines, and I figured if I followed it myself, I'd get over him. Or maybe even win him back. But all those tricks…they're not the answer, Mom."

Mom presses her lips together—they're quivering.

Judge Montrose glares at me. "Miss Wright, you don't need to explain this."

I hold my hand up at her. "Yes, I do. See, I answered this Craigslist ad and mostly I delivered stuff like donuts and theater tickets. But then they wanted me to help them get a photo of Sienna Hart. And you know how much I love her, Mom." I dip my head and my voice grows soft. "I should have told you the truth. But I was afraid you'd never let me go into the city." Since I sort of have Mom as a captive audience, I just go for it. "Even though there are some scary things in this city, like juvenile detention for instance, there are also so many amazing things and people. And one person in particular. Adam, my co-worker. Meeting him made me realize I can't control when love happens. It doesn't follow a list of rules. And it's because of him and spending the night in jail with Piper and her friends and Sienna Hart—all these people I met last night... I finally figured out all the things I *do* want, but one of them I want more than anything...I want to see you more, Mom. I want to talk about more than whether I floss or lock the windows or if I check my blind spot when I change lanes. I don't want to stay home alone and *record* your favorite shows for you...I want to watch them with you."

Mom pats her tears dry with a tissue and when she looks up at me, I see a wonderfully huge smile has filled her face—a smile like I've never seen before.

It's this look on her face—forgiveness, understanding—that I wish I could tuck away in a safe place so I can always remember it.

My insides do somersaults, and all I want to do is rush over and hug her. But the whole "about to be sentenced" thing is getting in the way.

I quickly turn back to Judge Montrose, my knees bouncing. "I understand if you have to arrest me and keep me here until I'm reformed, and I know this sounds rather silly, but honestly right now I really, really want to go hug my mom and tell her all about this boy I met."

Judge Montrose narrows her eyes, penetrating me with an icy stare. "I'm going to let you go. But it's not because you need to work on issues with your mother—most everyone who comes in here needs to do that. And it's not because some young man has clearly stolen your heart. So let me explain."

Oh, hurry it up! I don't care *why*, I just want out of here!

"I'm letting you go because Sienna Hart was in my courtroom just before you. She claimed you were..." the judge puts on a pair of fierce neon green reading glasses. She reads from her notes. "...

you were helping her get her dignity back. And she also said that you are, and I quote, 'the coolest chick she's ever met.' All charges have been dropped."

I practically jump out of my seat. Sienna Hart...that's my *girl*!

"And one more thing." The judge reaches down beneath her desk and pulls out a pair of shoes—Sienna's gorgeous gladiator wedge heels. "Sienna asked that I give these to some girl named Piper."

I can't help but laugh. "Take it easy on Piper if you can," I say. "She's in love and it can make you do crazy things sometimes."

Judge Montrose looks at me over her glasses at me. "That's right." She winks and adds, "You're dismissed, Tori. And I suggest you find a different line of work.

"Absolutely!"

Mom rushes over to me, wraps me in a hug and whispers in my ear, "You have *got* to tell me this Sienna Hart story!"

On our way out, I pass Piper in the hall. She sticks her fist out and I give her a quick bump. "No worries, okay?"

She nods. "No worries."

I sink into the front seat of mom's car and close my eyes, feeling relieved that I am no longer wearing a carrot-orange jumpsuit and old man loafers. And even though I'm certain Mom is going to ground me for a decade or three, I'm just happy that she is smiling, not crying.

Glancing out my window as we speed down the highway, I see the Hollywood sign up high on a hill overlooking the city. This city filled with millions of people. And out of all of them, I met Adam.

I can't help but think of the precise moment when I fell for him. In the bathroom at Club Bump when he wrapped his arms around my waist—I'll admit—was intoxicating.

But I realize now that wasn't the moment I fell for him.

It was the Jeep cover, on the first night we met, when he closed up the top just for me, one snap at a time. And with every snap, I fell harder and harder.

I turn to my mom. "I want to tell you about Adam."

She presses her lips together to keep them from quivering. Maybe it's a look of regret—for not being there whenever I needed her; for not being the mom I can whisper all my secrets to.

Mom reaches out and squeezes my hand. "Tell me everything, Tori."

Twelve hours after

CHAPTER THIRTY-FIVE

I've paced back and forth across my bedroom floor so many times I've probably completed a half marathon in brisk stress strides.

It's all figured out. Every word I'm going to say to him. The tone. The dramatic pauses. Everything.

"Adam, I was wrong," I'll say. And then he'll probably try to interrupt me with something about me not needing to explain myself but I'll cut him off mid-sentence. "No, no. Let me explain. I owe that to you." And then I'll dive right into how I've had an epiphany of sorts and I realize all these rules I was following were wrong. Wrong, wrong, wrong—I'll say it all dramatic like. What a fool I was! And then I'll tell him I want to go for it, forget about timing and stop trying to control every outcome. And then I'll tell him about the moment when he fastened the top to his Jeep. And when he wrapped his arms around me. I'll tell him that I know he's busy with work, but we should try to see each other. Except I'm grounded and can't go anywhere except for school and the BP gas station a block away, which isn't as romantic a gas station as he may think. So can you come over? That's what I'll say.

One more final deep breath. Aaaaand dial.

Before I can finish dialing his number, my phone buzzes. An incoming call. My heart pounds.

But it's not him. It's Lizzie.

This is disappointing.

But wait! It's after seven o'clock. He's probably there right now!

"Hello? Lizzie? Hi!" I am the definition of overeager.

"Tori! Adam told us you want to quit. What happened, hon?"

"I was arrested last night." I don't tell her the real reason—that I made an incredibly dumb proclamation to Adam, which involved us needing space from each other and then me walking away, like a tool.

"Arrested?! I had no idea. Adam didn't tell us that."

"It happened right after he left. Sienna's assistant, the one you warned me about, she thought I was stalking."

"Oh, that girl. She makes me boil. This is so ridiculous. I'm sorry about this, Tori. But why on earth did Adam leave you there alone? That's not like him."

"No, no...I walked off on him. I was stupid, said some stupid stuff...but I was wrong. I need to talk to him. Is he there?"

"I'm sorry, but when he came by last night to tell us about you, he quit, too."

"What? He can't quit. His Dad—"

"He said he had something to do and he wouldn't be able to work anymore. And to tell you the truth, he looked pretty sad. He wouldn't tell me why."

I know why. "Lizzie, I have to go."

"I understand. And for what its worth, you were awesome at this job. You two were the best team we've ever had."

I tear up at this thought. She's right. We are a good team.

When we hang up, I quickly dial his number. I pace the floor. Come on—pick up, pick up.

He doesn't.

And he doesn't pick up on my second call or my third call. By my fifth call, I collapse on my bed.

Mom pokes her head in my room. "You okay?"

I shake my head and look away, not wanting to let her see me cry.

She lies down on my bed and curls up next to me—something we haven't done in a very long time. She tucks my hair behind my ear. "He didn't call?"

I bury my head in her shoulder and the tears come, mean and strong. She holds me, rocks me, and pulls her fingers through my hair. I pull back and wipe my nose with the back of my hand. Looking her over, I notice her freshly highlighted hair and perfectly manicured nails. She really has managed to pull herself together beautifully since she and Dad split. The woman has rocked this divorce.

If I take anyone's advice on relationships, it should be from her. Not from some book.

I loop my arm in hers. "What should I do, Mom?"

She winks. "The bachelor is going on a rollerblading date with twelve girls. Wanna watch it with me?"

"Absolutely."

Eight days after

CHAPTER THIRTY-SIX

"So? Are her teeth really that white or do they photoshop her?"

Amanda Hawkins is bouncing in her neon pink Converse tennis shoes, surrounded by her equally peppy group of friends. The news of my arrest and connection to Sienna Hart has caused crowds of people to gather around my locker, incessantly asking questions about all the details of Sienna's life.

"Seriously, are her teeth that white? Is she short? I'm sure she's short."

I shake my head, trying my best to ignore the questions and retrieve my Spanish textbook.

"I heard she was on meth to impress her boyfriend."

"No—"

"And when she got arrested, she tried to slap the cop—"

"Stop," I slam my locker shut. "None of that's true. She's not dating that guy anymore. She got drunk one night and stole a street sign. That's it. Sienna's a perfectly nice person, she's taller than average, and her teeth really *are* that white. They're pretty amazing, actually."

I'm sure I sound annoyed and yes these questions are completely annoying. But what's bothering me most is the fact that Adam hasn't called. Lizzie said he quit because he's busy. With what? Lana?

With moving on?

I told him I wanted space, but I never told him about my thirty-day rule. My own ridiculous advice caused me to lose the guy. Yet again, IRONY…blinking above my head.

My phone buzzes. It's a text from Sienna. Yes, I just said that sentence all casually. After our court date, she got my cell number from Lizzie and started texting me daily. Sometimes it's a horoscope, sometimes it's an update about what she's doing on set that day. Since she fired her assistant, Maddie, she is downright approachable. And they didn't fire her from Werewolf Angel because of that unfortunate photo that landed on the front of every tabloid, lucky girl. In fact, someone made a funny GIF of her falling down in front of the X-Bar and it went viral—she's more popular now than ever.

Today's text from Sienna is a positive affirmation. She likes sending those the most. She's a regular Dr. Phil.

I lean against my locker and read it to myself, not telling the gossips around me who had sent the text.

HEY SWEET FIRECRACKER. SI SE PUEDE. ☺

Luckily, I have an A- average in Spanish and I know what it means. "Yes, we can!"

Shannon marches up and waves the girls off around my locker. "Let my convict breathe. We're waiting for a phone call from Nancy Grace. Give her space, people."

They scatter, not really sure if she's serious or not.

"Thanks, Shan." I lean my head on her shoulder. She's the rock who always has my back. If you don't have one of those kinds of rocks, get one.

I loop my arm in hers, and we head down the hall to our next class, her with a giddy smile on her face and me with a fake one. There's an Adam-shaped hole in my heart that I don't know how to fill.

So I trudge through my day, not even giving Joel a second glance as he puts his arm around Carly. Word is they've already broken up and reconciled twice this week and I'm relieved to be out of the picture.

By the end of the day, I'm exhausted from answering and deflecting all the Sienna questions and jail questions. Luckily, Margaret

Thatcher is waiting for me in the parking lot—my rusted ray of sunshine.

As I shuffle through the parking lot, I hear a car pull up behind me. "No one makes Puppy sad." My heart speeds up.

I whirl around and see a red Mini-Cooper. Taylor is leaning out of his window with a heart-melting smile on his face. He throws it into park, jumps out and rushes up to me, smothering me with a hug.

I can't control them—the tears start to flow. "Puppy's sad," I say into his collarbone. Thank God for this boy. And thank God he's the type to let me soak up my tears with his polo shirt.

"Shannon told me everything that happened." He pets my hair and when he can sense I've stopped wetting his shirt, he grips me by my shoulders, looking me in the eye. "I know you liked that boy. I'm sorry he disappeared. But there are other fish in the sea, so they say, and I'm still waiting for mine, too. We'll wait together. Or better yet..." He starts to bounce on his toes. "...we'll just go dancing and not give it another thought. We have each other. And there is fun to be had!"

I nod. Coming from him, this helps bring my life in focus. Just go dancing. So perfect. It's Shannon who always has my back, but it's Taylor who meets me head-on. Between the two of them, I am sandwiched with support. Just call me the luckiest girl on the planet.

Taylor cups my chin, lifting my face. "Listen. I'm not going to make-out with you or give you The Sex, but I want you to know I love you. You always have me, sweets."

"Man, you know how to make a girl happy. I just wish I had a pocket-sized version of you so I could carry you with me everywhere."

He laughs and grabs my hand, leading me to my car. We hug then he steps back, taking in my face. "You go do your thing, Puppy. Go on now." He winks then takes off.

"Thanks, guy," I call out behind him. As I pull my keys out, a flapping sound catches my attention. It's on my windshield...a flier.

I yank the paper off, reading the words faster and faster, gobbling them up. I can't believe my eyes.

INTERNSHIP AVAILABLE AT K107.7

COME WORK FOR JO-JO LOPEZ AT THE BEST RADIO STATION IN L.A.

NO EXPERIENCE NECESSARY, JUST A GOOD VOICE AND ROCKIN' ATTITUDE

Oh my God. Taylor put this here. He knows how much I love Jo-Jo Lopez. And now here's a chance to work with him! A dream come true!

I whip my head up to see him pulling out of the parking lot. He waves and beeps his horn as he pulls away.

That boy, I swear.

There won't be hot, deep kisses for us, but at least I know that one amazing guy loves me.

What more could I want?

I'm not sure how many days after. I've lost track. This is a good thing.

CHAPTER THIRTY-SEVEN

The job didn't pay—not at first. For a week, I ran around the office at 107.7 and fetched coffee and Red Bulls and Cheetos for all the staff.

But here's the moment that changed everything: one night Jo-Jo Lopez suddenly had a hankering for some donuts. I told him, "No problem," and rushed over to the Krispy Kreme, the same one Adam and I went to, and grabbed a dozen, fresh from the oven. For Jo-Jo, this tiny detail—*warm donuts*—impressed him because I was their first intern who'd ever come back with donuts that delicious. I'll be the first to admit Jo-Jo was probably on a sugar high when he said it, but nevertheless he said it. He asked me to read live on air.

Live? On air?

Holy, heartbeat! All those years as a kid holding a microphone hairbrush and introducing pop star Shannon have paid off. This is it...my dream come true!

Jo-Jo had me read a short gossipy article from a celebrity magazine and then he'd make his prediction. And then we did it again. And again. Then I started giving *my* opinion, and we'd play off each other in a sparring bit. Until this started to become a regular thing with us.

A couple of weeks later, Jo-Jo told me they'd gotten so many tweets and Facebook comments about my "cute, raspy voice" and "adorable upbeat attitude" that they wanted to give me my own ten-minute spot each week. With a paycheck, too. I repeat: A PAYCHECK.

So now, every Monday when you tune into 107.7 at exactly 8:50 p.m., you'll hear "The Tori Ten-Spot." Cute, right?

Mom agreed to let me work in the city as long as I take the back roads, stay out of jail, and text her with pictures of any celebrity I see.

Deal.

My radio show has a different angle on celebrity gossip—no drinking and rehab talk. I feel it's time to put a new spin on things around here. Since I get daily updates from my dear friend Sienna, and since she's been hired to star in the highly anticipated Zombie High School! (with an exclamation point in the title!), I get all the latest news on where scenes are being shot around town and whose been cast in which role. So my show is all about the movies and the actors. No gossip.

And unbelievably, it has become one of their most popular segments.

Strangely, it was Sienna Hart who'd caused my arrest, but it was also Sienna who gave me a chance at what I loved most. I had officially found my thing.

Si se puede, Sienna.

. . .

It's a Monday night, and I've just finished my show. I wave bye to Jo-Jo and the rest of the staff and head out to my car. As I push through the glass doors, my phone buzzes.

I answer quickly without even saying hello. "You're at the club, aren't you?" There's loud music in the background.

"You're not going to believe this," Taylor says sounding a little breathy.

"Argyle is out of fashion?"

"Worse. It's '90s night and I'm in *flannel*!"

"Be careful. Next thing you know you'll be wearing jelly shoes and a scrunchie."

"There's one more thing," he yells into the phone and I have to pull it away from my ear so it doesn't do damage. "I found my fish, Tori! Dustin, that love of a bouncer...he changed his work schedule. We've been dancing all night!"

"Wow. Is he—"

"Yes! He's *perfect*!!!" I can tell he's bouncing.

"I knew he would be, honey." There's a spark in his voice, and I get the feeling Dustin is going to be sticking around for a while.

"So did you catch my show tonight?" I ask.

"Recording it. Like I do every Monday, sweets. Call me later."

"I will." I take in a deep breath feeling so overwhelmed with how filled my life feels in this moment. If it hadn't been for Taylor nudging me to try for this internship, I might actually be torturing myself with dairy products. "And one more thing Taylor," I say just before he hangs up. "I want to thank you."

"For being brilliant?"

"Yes."

"And for being the most humble person in the *entire world*?"

"Of course. But also for putting that flier on my car. I wouldn't be doing this if it wasn't for you."

"What flier?"

"About the radio internship, silly. The one you left on the windshield of my car."

"I don't know what you're talking about, lady." He gasps. "Oh, sweet cupid. Dustin is break dancing. How did my life get this good? Call me later, love!" And then he hangs up.

I stand motionless on the sidewalk under a bright streetlight, hardly able to catch my breath. He *didn't* put that flier on my car? But who else would've—

My eyes drift up and that's when I see it. Parked on the street directly across from me is a Jeep—army green, no roof, just a roll bar.

"Tori!" He calls my name, and I frantically look around but see no one. Until I realize his voice is coming from above. Across the street, in the L.A. County Water & Public Utilities building, I see Adam's silhouette waving at me through the window on the sixth floor.

He quickly descends down, the outline of his body flashing by the window as he passes by each even-numbered floor, and with each glimpse, my heart pounds faster.

I sprint across the empty street and get to the sidewalk just as he emerges from the stairwell. We stop just inches from each other, our breathing heavy.

"I'm late," he blurts.

"Late?" I fidget with my sleeves to keep myself from throwing my arms around him. *Stay calm, Tori.*

But then I notice that he's fidgeting with his sleeves, too. "It's been thirty-four days, nine hours," he says. "I wanted to show up on exactly the thirtieth day but I thought it'd be cool to show up when you were working, but that's only on Mondays so..." Even in the dim light I can see his face blush. "I'm four days and nine hours late. Sorry about that." He smiles and it shoots through me, piercing my heart.

A guy will show up, later than you'd like, but you should wait. I can't believe it, but that psychic was right.

But there's one thing that doesn't make sense. I step back and look him over. "How did you know about my thirty-day rule? I never told you—"

"The blog. You told me the name of it, and I found the posts you had written. It was pretty obvious which ones were yours because of your frequent use of exclamation points." He steps closer. "You aren't my rebound girl. Not by a long shot."

My hands are *really* fidgeting now because I desperately want to throw my arms around him. But there's another question I need to ask. "Were you the one who put that flier on my windshield?"

He dips his head and says in a soft voice, "Of course." He slips his backpack off his shoulder, bends down next to me, and starts rifling through his stuff. "My dad gave it to me, thinking I needed a new job. But I told him I couldn't—I was busy."

I fold my arms. "Busy with what?"

"This." He pops back up and hands me a thick stack of papers. A manuscript.

"It's a story about a guy and a girl who take a night job running bizarre errands for a couple in L.A." His eyes light up. "But I'm thinking of adding some time travel and a dragon fight scene—you know...for commercial appeal."

I look up at him and our eyes connect; neither one of us can look away. "Will it be a love story?"

He leans in, and I can feel his breath on my cheek. "Man, I hope so."

Our lips are close but don't touch. "Do you know how it ends yet?"

He shakes his head then raises a brow, "I'm hoping it ends on a sidewalk under a streetlight in Los Angeles." He wraps his arms around me and pulls me in. My body fills with warmth as our lips meet. I throw my arms around his neck and kiss him deeply.

I wish I hadn't waited so long to do this. But here, on this sidewalk next to radio station...it's perfect. I'm glad I waited.

And after a moment, I step back—my head spinning—and say, "It's going to be the best story ever."

He takes my hand and leads me toward his Jeep. "It's close to 10:45. Want to..."

"Of course. The donuts will be warm."

I must say, this guy has perfect timing.

Los Angeles County Juvenile Detention Intake Report

Name: Maddie Stark   Age at booking: 22

Eyes: HAZ   Hair: BRN

Height: 5'7"   Weight: 134

Sex: F   Charges: Rule 594

Charging Officer: Ortega

Court date/time: To be determined

Intake Notes:

Suspect arrested on set of Zombie High School! for stalking Sienna
Hart. When asked why she was found hiding behind a zombie stunt
double trying to get closer to Sienna, suspect states emphatically:
she's her former assistant, NOT a stalker.

Suspect demands a bottle of Perrier water, not tap. Request
denied.

FOR YOU, DEAR READER

First, hello! You look adorable today. And thank you for reading PERFECT TIMING. Seriously…thank you.

A little history on the writing of this book:

It required some fun research…I visited a psychic. I went to late night donut shops in Beverly Hills. I managed to get a private tour of the Los Angeles Juvenile Detention Center (a very eye-opening experience). And I ate licorice.

All for you, book.

I loved writing this book and I hope you loved reading it. If so, you would get a virtual hug/chocolate/gold star from me if you took a moment to write a review and spread the word.

So what's next?

For those of you who have read my first teen novel—DITCHED—it has been rewritten and is now called PERFECT KISS. I've made a few changes. I took some stuff out. Put some stuff in. Gave it a hug. Pinched its cheeks.

I love it more than ever. To get you excited…following this letter is the first three chapters of PERFECT KISS. And you'll get to read the entire book within the month. So keep an eye out for it!

If all goes smoothly, I plan to publish my third rom-com, PERFECT ENDING.

Yep, I'm making a group of books that are THE PERFECT PACK. (I'm over here bouncing on my toes—so excited about this project!)

And please write to me. Tell me what you like. Tell me what you want more of. I'd love to hear from you.

robinmellombooks@gmail.com

And come find me on the web:

Twitter: @robinmellom

Facebook: https://www.facebook.com/rmellom (I share lots of pictures of my Labrador retriever, just FYI)

Instagram: robinmellom (pictures of my dog with funky filters, FYI)

I hope you enjoy the following sneak peek of PERFECT KISS. Virtual Rom-Com fist-bump, y'all! (Was that weird?)

Hugs,
Robin Mellom

PERFECT KISS

~A night to remember . . .
a prom to forget~

A romantic comedy of errors
By Robin Mellom

A PROLOGUE, I SUPPOSE

Food, a cell phone, and my dignity . . . all things I do not have

I DON'T KNOW how I ended up on the side of Hollister Road, lying in this ditch.

This moment, last night, the details—all fuzzy. A reluctant glance down and I see I'm covered in scratches and bruises. The bruise on my shin appears to be in the shape of a french fry. French fries cause bruises? And I have at least seven stains on my royal blue iridescent dress—two black, one greenish-bluish, and the remaining are various shades of yellow. *What are these? Mustard? Curry?*

Wait. I don't even want to know.

What I *do* want to know is why I just fell out of a moving Toyota Prius and was left here in this ditch with a french fry shin bruise and unrecognizable stains. Especially the yellow ones.

Please, please be curry.

Looking down the road, I see two things: the sun coming up behind Hollister Peak, and the car lights on Brian Sontag's Prius getting smaller and smaller in the distance.

The jerk.

I start to think about last night, but the past twelve hours are a total blur. Like, for instance, how and *why* I got into Brian Sontag's Toyota Prius.

I touch my forehead, which is already swelling from the fall, and I realize this must be why I can't remember a thing from last night. I look down at myself again and wish I hadn't. Gross. If Ian could see me now, he would ditch me for sure.

Except that he already has.

I even wore blue for him. Not all black, as usual. It was an actual *color*. Not that I wanted to wear it—but I guess even wearing something that went against my better fashion sense couldn't change his mind.

You are now officially on my list, Ian Clark. And not the good one.

The conversation. I suddenly remember the conversation we had two weeks ago.

"It will be amazing," he said. "I can't wait to walk into that room with you," he said. "It will be the best night of our lives," he said, as if he were reading straight from a Hallmark card.

So I told him I would go. I even told him if a Journey song came on, I would dance with him, and I imagined my arms draped around his neck, and his breath on my cheek, and my hip brushing up against his. I didn't explain I had been imagining a lot of things about him lately.

He made fun of me for organizing all the special moments in my life like I was a professional wedding planner. "The toast will happen here . . . the dance will happen here . . . and voilà! Happiness!"

That's when I punched him on the arm.

But he was right, actually—I did have that special moment all planned out . . . the kiss, of course . . . that kiss. Every detail of our first kiss that I hoped—hoped beyond measure—would finally happen between us. And change everything.

I even hoped that when we kissed, we'd be standing next to beautiful lush foliage. And a water feature. It's possible I've watched one too many romance movies.

But so much for acts of extreme hoping. Look at me now. There is nothing special about this moment. No foliage, nothing lush—just dried weeds and gravel burrowing into my legs. And butt, honestly.

The glamour of this moment is stunning. Thank God my lovely sense of sarcasm is still intact. It feels like the only thing that is.

There's an aching pain on my right upper arm. It's because of the tattoo. Wait, I have a tattoo? Who let me get a tattoo?! It's a Tinker Bell. Which could be cute if it weren't for the fact that she's a *punk* Tinker Bell. She's wearing combat boots, her wings are ripped, and her eyes are bloodshot. Great . . . Tinker Bell on a meth binge.

I stare up to the heavens.

Please, please be temporary.

I wipe the dirt from my face and shake my head. I can remember every detail of that conversation two weeks ago, but I can't remember a thing about the past twelve hours. Seriously?

A couple of deep breaths and I accept that I am now keenly aware of only three things:

1. It is 6:15 in the morning and I am a heap of a mess sitting in a ditch on the side of Hollister Road. I know this because my watch—the one that matches my dress and purse and shoes (thank you, Mom)—is still ticking despite the impact. *Ouch . . . my head hurts.* And I know it's Hollister Road because this is the back road that Ian always uses on the way to school when there's construction. I'd recognize that billboard anywhere. The one that says "Peg Griffith—Philanthropist of the Year!" and Peg is holding a metal statue in the shape of a heart. And Ian always asks, "Doesn't your mom get queasy around all that blood?" And I always answer, "She's a philanthropist, not a phlebotomist." And he lets out that sweet, goofy laugh that gives me butterflies. I hate this stupid road.

2. I still don't remember anything that happened last night.

3. I am starving.

My forehead is pounding, and I grab it, but it's not the pain I'm trying to stop; it's the memories that suddenly come rushing in.

Oh, no. No, no, no. The dinner. The dance. Allyson Moore. Jimmy Choo heels. That broken safety pin. In-N-Out Burger.

Tinker Bell. The Hampton Inn. The three-legged Chihuahua. Brian Sontag. Toyota Prius. Ian Clark.

Ian, who brought me a blue corsage, dyed to match my dress (and shoes and purse and watch).

Ian, who bought me a Mrs. Fields peanut butter cookie and stashed it in his glove compartment because he knew I would need a snack at some point in the night, given my low blood sugar problem. And my love of peanut butter cookies.

Ian, who promised we would dance to our song. Who promised prom night would be the best night of my life—his Hallmark promises.

And I believed him.

I glance around, looking for cars. But it's a Sunday. No traffic. No one to take pity on me and drive me home. Or at least lend me their cell phone so I can call my mom.

Mom!

She's going to kill me. I was supposed to be home by two a.m.! She must be panicked. But then again, she's probably asleep. It's going to be okay. Mom is a deep sleeper. People who do good deeds sleep very well.

And, oh man, she trusted him. "I wouldn't feel good about Justina going to prom with anyone but you," Mom had said. She even dusted off his tuxedo sleeve when she said it. And he gave that laugh.

I hate stupid tuxedo sleeves.

I have to get out of here. Find a phone. Something, *someone* to help me. I push myself up off the ground, but the sudden movement causes my head to swirl and I feel light- headed. Low blood sugar— it always makes me dizzy. And grumpy. And yes, even irrational. But right now, I'm entitled.

I take a slow breath, and the balance comes back. I put one foot in front of the other and manage to hobble down the road. But my feet are heavy, clunky, like submarines in a sea of taffy.

I need help. Where is Anderson Cooper when I need him?

Of course I know Ian would laugh at that if he could hear me. And yeah, maybe I should be obsessed with a hot musician or a movie star. But crushing on a CNN news reporter just makes more sense.

I'm into reliability, Ian.

Plus, Anderson Cooper's totally cute. I don't mind the ears.

But even *he's* not here. No one is. The road is deserted. I'm going to have to figure out a way to get out of this myself.

I'm going to pray for a miracle.

Please, please be erased. Make Worst Night Ever slip away from my brain.

But luckily, before I get too far in my pleading and have to start kneeling and ruining this dress any further . . . I see them. In the distance are familiar glistening fluorescent lights. I smile because I know those lights mean I have found the answer to all my problems.

A pay phone and a candy bar at the 7-Eleven.

CHAPTER ONE

FINALLY, A SNICKERS

I SUPPOSE IF I have to get ditched somewhere, I'm glad it's at *this* 7-Eleven, not the sucky 7-Eleven near downtown. This is the awesome one—the one on 4th and Hill with the nacho cheese bar and the endless row of magazines. Ian and I would stop by here on Fridays to celebrate. "No homework. No track practice. Time for jalapeño nachos!" he would always say. And I'd say, "Just a Snickers."

It's not that I don't love nachos . . . what's not to love? But I never got them on our Friday 7-Eleven stops because that was the day my weekly thimble-sized allowance was hovering in the cents column, and a candy bar was all I could afford. Ian would've bought nachos for me—he's a carefree buyer with an unlimited allowance, along with most of the student body at Huntington High School, but I didn't want him to worry that it symbolized more. The last thing I wanted was to weird out our friendship because of a plate of convenience-store nachos.

As I cross through the familiar gas station parking lot, my chest discovers gravity, and my organs and bones weigh me down with sadness, my feet barely moving forward.

Of all the 7-Elevens, *this* one.

Where are you, Ian Clark?

Then music. It's blaring through outdoor speakers, which seems odd this early in the morning. There's no one to listen to it because there are no customers. Except for me.

The bell rings as the sliding glass door opens and a gush of stale air-conditioned air rushes over me. Country music blasts through the indoor speakers, too.

"Need something?"

The cashier stares at my shoes. My two-and-three- quarter-inch heels are covered in dirt and mud—the same ones I had proudly dyed iridescent royal blue just two days ago. But that was before I found out *nobody* dyes their shoes to match their dress anymore. And before I realized listening to the advice of a relative—not my best friend and not an enlightened editor of a prom magazine—was an unwise idea.

Thank you, Mom.

It makes sense that the cashier would stare. I'm guessing not too many girls waltz into the 7-Eleven at 6:15 on a Sunday morning wearing heels that match their shimmering iridescent blue dress, looking like they'd just lost a match with a vindictive sewer rat.

"Got any Snickers?" My voice is weak.

Her eyes drift up to mine. She softens. She must notice my extreme lack of lip gloss. "You hungry?" She looks over my shoulder, probably to see if I am alone.

"Very."

She is wearing high-waisted jeans, a belt with a large silver buckle, and a long-sleeve white shirt tucked tightly into her jeans. Her ultra-long hair is pulled back in a perfect French braid—totally symmetrical—with hints of gray peeking through. She looks like she belongs in a music video for the country song playing over the speakers. Like she'd play the part of the consoling wise aunt who doles out good obvious advice: *Stop drinkin' and smokin' and bringing home stray dogs, honey!*

I can already tell I like her.

She reaches into a box in front of the counter and lays a jumbo-size Snickers on the counter. I was right—there really is kindness in the world. I glance at her nametag.

"Thanks, Gilda."

I give her a big smile and reach for the candy bar. "That's $1.09," she says. "I...I..." I can't believe Gilda isn't going to take some pity on me. Do I look like a monster?

I keep my mouth shut about her lack of human decency, and pat my dress down as if my purse will suddenly appear. But it's gone and I have no idea where I left it. Of course all my money is in there. And my lip gloss. And those directions to Lurch's party. The one Ian and I were supposed to go to the next night. He said he wanted us to go do something fun, just to make sure there wasn't any weirdness after prom. He even said *weirdness* with air quotes, like I didn't know what it meant. I had hoped "weirdness" referred to all the kissing we were going to do—so I guess I didn't know what it meant.

I had no idea "weirdness" to him meant actual weirdness. Dang it.

But in thinking over what happened last night, I have to say, "weirdness" was an understatement of epic proportion. Unreasonably huge . . . an understatement that is Hummer huge. Because Lurch's party—and especially the excessive kissing part—is *never* going to happen.

Which is a pity. Lurch always has the best parties.

"I don't have any money." My voice cracks. It sounds pitiful. Like someone you might even want to take mercy on. But it doesn't sway Gilda.

Gilda places the Snickers back in its box. Then she looks me up and down and tilts her head. "You need a phone or something?"

"Yes! Where?" I feel like a Jack Russell terrier—yippy, anxious.

"Out back. By the hoses. Fifty cents a call."

I'm not exactly sure why she thinks I can suddenly come up with fifty cents if I couldn't afford the Snickers. "Thanks." I wince at her. All I really want is to get home, so I retreat and hobble back through the sliding glass doors, across the parking lot.

The pay phone is *right* next to the hoses, just like Sorta Rude Gilda said, and I have to hike up my disgusting dress to get around them. I'm not sure why I care about saving my dress from any further grossness. This is absurd.

As I step up to the phone, I hear a car—the rattling, knocking sound of a diesel engine. I whip around, hoping it's Ian, but deep down knowing that he's never coming to get me. A man pulls up in a Mercedes to pump gas. His car is old, just like Ian's, but it's a coupe, not a sedan. He doesn't even notice me. Good.

I start to read the directions on the pay phone, but the words turn blurry. I can feel the tears gaining momentum—I press my temples with my palms, trying my best to contain them.

Get it together. You've gotten this far without falling apart.

My pep talk starts to work—the tears dry up and I glance back at the building to see Gilda planted at the window, glaring at me with her arms folded, standing firm like a redwood tree. She must think I'm going to steal these hoses. Gilda might be the type who takes her job too seriously.

I quickly turn back and finish reading the directions on how to make a collect call. I've never made one and it looks complicated.

I dial wrong three times, but then finally push all the right buttons in the right order and the phone rings.

Come on, Mom. Pick up.

"You've reached the Griffith residence. Please leave a message. . . ."

I can't believe this. She's still asleep. Doesn't she know I'm not there? No, this can't be right. Maybe she's out on a hunt with the police. They're probably using drug-sniffing dogs and everything. Given the people I've been hanging out with the past few hours, those drug dogs will sniff me out for sure. Should be rescued any moment now. . .

But I try the collect call one more time. "You've reached the Griffith residence . . ."

This can't be happening. She's asleep. She doesn't even know Ian just ruined my life. I never wanted to go to this stupid prom at that stupid hotel. I told him that: I like running, not dancing. I like veggie burritos, not rubbery hotel chicken. And definitely not rubbery hotel salad. But he convinced me that prom would be different. It would be a night I would never forget, and he promised I'd love the food. Well, he was right about one thing: I will *never* forget this. But the food? I'm freaking starving. All of a sudden, I can't hold the tears back anymore, my eyes feeling like the Colorado River after a spring melt—the flow just keeps coming. No pep talk can fix this. I fall to the

ground, sobbing.

Why me, Ian? Why couldn't you have—

"Eat this."

There's a tap on my shoulder. Gilda drops a Snickers on my lap.

She reaches out and gives me a hand, helping me to my feet. "Here." It's a scratchy paper towel from the bathroom— she motions to the tears flowing freely down my face, and I wish she had brought more scratchy towels.

I try to explain, not really sure what to say, and the words come out as a blubbering mess. "Why did you . . . Are you—"

"You look like you could use a snack. That's all." She leads me back to the store. "Come inside. We'll figure out what to do with you."

I knew there was kindness in the world. Sometimes I guess you have to turn into the Colorado Snot River before someone shows it, but I'm just relieved to know it's there.

Gilda pulls a stool up to the end of the counter and lets me sit while I scarf down my candy bar. She takes a plastic to-go bag and fills it with ice from the soda machine, then spins the bag to close it and hands it to me. "What happened to you, anyway?"

I hold the ice to the knot on my head. *Ouch!*

She waits a moment. "So?"

I look down at my dress. "You mean the stains?"

She nods. "And the scratches and the bruises and the bump on the head and the new tattoo."

I shake my head. "I know. So cliché to go to prom and end up with a tattoo, right?"

"That's your *prom* dress?"

"It looked better without the filth."

Her face is blank. "It's just all so . . . *matching*. I thought maybe you'd been in a play. Or a pride parade." I almost laugh—like she even knows what a pride parade is, but I don't feel a need to educate her on this matter. "Nope. Mom's idea."

"You didn't get a friend's opinion?"

I shake my head. "Didn't even read a magazine. I just wanted to impress him—"

"With your matching skills?"

"Color. But Mom dressed me exactly the way she did at her own prom . . . secondhand dress, dyed shoes, matching purse." I lower my head. "It's not like I'm proud of this."

Of course I would much rather be wearing my regular clothes: all-black everything, as Ian calls them. True, I only wear black: black shirt, black jeans, black boots, every day, without fail. Because no one asks questions. They just assume I've gone to the dark side— and lately that would not be too far from the truth.

But I get wild sometimes—with my nail polish. Black Cherry.

Gilda gives me a look like she's in pain—physical pain. "You mean you let your *mother* dress you the same way she dressed for prom?"

She must not have a daughter. Otherwise she'd understand how hard it is for a mother to let her daughter just "be." At least for *my* mother. I consider explaining this to her, but I figure I should zip it and be thankful for the Snickers. Plus, the rush of chocolate is calming me down, and the balance of blood sugar suddenly makes me a much more reasonable person. Unlike most of last night.

I shrug. "Mom's eager face—there's no escaping it."

Gilda scratches her hair, digging in delicately with her long red fingernails, being careful not to mess up a braid. I can tell she wants to let loose with some sort of hand-flailing lecture on being myself and not letting my mother's eager face control my life, but all she says is, "Huh."

I take another bite of my Snickers and swallow hard. Here comes the energy. "Look, if I had known my dress was going to cause this much pain, I would've worn a sleeping bag. No . . . I wouldn't have gone at all."

She narrows her eyes. "Spill it then. Why'd you go?"

Of course that's when his face pops into my mind. And all the amazing things he said to convince me to go to prom.

"Ian Clark," I say, as if that explains everything. But she doesn't know him. How could she understand his powers of persuasion?

Gilda looks around the store. "Ian Clark isn't here now. Did he do something bad?"

"Yeah. Very bad."

"Did he—"

"Hurt me?" I ask, because, looking at me, I'd wonder too.

She wrinkles her nose. I can tell she doesn't want to ask, but she knows she should. "Did he?"

"No, no. He ditched me." I adjust the ice pack on my forehead. The pain is lessening. I'm starting to think more clearly. "I was ditched. Figuratively and literally."

"He sounds like a real jerk."

I twitch. That word: *jerk*. It confuses my nervous system because my body wants to react with my first instinct . . . defend him.

Because even though *jerk* is the only word I can imagine to describe him now, it's not a word that ever entered my mind as being synonymous with Ian Clark. Ever.

I have always known *of* him—Huntington High isn't huge and it's the type of place where everyone's business is just known. It's

almost as if we're all distant relatives— people you've heard of and
you know their basic story—or the Lifetime movie version of their
story—but you don't *really* know them.

Ian became more than a person I knew basic facts about back in
sophomore year, spring quarter, P.E.: softball. I remember my first
words to him. "Have you seen that silver bat around?"

He turned and walked off on me. Sorta rude. But then he popped
back into my vision a moment later, the bat in hand. "Silver bat's my
favorite too." He gave it to me, but not in just some ordinary handing-
over-of-a-bat type of way. He flipped it around in a highly coordinated
maneuver and presented it to me, handle first. Just to make it that
much easier for me. "Whack it good," he said with a little smile.

I struck out.

But I stuffed that little moment away in my mind— the impor-
tance of it seeming like something that needed to be noted, filed,
remembered. I now knew Ian Clark was a handle-first kind of guy.
Why did this matter to me?

But time passed and the silver bat always seemed to be around
and I couldn't think of any other questions to ask him. So I didn't.
And that memory started to fade. Ian remained merely an unexam-
ined file in my brain.

Until last summer. The pool party.

Gilda opens up a bag of gummy bears and chews the head off of
one, then hands a piece to me, an indication she's ready for the story.
"Why'd you go with this guy?"

I twirl the gummy bear in my fingers. "Operation Lips Locked."

"What type of operation is that?"

Breathe in. Breathe out. Here we go.

"It's the type where you get ridiculed at Jimmy DeFranco's pool
party for hooking up with two different guys even though it was
accidental because one of them was a dare

and one of them was due to drinking too many Jägermeister
shots—him, not me—and get publicly humiliated when those two

guys claim it was much more than kissing—which is all you remember happening—but the glares from people you hardly know pierce your skin and jab your heart, so you declare to your best friend you are never *ever* going to kiss another boy again until you know deep in your bones, in your marrow, in your cell structure—one hundred percent—that he is boyfriend material."

"Okay," Gilda says. "I mean . . . *what?*"

I shrug. "No kissing allowed until the guy proved he had the material. Until then, lips locked." I press my lips together, reminding myself what they feel like. "It's been eight months and twelve days since I kissed a boy. I was going to finally unlock my lips for Ian. At prom."

The bell at the sliding door rings. The man who was pumping gas in the old Mercedes strolls around the store.

Gilda holds her hand up to me and whispers, "Hold on a sec."

She helps him find some individual packets of Tylenol, then rings him up. He's older with a pudgy middle and a rumpled shirt.

While he fishes through his leather wallet for money, he glances my way. And as he hands Gilda a twenty, he's still looking my way.

I shift on my stool. What's this guy's problem? "You need a lift?" he asks.

I laugh. A nervous laugh. Not really a laugh. "Me? No." "Her ride's coming," Gilda lies.

He puts his wallet away and gives me a smirk. "Looks like you worked a rough shift last night. Hope you made enough to buy yourself a new dress."

Oh my god, the guy thinks I'm a—oh, I can't even . . .

He scoops up his bag of Tylenol—hangover medicine, I'm sure—and saunters out before I can tell him he's so rude for assuming something I'm NOT. I'm only sixteen and this is my prom dress and my boyfriend who is not my boyfriend ditched me, and no, I do *not* have a ride home!

But I've gotten good at not confronting people. I let out a deep sigh instead.

When he's gone, Gilda turns to me with big eyes. "He doesn't know you haven't even kissed a boy in eight months. He's a jerk."

I shake my head, thinking about school and the reputation I managed to create for myself. "He's probably not totally off base. I've kissed a lot of guys in my past."

She waves me off. "Oh, who hasn't."

"A lot." I clear my throat and hope she doesn't ask—

"How many?"

Of course she asks. I clench my fists and look away. "A little more than a dozen." Silence, no response. "Or so," I add quietly.

"Or *so*?!" Her eyes are satellite disks.

"It's not like it's triple digits or anything. And it's not something I'm super proud of, except at first . . . I kind of . . . was."

Which is true. When I first started my excessive lip landings, I was a freshman and I was so excited about my success rate I wanted to put it on my résumé—in bold, italics, everything. I was *proud.*

"But nothing ever materialized. No boyfriend," I explain to her. "I just really, really like kissing. But now it's like I have a kissing disorder—I've overdosed on it and now I can't even get one simple smooch from my prom date. I mean, it's *prom. Everyone* gets kissed on prom night! What is wrong with me?" I look down at my muddy feet.

I feel like a non-human at this point. Realizing that it's come to this. Me without any dignity—completely alone and thinking only about the feel of his lips—and he's probably off with Allyson Moore doing whatever he's doing. I take a breath and look up at Gilda. "I'm always The Girl At That Party, never The Girl."

"Sounds like you've kissed one too many toads."

"And toads never turn into boyfriends. Not in my case."

"But Ian proved he was boyfriend material?"

"Yeah. Except it took a long time for me to realize it. We were . . . friends. For a long time. Like, almost nine months. I mean, that's how long it takes to incubate a baby, or whatever." I take a bite of the gummy bear, feeling more settled. "Ian drove me to school every day. And he'd remind me which color uniform I needed for a track meet. I trusted him." I stare at the half-eaten gummy bear, getting lost in the memories of him. "It's strange how you can be friends with someone for so long and then one day he brings you licorice and Motrin because you're whacked out from heinous painful cramps straight from the devil, but you notice he's wearing a new shirt that's a certain shade of green and . . . whammo! Your insides turn to pudding and all you can do is think about kissing him. He's the same guy, doesn't change a bit from one day to the next"—I start to think about his eyes, his mouth—"but because a color brings out his eyes, you suddenly realize . . ."

Gilda finishes my sentence. "Boyfriend material."

I sigh. "Totally."

That green shirt. None of this would have happened if it weren't for that stupid color. It's like some nightmare *Sesame Street* episode: *This month's gut-wrenching, painful heartache brought to you by the color green!*

But I quickly snap back to reality and remind myself that I am telling this story to the cashier at the 7-Eleven due to the fact that Ian Clark left me on prom night and I ended up in a ditch on Hollister Road.

Screw the color green.

I sit up and clear my throat. "He totally *was* boyfriend material. At least I never kissed the guy."

"That's good. I guess."

Maybe Gilda is right. It is good we never kissed. That way we don't have to worry about any "weirdness." Except that our friendship has come to a complete halt, and I'll have to find a new ride to school. Which is a total pain. So I should've just kissed him and gotten something out of this ridiculous mess. Plus, I still can't help but wonder what it would've been like.

Curse you, wonder.

"Or maybe I should've kissed him. Just once? Like maybe I should've done it a long time ago, not sat around waiting for the perfect moment. I could've gotten it out of the way."

"Like a chore?"

I laugh at that. I've never thought of kissing as a chore. More of a sport. "I just don't want to have to wonder anymore."

"Wonder what?"

"If he's the perfect kisser. Some guys are—they know exactly how much tongue to give, when to be gentle, and when to put on the deep pressure."

She quickly pops another gummy bear in her mouth and fake coughs.

"Sorry. Too much?" I wince.

She gazes off in the distance toward the hot-dog cooker. "No. Actually, I know exactly what you mean."

I snag another handful of bears from the bag and start gnawing. It really seems to calm the nerves. "Okay then, so you know that there are also guys who are awful kissers. Too wet. Too toothy. Too much tongue. Too much breathing. Too much coloring outside the lines, you know what I mean? I want to know which category he falls in."

"You still want to know?"

Immediately I picture him talking to Allyson Moore next to that pool and then overhearing that phone conversation in the In-N-Out Burger bathroom. "No. Not anymore. All Ian Clark got me was a ruined dress. And the worst night of my life." I straighten out my stained dress.

Allyson Moore.

Just *thinking* about her almost makes me throw up in my mouth. I mean, what was it exactly that he couldn't resist? Her strappy, silver Jimmy Choo pumps? Or her pale pink lip gloss with a hint of glitter? Surely it wasn't her remarkable intelligence—the girl thinks monogamy is a type of dark wood. Maybe he found her lack of common vocabulary terms adorable?

None of this makes sense. Ian is not the kind of guy who would leave me alone in a ditch. And somewhere deep in me, maybe in some file buried in my brain, I know this is true.

At least, I *hope* it's true.

This picture is so fuzzy . . . no crisp black and whites . . . just grays . . . and unanswered questions.

Gilda leans toward me to get a better look at my stained outfit. "What *are* all these?"

Looking them over, I realize each one tells a little piece of the story of what happened to me last night. Like a quilt—a stain quilt. A disastrous, heartbreaking, nasty stain quilt. "You really want to know?"

Gilda looks around at the empty store, another sad country song blaring in the background. She shrugs. "It's real busy, but I guess I could spare some time." She winks then tosses another gummy bear at me. "I gotta hear about this Ian Clark guy."

I point to the very first stain of the night—the one near the hem of my dress. It's the greenish-yellow one.

The one I got from him.

CHAPTER TWO
YELLOW CURRY, EXTRA CORIANDER

IT WAS YESTERDAY. 5:30 p.m. I had just gotten back from a jog over to the CVS to pick up the perfect color of nail polish: Barbados Blue. The same color as my dress, true, but at least it wasn't Black Cherry. Tonight, I would be daring.

I had carefully instructed my mother not to answer the door with a spoon full of lentil stew or barley goop or whatever vegetable concoction she had created and force it into Ian's mouth. He might not like it. Or he might not be hungry. Or he might be nervous and not want to make small talk with my mother about how tasty the lentils were. I happened to like lentils, but—let's face it—most people think they taste like clods of dirt.

Of course Mom didn't pay attention to my request. She was making a big pot of curry. And I could sense it was going to end up in Ian's mouth.

"Why are you making me dinner?" I was still in my running clothes, crunching on a Honeycrisp apple, talking with my mouth full. "We're eating dinner at the hotel."

Mom could make a mean lentil stew, and her curry was even more amazing. She never forced me into being a vegetarian, but when I was nine I watched a science show on how things are made. Once I found out how they *really* make hot dogs, I joined her and never looked back. Meat and I formally divorced. But even though she was a fantastic vegetarian cook, it didn't mean she should force it on Ian.

She blew on the stew to cool it down, and took a bite. "It's not for you. Fundraiser tonight. Remember?"

Uh, no. I didn't remember because Mom's schedule is full of fundraisers. And committee meetings. And action planning groups. And committee meetings about the planning groups for the fundraisers, or something. It's exhausting. For me, anyway.

"Wanna taste?" Mom wasn't asking me. She was asking Sol, our chocolate Labrador retriever. She always treated him like he was royalty—like he was just as important as the President's dog, or Oprah's dog.

Sol licked the spoon, as well as all the drops on the floor. "Don't tell Daddy," she said as she patted him on the head.

I crossed my arms. "You know Dad would throw you into the backyard if he saw you feeding Sol people food."

"But he doesn't understand how much Sol loves my curry." She leaned over and whispered, "It's the extra coriander."

Since Dad was out of town, Mom was using Sol as a taste tester for her fundraiser curry instead of me, which was fortunate because it didn't do any favors for people who wanted kissable breath. It was also fortunate Dad was out of town because he wouldn't be able to greet Ian at the door and use his psychology on him.

Calm, assertive voice.

Confident stance.

No means no.

And by psychology I mean *pet psychology*. Dad calls himself "Dog Trainer to the Stars!" He once happened to meet Meryl Streep at one of Mom's fundraisers and had an impromptu dog training session with her Irish setter in the parking lot of the Hyatt. He immediately updated his résumé. Only he rarely trained celebrities' dogs; it was the hairstylist or massage therapist or dermatologist of a star who called. But because of that little line on his résumé, he now got called off to Los Angeles and Palm Springs whenever a person who knew a movie star needed dog training.

The weekend of my prom he was training Halle Berry's manicurist's pug how to heel.

While my dad's job may sound glamorous—or not— it's not like we're rich. But we aren't poor, and we don't go without food or anything, and I always get stuff like fuzzy slippers and watches every Christmas, so there really is nothing to complain about.

But the one time I did consider complaining was a week ago when Mom took me shopping for my prom dress at a consignment shop, not the mall.

"This way, part of it will go to the person who donated the dress. Someone who *really* needs the money. It's a win- win," Mom had said.

Not that I wanted an expensive dress from the mall— it seemed like an excessive waste of money for something I was only going to wear once. But the secondhand shop didn't feel quite right either. It was fine for normal everyday clothes, but *formal* wear? Weird things happened to people dressed in formal wear, especially when worn to a party that more than likely got out of control. I couldn't be sure what that particular dress had witnessed.

I kept my mouth shut, though. Mom had a cute look on her face, and she was so excited that I'd agreed to wear a dress and not a pantsuit, which I had threatened to do.

Plus, truth be told, Ian once told me when we were sitting in the front seat of his car before school, listening to AC/DC—me decked out in black, of course, wool even, if I remember correctly—that he couldn't wait to see me in a bright, happy color someday, to match my insides. And I said it'd have to be red since my insides were sorta bloody. Then he gave that butterfly-inducing laugh.

Ian didn't know the real reason I wore black all the time.

But I liked that he wanted to see me bright and happy. So when Mom was standing in the half-off orange-dot aisle, holding a bright iridescent blue dress, wiggling with excitement and saying, "Go for the pop of color!" I gave in to her eager face.

I doubted my decision. Ever since Jimmy DeFranco's party, I doubted everything. But at least the dress didn't have a high slit that might further the reputation I couldn't seem to shake.

Maybe this dress—classic, traditional, colorful, and yeah, unsexy—would be just the thing to remind everyone I was no longer a kissing addict. Ian might not find me super hot and sexy, and the dress was rather a failure in the good-taste department, but he'd notice the color.

He'd know I did it for him.

"Go get ready!" Mom pushed me out of the kitchen and went back to stirring her pot of fundraiser curry.

I bolted upstairs, finishing my apple just before I jumped into the shower. It was a two-minute blur. I quickly combed and dried my hair, long and straight—an expensive sleek salon updo seemed silly given all the dancing we were going to do. Plus I wanted to leave my hair wild and open for business in case Ian wanted to run his fingers through it when I laid that kiss on him. I mean, what guy would get excited about his date pulling her hair back tight and shellacking it with hair spray? It'd be like kissing a dodgeball.

I quickly slathered the Barbados Blue on my nails. I was fast, but I was accurate. The nail drying—*that's* what took time. I paced around my room and blew on my nails. *Dry, come on, dry.*

My bedroom looks like a museum dedicated to daisies. I have daisy wallpaper, daisy pillows, even the trim on my lamp shade has a daisy print. I happen to love flowers, any flower, but I *adore* ones that symbolize something. Like how lilies represent friendship. And a tulip means forgiveness. Or how a rose is supposed to mean love. Except that I hate roses. Maybe because love is too complicated to express with just a flower.

Or maybe because I don't like red or pink.

Or maybe because Ian's ex-girlfriend, Eva, was wearing a rose in her hair the night she cheated on him—yeah, at that pool party at

Jimmy DeFranco's. It was an epic night, that's for sure. Ian caught Eva making out with Jimmy in his parents' bedroom. She ran after him wearing a pink bikini, the rose in her hair flopping around, about to jump ship. "It was only a kiss!" she screamed. But he dumped her. Wouldn't even give her a chance to explain.

That was the first night we talked about more than silver bats. My darkest moment. And his too. I was outside on the curb, crying because guys were saying they heard I was making the rounds. The jerks. Jason Harper was my only intentional kissing act that night, but Aaron Becker, drunk on Jägermeister shots, dragged me by my elbow to show me a dent he'd gotten in his dad's BMW but instead stopped me in the hallway and gave me an unsolicited hard sloppy kiss. I actually had to stomp on his toe to get him away from me. Thank God his toes were vulnerable in those flip-flops. And then all I could do was run.

So next thing I knew, Ian had plopped down next to me on the curb, right after Eva had taken off sobbing. "Epic night, huh?" he said with sarcasm, but it was the sad kind, not the rude kind, and I instantly felt at ease.

I looked him over and remembered who he was: the handle-first guy. I wiped my face. "I'm never kissing another boy again."

"O-kay. I'm Ian."

"I know. I remember you," I said. "I hate boys. You included. You should probably know that up front."

He nodded. "And I hate girls."

We shook hands, and that was it. We were perfect together.

As friends.

Months went by. We were friends and then even better friends. We carpooled. We shared history notes. We drove around and screamed AC/DC songs. Then we talked about the important things.

"Seriously, Lay's are the best," I'd say.

"Ruffles, you goof."

"Texture?"

"Yeah," he'd say. "There's something *there*. Something to hold on to."

"So you don't like *flat* things?" I'd wiggle my chest, strangely unafraid around him to be proud of my less-than-impressive chest.

"Are we comparing chips to the female form?"

"I don't know." I'd squint my eyes. "Are we?"

"Yes, Justina. That makes perfect sense. I only eat Ruffles because they make me think of a girl's chest, and I'm the type of guy to base my food preferences on girly parts. I prefer grapefruit to apples, you know."

"And the truth comes out."

We always teetered on the edge of flirtation—delicately dipping our toes in, but never fully plunging. That was the best part of our friendship, the unsaid part—the playful looks, the teetering, the toe-dips.

But there was one part of his friendship I couldn't live without.

When we took our conversation to the point of "almost too far," he'd pause, his face would flush, and he'd pull up the right side of his mouth into a smirk. No words, just a smirk. And it was then—when his mouth was pulled up to the right—that the most heavenly, lovely, tiny crease would appear.

That crease.

It made me drunk.

And what he didn't know—or maybe he did—was that I spent most of my time figuring out how to get another one.

That crease became air—I needed it.

But I think he loved the feel of that elusive crease on his own face just as much as I loved looking at it.

Even with all that delicate toe-dipping, I kept to my promise and didn't come close to locking lips with him for a long, long time. Having Ian for a friend was just what I needed.

But everything changed in an instant when he brought me licorice and Motrin, wearing that green shirt. But I never told him. I just kept treating him like a friend and silently imagining us being so much more.

After his breakup with Eva, it took him eight months before he got up enough nerve to ask another girl out.

Me.

And even though we were only friends, I couldn't help but hope he'd asked because he wanted to be more. But then again, maybe I was just a distraction from a rose-loving girl like Eva.

All I knew was, to me, roses couldn't handle the weight of their symbolism. But a daisy never took on more than it could handle. It was a simple flower. It wasn't complicated. And it symbolized more than just "Peace, man." It meant innocence . . . gentleness.

Ian Clark was all daisy.

Nails finally dry, I leaned in to my mirror and took an extra moment to pile on the lip gloss. Attached to my mirror was the invitation Ian had left for me in my locker. Of course it had a daisy taped to it. He was persuasive in *many* ways.

The Senior Class of Huntington High School
request the honor of your presence at the Junior/Senior Prom
on Saturday, April Fifteenth at Eight O'clock in the evening
The Grand Riverside Hotel

"The Grand Riverside Hotel," I said out loud with an accent dripping with royalness as I looked at myself in the bathroom mirror. I couldn't wait to walk into that ballroom with Ian. And I was wearing a sparkly, iridescent blue dress that matched the bright happiness of my insides (my emotional inside part, not my bloody inside part).

He'd better notice, because everything about tonight was going to be different.

I hadn't had the guts to tell him that my feelings had changed since green shirt day. But hopefully a kiss would do the talking for me. For some reason, I just couldn't say the words. Maybe that's what had happened to him the day he'd asked me.

"It'll be amazing," he had said. "No, um, pressure. We'll just . . ."

"Just what?" I'd leaned in and caught his eyes to get him to finish his sentence.

"We'll go . . . as friends."

"Friends."

"Right?"

He'd winced when he said it. He wanted *me* to decide?

"Right." The word came out without thought, and I'd regretted it the second it fell out of my mouth. This had been my opening to tell him how I felt, all laid out before me like a red carpet. But the words hadn't come for either of us—just a lot of wincing and throat clearing and shirt readjusting.

That's when I decided it was *action* that was going to take this to the next level. Not words.

I knew that the kiss I was going to give him was like putting all my cards on the table. I didn't know if he felt the same way—maybe he really did want to just be friends, which meant this could all end badly.

But oh, lordy, that green shirt.

He was worth the risk.

"Are you ready, Justina?" Mom called out. "Let me see your dress!" She was getting anxious.

So was I.

I slipped my shoes on, the ones Mom had convinced me to dye blue, and I spent a moment staring at my outfit, now all finally pulled together.

Wow. I suddenly felt overwhelmingly . . . blue.

I decided I would show Mom the dress before Ian got there—let her get all her overbearing giddiness out of the way. But it didn't turn out that way, because he was standing in the kitchen when I walked in, and there was my mother, cupping her hand under his chin, trying to stuff him with fundraiser curry.

"The secret is extra coriander," she was explaining.

I quietly stepped into the room and cleared my throat. I had hoped for some smiles, maybe some hugs and a gorgeous flower corsage—a daisy, of course. But the overwhelming color of my dress and matching shoes must have taken them both by surprise, because Ian threw his hands in the air and yelled, "Holy Blueness!"

And Mom threw her hands up too and squeaked, "Beautiful!"

Which wasn't initially such a horrible series of events, but then all the hand flying caused the curry to fly through the air and land just above the hem of my dress.

Mom squealed at first, but then pulled herself together. "Let's get this mess cleaned up," she said in a calming voice.

I should've helped, but all I could do was stare at Ian.

He'd noticed the dress, but did he *notice* it? But then all I could do was notice *him*. He was wearing a black tuxedo, and it made him look powerful. Rugged, tall, and a bit lanky, too, but he looked so . . . manly. But then I glanced down and noticed he wasn't wearing dress shoes—he was wearing Converse high-tops. Turquoise.

His long brown hair flopped in his eyes as he looked down at his shoes. "I couldn't find the right shade of blue. I thought we could match. Sorry."

I leaned in and made him look up at me. "We match." My instinct was to reach out and gently tuck his hair behind his ear, but Mom was watching. Plus, we had a whole night ahead of us—there'd be plenty of time for playing with his hair.

Mom apologized over and over while she scrubbed the floor with lemon-smelling cleaner, which always made my nose itch. And Ian just smiled as he scrubbed the bottom of my dress with a wet washcloth. I smiled back at him and scratched my nose.

He managed to get the chunky parts off, but the stain was forever. At the time, I didn't mind one bit. Ian Clark, with adorably floppy brown hair, was on his knees, washing my dress.

Butterflies.

If Mom hadn't been in the room, it would've been the perfect time to plant that first kiss on him. The Moment of Lip Lock Bliss. I had been deprived of lip lockage for eight months, twelve days. My whole body ached, starving for boy contact. But this kiss was going to be worth the wait.

Ian would hold my gaze, I imagined, then run his fingers through my wild, un-hair-sprayed hair and press his lips against mine. And I would know once and for all which category he belonged in.

But I was an excessive fantasizer; plus, I already had a perfect plan for The Moment of Lip Lock Bliss and it didn't involve my kitchen, yellow curry, and certainly not my mother.

Ian stood up and turned to my mom. "We're going to Dan's for a pre-party. I'll try to keep her away from anything liquid and yellow, Mrs. Griffith."

I took a breath. "My personal stain fighter." I may have even twirled my dress a little when I said it.

Mom pressed her lips together tightly, trying to control her quivering lip. "I wouldn't feel good about Justina going to prom with anyone but you." She reached out and dusted his tuxedo sleeve.

Just then, I felt a lick. Sol was doing his part to clean up my stain. I guess he really did like coriander. "Could you put him in the backyard, Mom? He's going to eat my dress."

"Sol, baby. Come here." She patted her hip as if she were giving a command, but she had already gone back over to the stove and was throwing more spices into the stew. Mom always called the dog "baby," and she rarely made him obey. She didn't want him to be *uncomfortable.*

Ian snapped his fingers. "Sit."

Sol stopped licking me. And he actually sat. Ian rubbed him behind the ears and told him he was a good boy.

"Wow," I said. "Persuasive." I wasn't sure if it was the finger snapping or the forcefulness in his voice or the rubbing of the ears, but I suddenly couldn't wait to get to the pre-party and away from Mom. Ian seemed to know exactly when to be gentle and when to put on the pressure. I had to know if this would translate into a perfect kissing technique.

A low grumble in my stomach interrupted my Ian daydream, reminding me of another reason I was eager to get to the pre-party: Dan's parents were preparing appetizers. I wasn't sure I could make it until dinner without a quick snack, because without proper food intake I start to make bad decisions.

In addition to the food and the kiss I was going to rock Ian's world with, I was also excited because Hailey was going to be there, my best friend—my best *girl* friend—and she was Dan's date. I liked him because he was the second nicest guy on the planet, and also because he had a pool and Hailey and I had an open invitation to swim whenever we wanted. Dan always got us whatever we wanted to eat and drink (orange soda and licorice, thank you), then he'd go inside to play video games and let us have our "girl time" by the pool. Fabulous.

But it felt like over the past year Hailey and I had detached from the hips and only saw each other on rare occasions— those seven minutes when our lunch periods overlapped, the occasional *Buffy the Vampire Slayer* marathon, and when it was warm enough to swim.

And I hadn't been to a party in months. Operation Lips Locked was in effect, and parties were like meth to a girl in love with kissing. So Hailey partied solo. Lately, since I carpooled to school with Ian, and she drove with Dan, most of our friendship was spent waving at each other from the passenger seats of other people's cars.

I missed her. But not just that . . . I hadn't even told her that my feelings for Ian had changed. I wasn't sure how she'd react. Would she be happy for me? Or feel left out?

"Here's your corsage." Ian pulled out flowers, but they weren't daisies.

Roses. Not white, for friendship. Not red, for love. They were roses that had been spray-painted glittery blue. The *exact* color of my dress.

"Blue roses?" I swallowed hard. What was he trying to say to me with blue roses? "For . . . patriotism?"

"No. Yes. I don't know." He pinned it on my dress, then leaned in and whispered in my ear, "Your mom said it had to be blue."

"My *mom* said?!" I suddenly realized that all this blueness— his shoes, the flowers, the blue purse and watch now laid out on the kitchen table—had been Mom's doing. I was an only child, true, but her need to be involved was approaching Creepsville. She didn't need to drape me in matchy-matchy "just like she wore" garb simply because I was her only living offspring. I wasn't a dress-up doll. Put a sweater on the dog and leave me out of it, for crying out loud.

I quickly pulled away, searching for a time machine portal—the only thing I figured that might save me—but that's when the corsage pin, which seemed to be the size of a samurai sword, jammed into my collarbone.

It took both my mom and Ian applying direct pressure for five minutes to get the bleeding to stop. But during that time, Mom explained it was true she had looked up his number on my cell and given him a quick call to explain the beauty of roses that matched a dress.

She actually said those words. *Beauty of roses that matched a dress.*

"Mom, it doesn't match the dress. It looks like it's *part* of the dress!" I lowered my voice and said, "This isn't your prom, Mom. It's mine."

She nodded, looking embarrassed. I felt bad for saying it.

"It's my fault. I can take it off." Ian reached out, and that's when I noticed his face had lost color. He looked mortified. Crap. Whenever Ian makes a mistake he always feels nauseous. One time just before a track meet, he realized he had worn the wrong color jersey, and he puked in the bushes.

Mom didn't need to call him and get involved. He didn't need to feel this way.

This ship needed to get turned around, quick. "I don't mind. I like it," I lied. The color slowly came back to Ian's face. Whew.

Mom went back to stirring her pot of curry. Under her breath she said, "I shouldn't have gotten involved."

I walked up behind her. "It's okay, Mom." But it wasn't.

"I won't call him again," she said as she blew on her spoon and tasted. "I'll delete his number from my phone. I shouldn't have it." When Mom felt forced into a corner she suddenly became the founder of the Melodramatic Moment of the Month Club. Time to pull her back out.

"You should have his number." I stood behind her, resting my chin on her shoulder and whispered, "For emergencies. Okay?"

She blinked repetitively, which meant she was thinking. She stirred. Blew. Tasted. Then said quietly, "Just for emergencies."

I grabbed Ian by the arm and told him we needed to go, that we didn't want to be late for the pre-party, and promised Mom, again, that I'd be home by two, and reminded her to put Sol in the back-yard or else he'd pee on the carpet. Mom always chose his warmth and coziness over his bodily functions.

"But he'll get cold," she complained. "We'll both be gone for most of the night."

"Even if you come back by ten, he still needs to be able to pee, Mom. Leave him in the backyard. Lock the gate."

I couldn't believe Sol's well-being was always in my hands. And I couldn't believe we were having this discussion in front of Ian. Like he wanted to know these details.

My face flushed. I reached up and touched my cheek and realized what was happening . . . I was embarrassed! It didn't make sense. Talking about pee was making me embarrassed? Before tonight Ian had farted and burped in front of me countless times, and I may have done the same in an emergency moment here and there, but neither of us hardly even blinked.

Except we had now clearly moved past the Just Friends stage, because my face flushed when I discussed dog pee in front of him. Oh, lord. There was no going back.

"I worked at the dog pound one summer," Ian volunteered. "So be sure to lock the gate. I spent most of my summer chasing down lost dogs who got out because of a gust of wind."

"Now see"—Mom sunk her chin into her hand—"that is such a fulfilling job. Taking care of others." She was looking at me as if I were supposed to respond, *Yes, he's perfect. Let's gift wrap him.* But I already knew that. I didn't need her approval on this one.

I really couldn't stand and watch her dote on him anymore. Especially because I knew if she got any more comfortable, she might start in with her story about—

"Did I ever tell you I was elected prom queen?"

"Mom, no."

Ian's face lit up. "Oh, you *were?*"

I held my hand up. "Don't encourage her."

He ignored me and slid into a kitchen chair. "Go on."

Ian has this thing with listening to people's stories. He loves it when people talk about their past—it utterly fascinates him. Like if we are in a coffee shop, nine times out of ten he is able to strike up a conversation with a random stranger and get them to tell some bizarre story about how they once sat next to an NFL quarterback on a plane, or how they single-handedly got an entire room of stockbrokers to sing show tunes. The stuff he found out about people was always random.

When Mom started up with her "I was elected prom queen" story, Ian beamed like Rudolph on Christmas Eve.

And so Mom went on with her old, sad story about how she was chosen prom queen, but when she went up on stage she grabbed the microphone and made a public service announcement about the benefits of using public transportation and riding bikes, but this was the generation of the V-8 Trans Am with gold trim, so the only applause she got came from the chaperones.

Ian turned to me, smirking, which meant a setup. "What are you going to say in your acceptance speech tonight?"

I tilted my head and played right along. "My fellow students, as your prom queen, I declare that all future proms will be bonfires on the beach with veggie burritos."

He shook his head. "According to your definition, we had prom last weekend. And the weekend before that."

"Exactly. I'm a warm sweatshirt and bonfire kind of prom queen."

He looked me up and down, then raised an eyebrow. "Not tonight."

Toe-dip.

Mom cleared her throat. "You were nominated for prom queen, sweetheart?"

"I nominated her," Ian explained. "And so did Hailey, but Justina forced us to take her name off the ballot. And I mean *actual* force. Her nails are pointy. She broke skin, Mrs. Griffith."

Oh lord, he was cute.

But being prom queen was not an item I wanted to check off on my Things To Do Before I Die list. Queen of the Daisies? Queen of all Black Boots? Now that I could handle.

Even though deep down, deep in the dirty soles of my crusty boots, I secretly did want to wear that prom queen crown. Only because I wanted Ian and me to be the couple that slow danced together while everyone watched and swayed along and said longingly, "Oh my god, they are the cutest couple."

But the title of prom queen was always reserved for the most undeserving—whoever was enjoying the biggest scandal at the time would take the crown, it seemed. And I had my bet on Brianna or Allyson. Brianna had that recent champagne incident that ended up in an embarrassing viral video and Allyson was rude to *everyone*, so the prom queen bar wasn't raised very high at Huntington High.

So maybe I *would* make a good prom queen. But then again, if I did win, the entire school would be looking at me in this dress and these shoes. I glanced down at my outfit and suddenly became overwhelmed by my own blue-i-ness.

This may have been a very bad mistake.

I pushed the crazy talk out of my head—literally. . . . I pressed on my forehead with the palm of my hand to make the thoughts disappear. A technique that usually worked, but not always. And not in this instance. Dang it. But the night had already started—there was no do-over. Sometimes you just have to work with what you have. Thankfully I had watched enough *Project Runway* to know that.

I quickly snatched my purse and looped my arm through Ian's. "Let's go, Stainfighter."

We waved to Mom as we headed down the driveway. She stood watching us, still pressing her lips together tightly to stop the quiver. She didn't even notice Sol licking the spoon in her hand.

That's my dog. Badly behaved, but a resourceful little sucker. He's not just a dog to me, he's people. "Good boy, Sol."

Just before we got to the car, I turned to Ian. "You didn't *have* to get me a blue corsage just because my mom called. You could've said no."

"Like I'm going to say no to your mother. She's your mother. She's Peg Griffith! Phlebotomist of the Year!"

I shoved him. "Shut up, goof."

"I'm not saying no to Peg. Even though I wish I would've said no to that curry."

I smiled. "She was never going to give you a choice. Peg is eager."

Which was exactly why I looked like the Uni-Color- Bomber on my prom night.

"Can I talk now?" He was bouncing on his toes.

I folded my arms, preparing for what he was about to say, then nodded.

"Two things. One, we're going to dance to a Journey song tonight—I don't care how much you protest, I will dance you into submission—and second, I brought you a peanut butter cookie in case you get hungry and turn all old- man cranky on me."

This made me smile. I liked that he was prepared for my low-blood sugar moments. It made me happy with my decision to make this the night we would finally kiss.

"Oh wait," he added. "There's a third thing."

I looked up.

"The color." He gently lifted my skirt up high, but not *too* high, then let it fall back softly onto my thighs. "You look . . . nice."

Nice. Did he say *nice*?! What does that mean? Boring? Uninteresting? A dirt clod? A lentil?!

He must have sensed my ridiculous raging silent monologue, because he grabbed my hand, led me to the car, then leaned over and whispered in my ear, "You're not like any other girl, Justina. Thank God."

Oh my word, I have been kiss-deprived long enough.

It was time for me to put Ian in his correct kissing category. Most people wouldn't put this much forethought into a kiss, but I knew what it would mean for Ian and me. We wouldn't be friends anymore. And there would be no going back. But I was ready.

Hopefully he was too. And I knew the exact moment and place I hoped it would happen.

Next to Dan's pool, in the far corner, was a hot tub. It was surrounded by ferns and sweet-smelling gardenias. It was lush. It was quiet—other than the sound of bubbling water, but water features are totally romantic. It was perfect. My plan was to take him out there to discuss something, maybe tell him a story about my childhood, like a good Christmas story because he always seemed to love those, then we'd stare at each other for an awkwardly long moment, but neither of us would look away, and then we'd step closer to each other, tilt our heads in opposite directions, and at precisely the right moment, our lips would touch, and *whammo!* I'd have my answer.

But, of course, that's not what happened.

I did manage to get out to that beautiful spot by the hot tub. And I stood next to the lush ferns and sweet-smelling gardenias.

And I got kissed.

But it wasn't by Ian.

CHAPTER THREE

CORN DOG

"WAIT. YOU KISSED another guy?!" Gilda is poking at the hot dogs as they rotate on a greasy conveyor belt.

"Yes. No. Not intentionally." I readjust myself on the stool. "It's complicated."

Gilda closes the lid to the hot dog cooker, waits for the quiet click. "These things are."

I notice that she isn't offering me a hot dog; not that I'd eat one, but still. They are glistening—even the corn dogs have a thick warm glow about them, and I'm still starving.

The bell rings, and this lady wearing Bermuda shorts, a tank top, and a fanny pack attached tightly around her, well . . . fanny, flies through the door. "Morning, Gilda. Need my Red Bull. And my patch."

"Sure thing, Donna."

Donna heads off to search the refrigerators for her jumbo sugar-free Red Bull while Gilda digs through boxes next to the counter for a patch. A nicotine patch.

This feels like a routine these two have done many times before.

I can't help but stare at Donna. Her hair is transitioning to a light gray color, and it's so short it's spiky—almost dangerous look-ing, like a barbed-wire fence. She's strong, not like manly strong, but like garden-landscaping-rototilling strong. I say that because her nails are dirty, full of dark soil, or maybe pudding? And her arms are thick and tan, like a corn dog. I'm just so hungry!

Gilda starts ringing up Donna's order, and that's when Donna looks in my direction. She doesn't blink, doesn't pretend to be doing anything other than staring at me, and it's making me uncomfortable. "What happened to you, doll?" Her voice is strong and raspy.

I try to straighten out my dress, as if that will help. "I . . . I . . . ."

"This poor girl got ditched. At prom," Gilda explains.

"Ditched? What kind of scumbag would do that to a sweet girl like you?" Donna peers over the counter to get a better look at me, and gives me the full up-and-down once- over. "Do your shoes match your dress?"

"Yes." I fiddle with my hem. "Mom's idea."

"Not a good one."

I look down, feeling the tears well up as I think about Mom and her eagerness to make me perfectly color coordinated—in *every* way. And how sick it makes me feel, given all the suffering I went through because of these stupid matching shoes. And now Donna, who I don't even know, is making me nervous with her dangerously spiky hair and eagerness to remind me of my bad decisions. "I really don't need to have the obvious pointed out right now," I say, like I'm all confident or something. But I can't even look her in the eyes.

"Aw, doll, listen up." She leans over the counter, folds her arms, and gets comfortable. "I got dumped once. Homecoming. Jessie Saxton took off in his van and left me stranded at the Ledbetter Community Center. I had to walk a mile to a Piggly Wiggly. It was humiliating. I know what you've been through." She pauses as if she's remembering the details. Her face grows tough, like jerky. "True, I kicked him in the shin for eyeballing another girl who it turns out was the girl in charge of playing music and he was giving her the eye to start playing our song, which was sweet and all, but still. How was I supposed to know?" She shakes her head, trying to convince herself. "No, he was going to be a scumbag *someday*. They all are."

Before she goes on, I say a quick silent prayer.

Please, please, Lord, don't let me grow up to be this hard and crusty. And forgive me for using the word 'crusty' but I couldn't think of anything else more descriptive.

But then I realize there may be some slivers of truth to what Donna's saying.

There's no excuse for what Ian did. I guess I should've known he'd turn into a scumbag *someday*.

I just wish that day hadn't been prom.

My stomach growls.

Donna looks over at the hot dogs and corn dogs rotating under the warm glow of fluorescent lights. "You want one? My treat."

"Don't you have a meeting?" Gilda starts bagging her box of nicotine patches. These two seem to know each other well. Maybe Gilda listens to stories from lots of her customers.

"There will be others." Donna winks and says to Gilda, "This young doll could use a corn dog. Don'tcha think?"

Gilda scuffles over to get me a corn dog, and I turn to Donna. "What kind of meeting?" I immediately realize it's probably an AA meeting and I should keep my mouth shut.

"DA meeting."

I crinkle my nose. "A what?"

"Debtors Anonymous." She pulls out a credit card and slides it across the counter. "I'm a compulsive spender. And a professional under-earner."

Gilda holds her hand up. "Forget it. Put that thing away. This one's on the house."

I might be the type of person to end up in DA one day too, but Mom's monitoring of my credit card keeps me in check. Most girls in my high school have credit cards, but they don't have spending limits like me, and they don't have moms who read their statements, making sure they only spend money at thrift stores, not the mall.

I have a $400 limit. Per *year*. That gives me $7.69 to spend on clothes every week. Since Tuesdays are orange-dot half-price at the Huntington thrift store, it's the only day I shop.

If I had my credit card with me right now, and it wasn't lost forever in the back of Brian Sontag's Prius, I'd use it to pay Gilda for the glistening corn dog. But all I can do is thank her. I smother the corn dog with ketchup, then hold it up and look at it. I haven't eaten meat in years. And I know how hot dogs are made. And I am disgusted that I'm about to break my pact to divorce myself from meat. But right now I'm so hungry I'd eat a bunny.

My hand trembles as I pull it closer to my mouth.

"It's a tofu dog," Gilda offers at the last possible moment. "I kinda figured you were one of those."

I cram the dog into my mouth. "Fank you!" I say, relieved that convenience stores have now become convenient for *my* type, too.

Donna leans over the counter. "So who exactly is this scumbag?"

"His name is Ian," Gilda answers for me, explaining where we are in the story since my mouth is full of tofu dog. "He picked her up for prom, he dazzled her mom and trained her dog and brought her a cookie, and basically presented himself as a perfect guy." She looks at me for permission, wondering if this is accurate. I nod and chew and swallow and she continues. "So they're on their way to some pre- party at Dan's house and Justina can't stop thinking about kissing him."

Donna nods, as if this story is familiar. "So you got tongue-tied with the guy in his car."

I shake my head and make out a somewhat audible, "No."

"Sucked face in the driveway?"

"No!"

"At the party?!"

Gilda sighs. "She never kissed him."

"Oh, no." Donna stands up straight.

"What?" I swallow hard and clear my throat so I can finally speak. "Isn't it a good thing I didn't kiss him?"

"No, doll. It's bad, real bad. You'll always wonder . . . was he or wasn't he?"

I know exactly what she is getting at. And she is absolutely right.

I can't believe I never got the chance to kiss you, Ian. Now that we're non-friends. A non-couple. A non . . . everything.

Donna folds her arms and lifts an eyebrow. "So why did Captain Scumbag ditch you?"

That's the zillion dollar question. I shake my head. "It's one of those long, complicated stories." My voice fades away.

"I hear you." Donna picks at the dirt under her fingernails. "I have some long, complicated stories. But it's not such a bad thing—it's because of those stories that I can proudly say I am the cougar I am today. Look it up—cougar—in the wiki encyclopedia."

"Wikipedia," I correct her.

She nods. "You've seen me, then."

I turn to Gilda, looking for answers. She holds her hand up like she can take it from here. "Justina's story isn't all that complicated. Not yet," Gilda explains. "All we know so far is Ian tried cleaning yellow curry off her dress and she thought it was adorable and she planned to kiss him at Dan's pre-party. She got a kiss, except it sounds like it was from someone else."

"Oh, you gotta tell me this story." Donna's eyes sparkle. She approaches me and reaches out to touch my blue dress, but pulls back. "What are these stains?"

I take a deep breath and settle onto my stool. Then I start to explain how the stains represent a tapestry of memories, and how they tell a story—

"That's all fine and good," Donna interrupts. "But let's get to Captain Scumbag. And more importantly, this other guy you kissed—scumbag number two."

"The kiss happened right after I got this." I point to a long black stain, the shape of a thin, wimpy corn dog, just above my knee.

FOUR

DIPPING SAUCE (SOY, I THINK)

...

Made in the USA
Lexington, KY
01 June 2015